AND THE SEA DARKENED

VICKI LLOYD

The Book Guild Ltd

First published in Great Britain in 2020 by
The Book Guild Ltd
9 Priory Business Park
Wistow Road, Kibworth
Leicestershire, LE8 0RX
Freephone: 0800 999 2982
www.bookguild.co.uk
Email: info@bookguild.co.uk
Twitter: @bookguild

Typeset in 11pt Adobe Garamond Pro

PPrinted on FSC accredited paper
Printed and bound in Great Britain by 4edge Limited

ISBN 978 1913208 738

British Library Cataloguing in Publication Data.
A catalogue record for this book is available from the British Library.

For Duncan and Zoë

CHAPTER ONE

It was not the shock of a noise that snapped Magnus Bostock out of his deep sleep. More the lack of noise. An abrupt, profound silence that should not have been there.

One foot struck the cold floor while his hands thrust the duvet aside. He found himself staring into the hollow corners of the room, searching the blackness for what had woken him. His breathing was so loud it would have blocked out any sound anyway. But then he heard – what? A distant dog whining?

The ceiling beams groaned, as they did through every night, with the effort of keeping the old farmhouse together. The few dead leaves on the chestnut tree at the back of the house rustled in the salt-laden wind that blew in forever across the marshes. He heard the low breathing of Brenda, her face half-buried in the pillow beside him.

He reached for the discarded clothes on the chair. Downstairs, he headed straight for the back hall and switched on the light, which cast a dull yellow glow over the gun cupboard, the heavy jackets lined up, the row of muddy boots below.

Outside in the yard, Magnus stopped. His right hand gripped the shotgun; his left hand was clenched in a fist. He stared into the gloom, trying to see, trying to hear. He looked up – the palest of yellows in the eastern sky signalled the approaching end of the night. He set off towards the source of the noise he had heard, or imagined.

This was not the first time in recent weeks he had been out at this hour. Sometimes it was a false alarm and the shrieks and howls which echoed through the darkness and into his consciousness had brought him out in the night for nothing. Or sometimes he would come across drunken, would-be poachers from the caravan site, staggering back through the trees to the main road. This time, though, he was now certain, he had been woken by Toby. The old sheepdog never came into the house; he would find himself somewhere comfortable to sleep – somewhere right for the season. But now he was whining, crying out in distress.

It didn't take Magnus long to find him. He was in the old coal bunker round the back of the house. The flap allowed easy entry, but almost impossible exit. *Stupid bloody dog. How on earth did he get in there?* He'd certainly been there for a while, by the look of him, shivering and grimy. As soon as he was released, though, Toby headed off with determination away from the farmhouse and the shelter of the barns towards the fields. He paused, looked back, cocked his head, then trotted on again; so Magnus followed.

Yet he did not stride out at his normal, confident pace. At each step, as his boot crunched down on dry twigs and leaves, he paused, trying to walk more lightly. A tawny owl hooting off to his right in the woods made him falter and stare through the trees. He almost laughed at himself. *Fancy being scared by an owl. Ridiculous.* At the end of the lane he stepped up onto the stile and swung his leg over the top bar.

His family had farmed this land going back generations. It belonged to the Bostocks; but something was happening here that was outside his control. Any other man might feel like the king of the castle, but now he felt more like the ghost in the castle, able to move from room to room, field to field, but powerless, without substance, forced to watch in silence as life shifted around him.

He clutched at the rough wood – barely noticed the splinters forced into his hand. There was a sudden rustle in the undergrowth, but after a long moment motionless astride the stile he climbed down and pressed on. The open fields to his left glistened with silver dew, but the woods were oppressive, untouched by the dawn. Someone or something was shadowing him; moving when he moved, stopping when he stopped. He licked his lips – his mouth had gone dry. This was no badger or fox.

It was not far now to the fence where the wood made a sharp right-angled turn and the ten-acre meadow would stretch out before him, sloping down towards the marsh lands and then the sea. Magnus moved faster now, striding out. As he reached the next stile the moon peered out through a more thinly veiled cloud and, mounting the step, he turned again towards the deep wood, before looking into the field.

His sheep would normally raise their heads, give him a bored stare, then carry on with their listless chewing. On this night, however, he could make out only a hunched, defensive clump pressed hard against the hedge. As he neared, they shrank back into a tighter, uneasy mass. There was no bleating. *Why are you so quiet?* he thought, as he stumbled in the pits and hollows of the rough grass. Three darker, unnaturally still shapes appeared to him in the gloom. Veering now towards them, Magnus drew in a long breath. Three… no, five… no, eight mangled carcasses lay scattered haphazardly. No rhyme or reason was the thought that came to him. *No rhyme or reason.* He stepped from one to another and peered at each of them. Most had their throats ripped open and the black of their blood stained the paler grass. All had their bellies torn apart – their guts spilt untidily onto the ground by deep, parallel gouges. The stench rose up towards Magnus's face.

He retched and turned away, gasping. As he straightened up he looked quickly from left to right, his eyes wide. He snapped the gun shut with his clammy hands and raised it to his shoulder, slowly turning on the damp grass. But nothing moved; all was still.

By eight o'clock the weak January sun cast its watery light through the farmhouse kitchen windows. Magnus Bostock sat slumped at the table, still wearing his jacket and boots, the gun propped against the edge of the soft pine. The light switch snapped and the orange glow from the overhead light faded away, leaving the room stark and dull.

'No need for lights on all over the place.' His wife Brenda marched across the room and twitched back the curtains at the window that looked out over the yard. 'Here comes Balt now.' She lifted up the cover of one of the hotplates on the Rayburn, plonked the kettle in place, turned and looked at her husband. 'You'd better look sharp. He'll need to know. If he doesn't already.'

Magnus raised his head slowly and stared towards the door. His stockman was brilliant with the animals and Magnus lived in awe of the big Dutchman's ability to subdue, as though with one sweep of his arm he could bring a cow to its knees with its head bowed before him, if he wished. Baltasar had dumped his boots in the back hall and padded in in his thick socks. Magnus had always thought he looked like a bear, with his shaggy, dark ginger hair and powerful, rounded shoulders. And it was obvious, from the look on his face, that he knew all too well what had happened in the night.

—

Elaine Maple pulled back her bedroom curtains, saw the rawness of the morning and reached for her thick, fluffy dressing gown. The sky was only just starting to lighten. She looked out over the dark, flat landscape beyond the pub garden, intersected with bare hedges, ditches and gates, with scattered cattle feeding on it. The narrow leaden line beyond was the river; and the distant emptiness from which the wind rushed in was the sea.

She trudged into the bathroom. The mirror showed a bleary face, framed by a mass of frizzy blonde hair; the face of a forty-five-year-old who could do with more sleep, less fat, less sugar and less white wine; and a month lying under a palm tree on a white sandy beach in the Caribbean. She almost smiled.

As she gazed out, her eyes gradually focused on a darker shape emerging from the distant mists. Was that the same strange wanderer she had seen several times in recent weeks? Never close enough, never clear enough for her to make out size or gender, just a vague, menacing figure that this time, as before, left her wanting to close the curtains, hug a duvet round herself and turn on all the lights.

By midday, the sun was higher in the sky, but her mood had not managed to lift with it. She reached for a cloth and began to polish glasses, her lips clamped in displeasure. The lunchtime rush was starting, but did she have any help? Did she heck. That little bugger of a barman was off sick – again – with an upset stomach, so he claimed. And Alex? Fat chance of him doing anything around here. He might say he wanted to earn a bit of cash, but where was he now? Still in bed, of course.

The door from the car park swung open and a large man with windswept fair hair and a bold face marched in. His oilskin gave off a faint whiff of diesel and fish. Elaine put down the cloth and pasted a bright smile onto her face.

'Morning, Nick – what can I get you?'

'Pint of Broadside, please, Elaine,' he replied.

As she filled his glass, she came up with one of her stock phrases. 'Nippy wind out there today, I gather.'

'Playing merry hell with the boats. Had to lay up *Shadowbrook Star*.'

'You stuck in harbour, then?'

'Take more'n that. Gang I had out yesterday got totally soaked when the spray covers ripped. Right lot, they were – just sat there whimpering, all huddled up. What a laugh! Half of them wanted their money back. Dream on, I says.' He took a long drink from the glass Elaine had planted heavily before him.

'You're a shocker, you are. One day someone's going to pull the plug on you and your… enterprises.' She laughed. 'Then you'll get your comeuppance.'

'Don't you worry, Elaine. Don't you worry.'

Other customers started drifting in. Nick Bostock took his pint over to a table in the little bar, near the dartboard. Regulars arrived, ordered their usuals, settled down in their favourite chairs or perched on their favourite stools. A few families from the caravan site braved the weather and crowded in to fill up on scampi and chips or sausage and mash. Elaine was kept busy, when she wasn't pouring drinks, by running to the top of the stairs where she shouted orders down to the basement kitchen. The two grungies, Mark and Angie, were preparing the meals down there. Handwashing may not have been their priority, but they were quick, she had to give them that.

A couple more fishermen came in, hung their wet oilskins in the corner and took their drinks over to Nick Bostock's table. When she brought him his steak and kidney pie she found the three of them talking quietly, heads close together over their pints. One of them rose after a while to get another round in. Nick became more expansive – and louder – as the murky day slid into afternoon. Elaine moved round the room, clearing up the empties, and saw him and his companions leaning back, laughing.

The elderly couple from the Post Office were in today as well, indulging their habit of a Wednesday lunch out. They'd both had the scampi, chips and peas. Elaine hoped to God the grungies hadn't left the scampi lying around defrosting for too long in the warm kitchen.

The man – Elaine never could remember his name – *Mr James, was it?* – beckoned her over.

'You know it's happened again, don't you?' he asked in a stage whisper. 'More animals killed.'

She went closer.

'Oh yes,' he went on, while his wife, her lips pressed hard together, nodded, apparently wisely. 'Police up at one of the farms. Not sure which one, but I'll put money on it being Slegholm. You know they've got that strange man working up there. The Dutch boy, we call him, though he's no boy, of course.'

'Always carries binoculars,' added the woman, as though this clinched it.

The man nodded in agreement. 'And it's always on the island – never on the mainland. And I've heard it was the calves—'

'No, sheep,' the woman interrupted him. 'Definitely sheep.'

'Right. Sheep. And they were slashed to pieces,' his hand came up now and made a slow, clawing motion above the remains of the scampi, 'with these gouges. Ripped their—' He stopped, looked away, changed his words into a prolonged clearing of his throat.

Elaine turned and looked towards the door to see a couple walk in. The man was big, with brown, woolly hair, and was dressed in cords, heavy boots and a thick sweater. The other Bostock brother and his wife. What was she called? Barbara? Brenda? The woman was plumpish, with colourless curly hair and drab, baggy clothes. Elaine saw the aura of defensiveness about them – the barrier they put up between themselves and the rest of the world. They looked like the sort of people who were eternally middle-aged, though she guessed they were about forty, if not less. She moved back to the bar quickly, her eyes wide with curiosity. She needed to know if the rumours were true.

Then she glanced over to Nick's table. He was still laughing, but when he noticed the new arrivals he switched off, like a door had slammed. He leant forward; his face darkened and took on a scowl. Elaine saw him mutter to his pals, who both glanced towards the door, then sank their faces into their pints.

'Magnus, Brenda, it's been a while since we saw you in here.' Elaine drew nearer, as though to make their conversation more intimate. She brushed away Jaggers, the pub cat, who had jumped up onto the bar, his back arched. 'But I wondered if you might be coming in today. You've had some trouble…?' She tailed off and glanced from one to the other encouragingly. Her raised eyebrows and wide smile invited them to fill in the details. Neither husband nor wife spoke, however; just nodded slightly and looked down. Elaine held her ground, head tilted to one side, the expectant look fixed in place.

'We'll have—' He cleared his throat and started again. 'We'll have two glasses of cider, please.'

'Fine! And would that be pints or halves, Magnus? And then we've got…' She stretched out an arm to indicate the range of ciders on offer. 'There's Aspall's or Old Rosie.'

'We'll have two halves of Aspall's, please, Elaine. Thank you.'

As she filled the glasses she watched Magnus lean one elbow on the bar and look cautiously round the room; then peer further into what he could see of the smaller bar through the archway, where the dartboard was. If he expected any reaction, he was to be disappointed. Everyone in the place just carried on. They chatted, laughed, ate and drank as though their own little lives, and their own little problems, were all that mattered in the world. Everyone, that is, except his brother, seated over there and glaring at him. When he spotted him, Magnus snorted and turned his head away quickly. Brenda glanced up from fiddling with her large, brown handbag, then frowned more deeply when she recognised her brother-in-law.

Elaine returned with the full glasses, put them down in front of the couple and waited for the money. The farmer's rough, stained hands pulled a fistful of coins out of his pocket and he stared blankly at them, his mind obviously somewhere completely different. She reached across and helped herself to a few pound coins. By the time she came back from the till with his change, Magnus's face had grown darker, his eyes more fixed and his hands now bunched into tight fists. Even as she watched, he slammed his glass down on the bar and straightened up to his full height, taking in a deep breath.

His wife, looking increasingly uncomfortable, put a restraining hand on his arm. 'Leave it, Magnus. Best not start.'

'But look at him, just sitting there with his scummy friends, doesn't give a damn, doesn't give a damn about anything.'

He shrugged her off, strode across to the table in the corner and planted his large hands down heavily on its edge. Nick's two companions shifted their chairs back, not wanting to be involved in this confrontation, yet ready to enjoy the show, if there was going to be one. Nick looked boldly into the weather-beaten face glowering down at him.

'All right then, bro? Giving the missus a fancy day out then?'

'You scumbag – you must have heard about what happened last night.' Magnus's voice rose. 'But do I get any help? Do I fuck. All you care—'

Elaine stepped across swiftly and laid her hand on his arm from behind. 'Now then? Let's not have bad feeling in here, eh, lads? There's kids in here.'

Magnus turned and looked down. 'All right. Yes. All right.' He swung back round. 'Come on, you, we'll take this outside.'

'Outside? Who are you? Fucking Bruce Willis?' Nick's laugh was harsh, unamused. 'Anyway, there's nothing to talk about – far as I'm concerned.'

Magnus's arm shot across the table and he grasped his brother's shirt front. 'Out. Now.'

Nick stared hard at him, but rose from his chair, shrugging off the hand, and stepped out through the door towards the car park, his brother right behind him. Several customers stared, nodding and muttering to each other. Elaine took a cloth from her belt and started to give the small round table by the window a very good polish.

Once outside, Nick folded his arms and huddled against the drizzle and chilly wind coming in off the sea. He turned to face his brother. Elaine put down the cloth and cracked the door open a little. She realised Brenda had come up behind her and was staring silently out at the two men.

'What? What now, you miserable git?' asked Nick.

'You well know.' Magnus's fists were bunched in front of him, his face a deep red. 'I have to manage that farm all by myself. And sometimes – just sometimes – when the bad things happen, you could get off your lazy arse and give a hand. You don't give a toss about anyone but yourself.'

'Man – I didn't know—'

'Of course you knew! It was only a couple of hours before the whole damn island knew!'

Nick shrugged and Magnus moved closer. Elaine opened the door wider and stepped out. She held it tight to stop it smashing back in the wind.

'And where were you last night? Where were *you* when all this was kicking off?' Magnus went on.

'What d'you mean?' Nick unfolded his arms now and stuck his face out towards Magnus's. 'Eh?'

A fist lashed out, a pale blur caught momentarily in the dim car-park lighting. A swift jerk of the head and the rough knuckles skimmed the blond stubble.

'Stacey didn't know where you were!' Magnus shouted. 'Brenda called her.'

'Bastard!' Nick rushed in on him and they grappled, straining and grunting as their feet slipped on the gravel. Magnus was stronger, but Nick was younger, and he managed to wrong-foot his brother and push him to the ground. He stood over him.

'You need to get a life and get real!' he almost spat at him. 'You spend too much time with your livestock, you do. And what happens? They keep dying. Freaky, I call it.'

He turned and marched off, and was halfway down the road before Magnus had risen to his feet and brushed himself down, watched from behind the net curtains of the public bar by customers – some biting their lips in shock, others licking their lips in relish. Elaine opened the door wider and stepped out. She looked along the road to make sure Nick had gone, then turned to Magnus. 'Right then, perhaps you'd better get yourself home.' She headed back towards the door, where Brenda was standing, expressionless, motionless.

–

The wind whipped angrily at his hair as Nick trudged along the path which led on down between the houses, towards the sea. He reached the hut which was the centre – the official one, anyway – of his business. A tatty sign leaning against the wall announced: *All Year-Round Fishing Trips. Latest Safety and Navigational Equipment. Group Bookings at Discount.* He barged the door open. A woman in jeans and a pale pink hoodie stood with her back to him, bent over a laptop open on the rickety table. He strode up to her, put his arms round her waist and nuzzled her neck.

'Mmm. Is it good to see you!'

'That was a long lunch.'

He let go of her and turned away. 'Oh, don't start, Stace. I've not just been boozing – been fending off the attentions of my loving brother.'

She swung round and looked at him. 'Oh, Nick – you been rowing with him today of all days, have you? So what happened?'

'Nothing, nothing at all.' He leant over the computer. 'Anyway – what's new?'

'Plenty – since you went out.' She tapped some keys. 'Five more bookings for Tuesday – so that makes the boat full now. They're bringing their own rods, they said.'

Nick took out his phone and looked through it for a while. 'They'll have to take the *Lady* – the *Star*'s going to be out on another job Tuesday.'

'What other job?'

He didn't answer. Stacey turned and looked hard at him, hands on her hips.

'Nick – we need the *Star* to be out there earning us money, not skulking off—'

'Give it a rest, will you?' He slipped his phone back in his pocket. 'She'll be earning us money.'

Stacey sighed and turned to look out of the window. The tide was at its lowest, leaving acres of mud flats exposed. To the east stretched a graveyard of abandoned boats, high and dry with the sea so far out, all the rust and faded, chipped paint on view under the harsh white sky.

'Coastguard boat's been up and down again today.'

Nick came and stood alongside her and gazed out too at the flat landscape. A loose group of oystercatchers and redshanks waded gloomily amongst the frayed scraps of rope and broken plastic crates littering the foreshore.

CHAPTER TWO

Morgan Welland could hear the deep throbbing of the boat's engines, but she could see no vessel. She was never sure where the water ended and the sky began on this island. A bird soared high above the waves. Often, she became the bird. She would see with the bird's eye, spot a dark flicker in the water, size it up – gauge distance and speed – before launching into the downward plunge. The pointed beak would cut into the water so cleanly that the taut body and closely folded wings might barely be aware of the transition from one medium to the other. Those sharp eyes, fixed still on the prey, could see as clearly below the water as above. The fish would be seized and only then might the struggle begin – the need to breathe air, the struggle to breathe out of water; the need to spread the wings for movement, the need to thrust the tail through the dense water. The bird won, inevitably. It soared up above the waves, triumphant, the silvery scales of the fish glinting in the white light as it hung in a defeated arc.

Morgan sat huddled on the pebbles, exhausted by watching the struggle. At last she could see the boat, whose engines were disturbing the quiet of the beach. It was coming towards her, ploughing a white furrow through the steely waters. Not liking this intrusion, she rose, gathered up her shawl and wrapped it around her shoulders. She was eighteen but liked to dress in a way she knew other people of her age thought strange. She didn't mind. Today she had on a long, patchwork skirt, mainly black and brown, and a huge, baggy, cherry-red knitted sweater that clashed with her ginger corkscrew curls. This was all topped with an olive-green, ancient waxed jacket.

Turning her back now on the sea she started to make her way towards the road that skirted the edge of the village and led on towards the salt marsh. A trail of old, black, dried seaweed, mixed with feathers dropped from gulls and small bits of broken plastic, marked the centre of the rough path that separated the beach from the road. A scattering of people were on the pavements but none of them noticed her. This suited Morgan very well. A black and white cat on a gatepost stood up and stretched. It arched its back as she approached and invited her to stroke it. When her hand ran along its sleek back it raised its head, asking to be tickled under its chin.

As she moved on from their tacit farewell Morgan made her way past the last few straggling houses and the boarded-up carcass of the White Hart to where the road gave way to a track and then a badly trodden path leading out into the marshland. In just about the last spot where the ground was still firm enough to hold foundations, stood a small, stone cottage. She didn't need a key. The door was never locked; there was nothing worth stealing. Once inside, Morgan cast aside her jacket, pulled off her rubber boots and replaced them with her old sandals. She stoked up the stove and put the kettle on. While she waited for it she started to empty out the pockets of the tatty waxed jacket. There were several perfectly formed oval pebbles, which she added to her collection on the mantelpiece. Then there were shells of some large oysters and a couple of crabs, which she took over to the sink and washed thoroughly. She would polish them later.

Morgan took her cup of tea outside to the small garden – a tiny square of shelter from the wind. Those winds swirled bravely out over the North Sea heading for exotic, barren wastes with names that curdled on the tongue – Hurtigruten or Chechskaya – then lost their courage and swooped back in low over the mainland. They brought with them debris they scooped up on their journey and deposited a thin but steadily growing layer of sand. A monolith stood aloof in the far corner of the garden – a striated, narrow stone, a finger pointing up to the sky. She walked up to it and stroked it.

In front of the south-facing fence, which had long been bleached silver by the sun, rows and rows of clay pots stood in sheltering groups. Some contained the winter remains of recognisable herbs – thyme, parsley, rosemary, marjoram, mint – others had leaves or seedheads with a strange, alien twist to them that would have made a botanist pause, peer closer, then back off with a frown.

She perched on the back step of the house and wrapped her patchwork skirt tightly round her knees, watching her four hens who were scratching at the grass. Safe, safe for now; but for how long she could protect them, she did not know.

–

Magnus Bostock bounced the old Toyota over the last deep ruts in the lane and onto the main road. He ought to sort those out – get them filled in; but he had more on his mind than a few potholes. Brenda kept saying he never thought about her or even about himself. She said she would ask him over and over to fetch in the washing, take out the rubbish, wheel the wheelie bin down to the road on dustbin days or go to the supermarket when he was on his way back from town.

Did she say things over and over? He didn't know, really. Sometimes people's voices were coming at him through a dense blanket of cotton wool. He could hear the tone – get a vague sense of the purpose or emotion behind it – but he could not grasp the actual words. Or he would rise up from doing some mundane job, such as filling the sheep's feed tanks or drinking troughs or scraping the mud off the teeth of the cultivator, to hear her voice calling to him. And it would be as though he was under the sea with the last of the breath flowing out of his constricting lungs and his ears full of water. There were other times when he would find himself being shaken roughly by the shoulders and look down to find Brenda's sometimes anxious, but usually angry, face looking up at him.

He would find some sense of peace, on occasion, when there was nothing but him and the stock and maybe the old dog Toby and a few cawing crows over the fields and gulls swooping further out over the grey sea. One other place, one alone, brought him any tiny relief from the swirling confusions of his mind, and that was when he visited his grandmother at Laurel Dene.

He never liked the drive up the hedge-lined approach to the large, Victorian red-brick building. The neat flowerbeds and sloping lawn, the drooping figures in wheelchairs with rugs over their laps all depressed him. And the nurses and carers would always want to chat – to talk about the weather or small changes to his grandmother's medication. But Magnus was never keen to linger in the pale-green corridors with their smell of boiled beef and toilet cleaner; he preferred to head straight up the stairs to his grandmother's room.

Once there, he would flop into the spare armchair. Grandma was the only person who would simply let him be. Dorothea Bostock would not force him to chatter and she was not one for small talk herself. She would make him a cup of coffee and open the tin of ginger nuts. Today, however, the coffee tasted of cat's pee and the biscuit stuck in his throat. He put it down.

'We've had more trouble up at the farm.'

Dorothea looked up sharply. 'What is it? What's happened now?'

Magnus slumped in his chair and put his head in his hands, then ran his fingers through his hair.

'Eight sheep – ripped apart. Spread all over the field.'

Dorothea folded her hands in her lap and looked across at him with deep concern. 'Did you call the police in?'

'Yes, I called the police and yes, they're looking into it.'

'No need to take that tone with me!'

'I'm sorry… I'm sorry, it's just that—'

'They may even be able to help if they can find some connection with the other times.'

'They won't.'

Dorothea pushed herself up from her chair, made her way stiffly to the window and closed it. 'This can't go on, Magnus. It mustn't.'

'I know that!'

They sat in silence for a while, Dorothea staring at her hands folded in her lap, Magnus staring out of the window. Then she remembered something. She rose again, pushing down hard on the arms of the chair to lever herself out. She grasped her stick and made her way over to the little desk. From the drawer she took a letter. 'I received this.'

Magnus straightened up and turned round to see what she was holding.

She took the letter from its envelope. 'It's from someone at the University of Manchester. A historian. She's coming here to look into' – she sniffed and looked again at the letter – 'family background. Of families descended from officers in the Army at the time of the Indian Mutiny.'

'What?'

'I shan't speak to her, of course.'

They talked a little longer, then Magnus drove back towards the farm. The tide was approaching its high point and the causeway to the island was already awash with an inch or so of water, heavy with salt and sand. He paused at the fork in the road:

the right turn would take him down towards the farm – home and Brenda. The road to the left veered round past St Cedd village and on down to the cove where his brother's hut stood and from where he ran his fishing-trip business. *So-called fishing trip business*, thought Magnus bitterly. A lorry, which had come up behind him unnoticed, blasted its horn and stung Magnus into making a decision. He thrust the gear lever into first and swung the wheel to the left.

–

Nick gripped the phone and ground his teeth.

'I can't get out there by tomorrow night, man, it's not possible.' The voice was angry on the other end of the line – insistent and threatening.

'Fuck you, Rokesmith. Just fuck you. I'm not doing it,' Nick said. He pressed End Call and threw the phone down angrily on the desk. Then picked it up again and switched it off. He stood staring at the floor for a moment, then grabbed up his jacket and headed out of the door. A trace of after-sunset light lingered in the wide sky. A bland concrete wall, five feet high, separated the path from the beach. He stared across the hundred yards or so of sand dunes, pitted with prickly sea holly and sharp grasses. The coarse sand whispered angrily under his boots as he ploughed his way forward, heading for the shoreline. He needed to breathe. He needed to clear his head. His feet sank into the softer sand as he approached the water's edge. What was there for him on this godforsaken island? He looked up at the abyss above him, then out to sea, which was just as endless – never-bloody-ending. Why had he stayed?

Simply because he was born here – and all Bostocks had been, since Christ knows when – wasn't a need to stay. In fact – a good reason to get away. New Zealand. He liked watching programmes about New Zealand. Looked like a fun place. But there was still sea all round it. And though sea meant his living, his boats – he couldn't stay away from it. It was bad. Plenty of ships had gone down off these beaches back in the old days. Sometimes the sandbanks got them, sometimes the heavy seas and rip tides. Staring at the black waters that lapped at the shingle, it was as though he could hear the desperate cries of men tumbling off the splintered wrecks of their ships, see their arms and legs flailing against the malevolent water that wanted to suck them down into its depths.

And it didn't stop at wanting to destroy people who dared to go out onto the water. Every year it licked away at the land. It was snide, insidious, it crept up on you without you noticing. It played Grandmother's Footsteps so that every time you glanced back it looked so benign, with its gentle, little, white waves. But the minute you turned away they turned into snarling beasts that wanted to eat up more and more of what lay before them.

He should get away from the sea – and away from Patrick Rokesmith and away from his dismal brother, Magnus. Why did he have to be such a fucking misery?

Nick knew he himself had always been the cocky one – the one who didn't know the meaning of the word fear. As he stood staring out to sea there were the pinpoint flashing lights of some distant boat. But what he was seeing had happened way back in the past. He could picture Magnus standing on the front lawn of the old house, thumb in his mouth, other hand to his ear. One of Nick's earliest memories was of sitting on one of those little wooden bikes, the sort that had two pairs of coloured wheels, and zooming down the drive at Slegholm Farm, where he and Magnus lived with their grandparents. It was a long drive, the size of a mountain to a three-year-old. The very end part was dead steep and curving as it swept down towards the road. Magnus would watch wide-eyed as Nick rattled past him, pushing hard, getting up as much speed as he could. Nick loved the rush – always had – still did. When he got to the bottom of the drive he would twist the bike sideways, onto the narrow country pavement, and come to a halt before the slow business of getting it back to the top of the slope.

He could remember still how surprised he felt at the reaction of the grown-ups – when they finally stopped their chatting, came out of the house and realised what he was doing. How they had snatched him up, cuddled and scolded him, and taken the bike away, and how Magnus continued to stand on the lawn, watching and silent. He had always been like that – older, slower, heavier – but above all, envious.

Why Magnus filled his thoughts so much now, he didn't know. It was partly that stupid fight outside the pub; partly these freaky happenings at night-time. When it was only the odd cat or shedful of chickens that got mauled it wasn't too weird. But big dogs? Flocks of sheep? And now Slegholm seemed to be getting it worse than most. Magnus, as usual, did what he did best – being a victim and just brooding about it.

Nick started back over the sand towards the hut, yet the moment it came in sight he also saw his brother's old Toyota approaching, leaving a dust cloud in its wake. *Oh, not now. Give us a break.* He looked around him and for a moment almost considered running away. But the sloping expanse of damp sand, marram grass and low jagged rocks he saw before him offered no hiding place. He went inside. The car door slammed and Magnus stomped towards him, obviously squaring up for a fight. *Oh, well.*

However, the first thing his brother did when he entered the hut was to cross to one of the chairs by the desk and sit down. He slumped forward and rubbed his face with his hands. *No fight for the moment, then.*

'I've been over to see Grandma.'

Nick stuck his hands in his pockets and looked up at the ceiling.

'It's a pity you don't get out there and visit a bit more often,' his brother carried on. 'She's an old woman. She's not well.'

'Huh! She's still tough as old boots. And what's the good of me going to see her? What are we going to say? Eh? *Eh?*'

'She's a very old woman,' Magnus repeated, but with a tone of resignation.

So this was it, was it? The time had finally arrived when she could be considered so frail that no argument with her was worth pursuing; no resentment worth harbouring; no revenge worth wreaking. All past events could be forgotten as though they had never happened – simply because Magnus had decided that Grandma was now officially "old".

'I'll see her if I want to – whenever that might be. I can do without the extra hassle right now, for God's sake!' Nick kicked the plastic chair so that it slammed hard against the desk. His brother had no fight left in him, nor was he interested in whatever trouble Nick might have got himself into now. He rose slowly to his feet and without raising his head or looking at Nick he stumbled outside to his truck.

As the Toyota bounced back towards the main road Nick stood in the doorway and shouted after it: 'I didn't have to come back here! I'm not stuck in this place – not like some people!' And, sure, he had been away from St Cedd – for short periods – a few months here and there in London, Stevenage, Birmingham. Yet he'd always come back – drawn by the ties he had here, by links stronger than himself, and by the sea. This time he'd get himself out of this mess with Rokesmith and when he'd done that he'd leave for good.

But in the meantime he had things to do, so he grabbed up his phone, wallet and jacket and strode out of the hut.

CHAPTER THREE

Magnus walked out into the yard and watched Brenda heave open the door of the barn. The rotting wood dragged on the uneven concrete floor as it always did and she kicked at the base of it, as she always did. She was a big woman, not tall, but solid. She had broad shoulders, but rounded, as though borne down by some relentless weight. Her clothes were drab: stained waterproof jacket and shapeless brown woollen trousers tucked into rubber boots. She wore no gloves and her large hands were patched with rough skin and angry red blotches. Her face bore little expression. It was a round face, the skin uncared for, the eyes small, and was topped by short wiry hair that had once been long and luxuriant. A few years ago, he used to love running his hands through her hair. He watched her take a metal bucket and plunge it into the bunker of chicken feed. She straightened as she heard Baltasar call out a greeting as he arrived in the yard. She turned towards him, clamped her thin lips tightly together and nodded.

Magnus Bostock was worried about the silage. He and the one everyone called 'the Dutch boy', Baltasar – who had to be at least fifty – were going to check the silage containers, unsure whether there was enough feed to see them through the rest of the winter. He needed some thick gloves; there were definitely some in the tool barn, though he hadn't used them for a while. It was dim inside and he had trouble seeing what was tucked away in corners. He moved about, searching in boxes and bags. As he straightened up, a glint of something shiny caught his eye. Hanging up on a row of hooks on the far wall was a collection of hand tools no one ever seemed to use. They had been there probably since his grandfather's day – or even longer – so long that he never looked at them anymore. And yet there was a silvery gleam, a flash of shiny steel, amongst them. He walked over to the row of tools and took the implement down. He didn't know if he'd seen it before or not. It was the strangest thing: a shortish, wooden handle, worn smooth and grey over what must have been many years; an iron shank emerging from it, which divided into two narrow, vicious-looking prongs that curved as semicircles, ending in sharp points. Parts of it, towards the handle, were encrusted with rust; nearer the points, though, the metal shone clean and fresh.

'Boss.' Magnus turned. Baltasar stood in the doorway, his bulky silhouette blocking the light. For a long moment the two men stared at each other. 'We are going, yes?' said Balt eventually.

Magnus hung the tool back where he had found it. He gave up the hunt for gloves and followed Balt across the yard to the tractor. They were about to get in when they heard the shouting. Both turned to see Brenda striding towards them, waving a newspaper. Everything about her announced that she was angry and they swapped a nervous glance before Magnus stepped forward to meet her. Baltasar busied himself with checking the bolts on the back of the trailer.

'Worse than we feared,' said Brenda. 'The bastards have given them permission. Can't believe it.'

'Who's given what?'

'I said all along – didn't I? When they bought that field. They'd fill it up with their poxy tincans. Let those horrible screaming children run riot. Dumping their rubbish, tramping our crops. And those damn dogs running loose – barking and barking.'

Magnus turned towards the north, where a thin row of trees and the slope of the land hid the caravan site. But he knew it was there. They all knew it was there. It spread across the flat landscape, defying the gentle roll and curves of the land with its harsh, rectangular vans in unnaturally neat rows; the concrete bunker of a clubhouse. He took the newspaper, looked at the article. The picture was flattering. Little window boxes full of flowers softened the lines of the caravans; small children with bikes and trikes smiled up at the camera; a smiling dad stood nearby laden with buckets and spades. One field – Archie's Piece, they'd always called it – separated the caravan site from Slegholm Farm. This field had lain fallow for years. The old man who owned it had died, and Magnus and Brenda thought it had been inherited by daughters who lived in Birmingham. Brenda was always nagging him to try to find out who owned it now. But he didn't know where to start. And anyway, it was dry, thin soil that would take a lot of effort to bring up to scratch.

And now, according to the article in the paper, the Langeveldt family, who owned the caravan site, had bought Archie's Piece.

'They'll never get permission,' Magnus had said. 'Not for change of use.' Though he hadn't really believed that himself. He had been to a parish meeting when Ethan Langeveldt had bought the site a few years back and was outlining his plans. A tall South African, with an easy way of impressing people with his bold faith in his own abilities and obvious belief that those around him would fall in with his plans, he had won over the parish council. Magnus took against him from the beginning. Cocky bugger, was his verdict. Langeveldt would bring jobs for local people, he said, though that turned out to be little more than hiring a few local teenagers in their holidays. His own wife Margie ran the shop on the site. In their defence, they did clamp down heavily on littering and loud music, and were very firm about who they allowed in: families and couples only was the rule. No single-sex groups – so no stag or hen dos – and no groups of teenagers without their parents. Every evening in the high season Langeveldt would patrol the site on a quad bike with a powerful flashlight, flanked by his three Rottweilers, who barked constantly. Though Magnus hated to think that any living beast should suffer pain or violent death, he'd not felt much sorrow when he'd heard that one of those dogs had been found in a ditch, its throat slashed open. A horrible way to go for any creature; but why shouldn't Langeveldt suffer too?

And now, according to the paper, Langeveldt had bought Archie's Piece. Caravans would be right up to their fences.

Once the silage was checked, Magnus drove the tractor and trailer up towards the top field. He could feed the sheep and fill up the water tanks and still have time, just, to mend the broken fence before dark.

His mind wandered as he drove. His brother Nick didn't give a toss about anything. Nick hated the farm. He had walked out when he was sixteen and lived in bedsits – took on any dodgy job that came his way. So it was down to him alone, Magnus, to keep the place afloat.

And for what? He didn't have a son to pass it on to. Nor a daughter. And the pain of that thought brought the feelings it always brought, of a fist clenching round his heart.

Although he'd done it a million times, for some reason today, perhaps because his mind wasn't on the job, he took the gate into the field much too fast and steeply, and jammed the wheel of the trailer against the metal gatepost. *Bugger, bugger, bugger.* The wheel was badly mangled. He'd have to unhook the tractor and drive all the way back to the yard to pick up some tools, find the other trailer and bring back Balt to give him a hand.

He stood leaning on the post for a minute and stared up the hill at the low sun in the west. He used to love this time of day – making sure the animals were fed and watered and safe before night fell.

But now, nothing felt safe. Every morning he dreaded waking up to hear that some other awful thing had happened in the night. He had no one to turn to who really seemed to understand the horror of it.

He uncoupled the trailer, climbed back into the tractor and reached out to start the engine. But instead he closed his eyes and let his head drop forward, feeling like the last man left to bail out a sinking boat.

–

Down at the Dog and Whistle, Elaine had been cursing the bad weather, her truculent son and the lazy barman.

'Come on, Dave – get some glasses washed, can't you?'

'Not much point,' her shaven-headed, so-called assistant replied. 'Not exactly many punters in.'

Elaine gave up on the bottle of Bell's she was trying and failing to fit into the optic. She strode to the foot of the stairs. 'Alex! *Alex!* Are you out of that bed yet?'

Silence from above. After a moment she started to climb the stairs. There were three unpainted doors on the landing, and Elaine rattled the handle of one of them for a moment before turning it and flinging open the door. The warning had not been needed – her son was an immobile mass under the heap of black duvet.

'For God's sake, Alex, it's gone twelve o'clock.' She stumbled over the discarded clothes on the floor as she made her way to the window and pulled the curtains open.

'And it stinks in here,' she added, struggling with the rarely used window catch. Eventually she won and as she pushed the window outwards a stream of cold air, heavy with drizzle, weaved its way into the fug.

'No! Shut it…' came a muffled mumble from the bedclothes.

'I'm warning you, Alex, even if you don't go to school that doesn't mean you can stay in bed all day! There's stuff to be done, I could really do with a hand—'

'Oh, give it a rest—'

'No, I won't give it a rest! You spend nearly all your time in here – you never talk to anyone, you're always on that computer,' she pointed at the laptop on the floor from which a faint white light pulsed, 'and then you go off out at all odd times of the night—'

'All right, all right!' The duvet was heaved aside. Elaine glared at the skinny youth with dark, spiky hair and very pale skin who slowly emerged.

She folded her arms and watched him rub his eyes and blink in the unaccustomed light. She turned away. 'I'll be downstairs.'

She went back into the bar, grabbed up a cloth and started polishing glasses vigorously. The cat, Jaggers, hightailed out of her way. The lacklustre barman glanced across at her then inched further away. That job at Maccy D's was looking more appealing by the minute.

A large man emerged from the gents and came up to the bar, shirt buttons bulging over a paunch, his too-short tie a bit skewed. *Some sort of rep*, Elaine thought, *probably spends most of his day in his car.*

'What can I get you?'

'I'll have a pint of Guinness, please, love.'

She grasped the handle and started to pull. The guy had wandered over to the fruit machine – he knew how long it took to pour a pint of Guinness. How much of her life had she spent pulling pints? She didn't even want to think of that. As she poured she found herself gazing up at the cobwebs above the door to the gents. How had she come to this – without really noticing? This godforsaken island, which had become her home and where she had brought up her child, had seemed thrilling when she first came. Its flatness and wildness – the long beaches and the endless horizons were new to her. Truth to tell she'd never strayed far from

Peckham. Gone to school, gone to college. Then some of the girls had said about this folk festival in Essex. Folk? But then, when her friend Maz had added that there was this boy with a camper van who was going to take them all, she'd agreed.

And when she saw it, yellow and orange, probably painted that way to cover up the rust – but who cared? – and she saw him, Jeff Maple, well, that was it. He had flung open the door of the van and jumped down. *Wow.* Nirvana tee shirt. Floppy hair. Grungy.

Then he spoke: 'Hey, doll.'

That just creased her up.

She'd loved that journey. They were going somewhere new. Jeff had wanted her to sit on the bench seat beside him. There were three of them in the front, so every time he changed gear his arm had to rub against her thigh. And she loved his lanky blond hair, his tattoos.

When the clapped-out van finally got them to Essex, they had gone to a campsite – long gone now – and rented a pair of static caravans; not on the side of the site nearest the sea, but handy for the main road and the toilet block. This was back in 1985, or was it '86? John Martyn and Big Muff and The Pogues and Loudon Wainwright III were all playing. She hadn't heard of any of them. She was more into Dedringer and Iron Maiden. In fact, she might still have some of them on vinyl stashed away somewhere in the attic.

Elaine looked at the glass. Nearly full, but she'd need to let it stand for a minute for some of the head to go down. The customer was still at the fruit machine.

She and her friends Jess, Maz and Steph had been in one caravan. It was a bit crowded. Jess and Elaine were sharing the double bed and there was a lot of smirking about that. The other two were in bunk beds designed for kids. Steph took a picture of Maz climbing the ladder in her very short skirt and said later that when she went to collect the photos from Boots the man behind the counter frowned at her over his glasses. No Instagram in those days. Good thing too, probably.

They'd had a good laugh there. On their second night they'd taken some ciders down to the beach. It was the early days of a heatwave; a balmy, moonlit night. Yet as she stood on the shingle, gazing out at the blackness that was the sea, she felt the mournful bleakness of the place. And it drew her to it. It wasn't Peckham.

The campsite was amazing: loads of young people, no boring old farts. But it wasn't till the next day, after a night on the beach – a night of ciders and snogging and star-gazing – that Jeff told her that this was where he came from.

'Here?'

The Guinness was ready; the customer wandered back over and paid for it and took it to a table.

She leant on the bar and went back to her thoughts. Yes, she had asked the question, 'Does anyone actually live here? Does anything happen here?' And now, for the last twenty years or more, she had lived here. Was it ironic or was it just life that found her running the pub not half a mile from that beach, pulling pints? And where was he? Long gone.

The door opened from the car park and Nick Bostock walked in. He shrugged his jacket off as he came up to the bar. 'Hi, Elaine.'

'Hello there, Nick.' She flashed a quick smile. 'What'll you have?'

'Oh, just a half of Skippers.'

She started filling a glass. 'There's some of your crew-mates over in the Snug,' nodding her head towards the corner.

'Oh, right – yeah, I need to see them.' He took his drink and headed away from the bar.

The two men he wanted to speak to were nursing pints in a quiet, dim corner.

'Hi, Matt… Kev.'

They looked up and nodded at Nick as he pulled up a chair.

'How's tricks?'

They both grunted in reply, then: 'I can do both the trips on Sunday and Tuesday, Nick,' said the older of the two – a big, bony-headed man whose lined, leathery face indicated years spent on the deck of a boat. 'Is the *Lady* fit to go?'

'Eh? Oh, yeah, she's fine – just needs cleaning out a bit. And there's seven rods booked to come – five of them bringing their own gear. We've had them before. You can do some cleaning up in the morning, can't you, Matt? Get down there by eight, if you can get your sorry arse out of bed.'

The other man, young and skinny with a long, mournful face, looked affronted. 'Course I can.'

Nick drank from his glass. 'There's something else.' He leant forward and told them his problem.

Kev started shaking his head before Nick had even finished. 'I don't want no more to do with this.' He shifted in his seat. 'It's getting far too dodgy. It ain't worth it, man.'

Despite Nick's pleadings, he would not shift his stance.

'I know about fishing, Nick. That's all I know about and all I want to know about. My missus ain't at all happy—'

'What d'you want to go talking to her about it for? I'll bet she's happy enough to get the extra money.'

Kev shook his head, still not meeting Nick's eye. 'No,' he said firmly. 'No. You'll have to find someone else to help that Rokesmith with his dirty work.'

Nick was frowning now into his glass. He glanced up at the other man. 'Matt?'

'Sure, I'm up for it – no worries. But can we manage… just the two of us? I'll want a bigger cut, mind.'

Nick took a deep breath. 'Rokesmith's really coming on strong.' That was a bit of an understatement; Rokesmith had too much on him – too much leverage. He sat back. 'Yes, we can manage. We'll just have to be firm with them, get them moving fast. No arguments, no faffing around.' They arranged when and where to meet, and Nick left the pub.

As he walked back down the lane towards the harbour, the sun was low on the horizon; a few red streaks spilling across the sky suggested a dramatic sunset to come. The tide was getting high and he pushed off from the jetty in a tired little rowing boat to reach the *Lady*. She was pulling on her anchor and listing slightly. Nick climbed aboard and started to sort out a tangle of ropes on the deck. The *Lady* was an Aquastar 33 and her turbo diesel engine was running well, he knew, but the wheelhouse was a mess. He'd need to clear out a load of junk to make room for God knows how many passengers. He sat down and started to coil a rope.

Looking across at the shore in the fading light he noticed a shadowy figure with long, corkscrew curls that drifted on the breeze. She wore vague, floaty garments and was standing staring out over the water.

CHAPTER FOUR

Morgan had been there since the tide was low, when the knots had been down on the mud flats. They were searching for small molluscs, crustaceans and worms; each of them probing the mud, then running a few steps and probing again. As the tide rose the flock had taken to the skies – wheeling, twisting and turning. Her eyes were now fixed on one bird. It was slightly smaller than the others, flashing from dark to pale as the dying sun caught its pale underwings.

This display at dusk, a show of strength in numbers, took place every evening the knots were on these shores. Morgan knew she would have to say goodbye to them soon when it was time for them to return to the lands where they would breed, far away in the Arctic. Until then, she would carry on loving it, loving imagining the feel of the wind through her feathers, the soft warmth of the rising air and the companionship of the sisters and brothers. They circled in unison, collectively enjoying the feel of a full-enough stomach and the approaching end of another day.

As she stared, Morgan's body started to sway and her shoulders rolled, one way then the other, with the wheeling and diving of the flock. With the keen eye of a bird she could make out every detail of the last band of muddy shore as it was lapped by the incoming water. The bird she was watching, with its grey and white wings fully extended, her head steady and long, her waders' legs stretched out behind, swooped and turned in tune with the others, relishing the swirl of the rising thermal stream.

Then gradually, as the sun spread itself wider, as it prepared to sink below the distant fields, one of them would take the initiative and dive gracefully down towards the roosting ground. The others – in one and twos, then dozens and scores – would follow, until the whole flock was settled for the night.

The smaller bird, the one Morgan was watching, was among the last to turn and descend, and as she did she swerved towards the motionless figure of the young woman waiting. Finally, she settled.

Morgan came to herself, as she always did, unhurt but cold right through to her heart. It was almost dark and she knew that this time she had been gone for quite a while. It must be getting worse. But as she climbed stiffly to her feet her greatest fear was not of breaking bones or freezing to death or drowning. No, it was of what she did while her mind was gone, or her body was gone – she couldn't really work out which it was. Her fingertips and nails might be ripped – bleeding. She bit her lip as she looked at these quivering fingers now, but they were simply muddy.

–

By the time Nick got back to the road, the sun had gone down and the streetlamps struggled to break through the murky darkness. He walked quickly along Western Road and into the Co-op. The bright, stark lights made him wince and the chill cabinets, humming and emitting a low, white mist, made him shiver. He picked up a six-pack of beers and waited in the queue behind a large woman. She looked like she was buying one of every type of chocolate bar you could get, and when it was her turn at the till she unloaded them one by one. *For Christ's sake, get a bloody move on, can't you?* he thought. He shifted from foot to foot, staring at her broad backside. He had the urge to tell her she didn't need to eat more sweets but stayed silent. It wasn't worth the bother. Her basket was topped off with a bunch of deep-pink carnations. *Nice fucking touch.*

It was completely dark by the time he got to the flat. The faint aroma of soap powder mingling with mould filled the stairwell, as always. When he opened the door he could smell onions and bacon frying.

Stacey was stabbing at the pan with a spatula. She glanced over her shoulder, then turned back to her cooking. 'I suppose you're hungry.'

It was never a question, so he didn't bother answering. He just wished that sometimes, when he walked through the door, she would come up to him with a smile on her face and give him a big hug. She used to have such a cheeky grin. But then he supposed he wasn't a barrel of laughs these days, either. He slumped on the sofa and cracked a can.

'I'm having a right load of trouble with Kev and Matt. Bloody useless, the pair of them. Need to find some more help – someone with a bit more balls.' He took a swig and looked over at her. 'Nearly ready, is it?'

Stacey slammed down the frying pan and put her hands over her face. He sat up a bit straighter and looked at her as she went into the tiny bathroom. *Oh, Christ – what now?* She came back with a white plastic stick; he ducked as she threw it at him. He picked it up and stared.

'Yeah… and there's some people around here with too much balls,' she shouted. 'Bloody positive this time. No doubt.'

'Fuck.'

'Is that all you can say? Eh? *Eh?* She was shrieking now. 'How we gonna manage, Nick? No sooner we have a bit of money come in, you're off spending it on God knows what! There's no space for a baby in here...' She looked round in despair at the room. The off-white walls were dotted with faint, rectangular, paler patches – the ghosts of pictures taken down by previous occupants. The sofa, which still bore the imprint of its original blue and grey diamond pattern, worn away now by years of different arms rubbing on it, different bodies thrashing in urgent sex, sagged unhappily. The fitted carpet was the colour of rusted iron. Only at its edges, where it bulged against the walls, did it show signs of its original pale orange. The two upright wooden chairs failed to match each other or the table.

Nick stood up, staring at her, through her. He lifted his arms, then dropped them. Whatever he said, it would be wrong.

She swung away and stormed over to the window and gazed up into the darkness. Then she leant forward as the lights of a car below caught her eye. 'Oh, Christ, Nick, that's all we need. What you done now?'

'What d'you mean?'

'Fucking pigs. Coming up the stairs.'

Nick jumped to his feet, put his hands to his head and looked around. 'Bloody hell!' No time now to flush anything down the toilet.

Stacey looked hard at him as she marched to the door, which she wrenched open just as the constable was raising his hand to knock.

'Come in, why don't you?' She left the door wide open, stared again at Nick and stomped off into the bedroom, slamming the door.

'Mr Bostock? Nicholas Bostock?'

'Yes.' Nick thrust his hands in the pockets of his jeans.

'It's about last Tuesday night.' The policeman stepped in. He was as tall as Nick and looked him squarely in the face. 'We were wondering if you could shed any light on what happened?'

'Er… Tuesday?' Nick's mind was racing.

'The incident on your brother's farm. Several sheep were killed, with a great deal of violence.'

'Oh… ah, yes.' Nick sank down onto the sofa, trying to look concerned rather than relieved. The policeman took the chair opposite and pulled out his notebook. His boots were dull, with mud drying round the edges. Looked like he'd had a long day, too.

'So if you could tell me if you were over there that night? If you saw or heard anything?'

'What? I never go there.'

'Never? You don't visit your own brother?'

Stacey flung open the bedroom door, marched forward and thrust her face at the officer's. 'He weren't up there that night. He never goes there. Get that? There might be something wicked on this island – some fucking nutter out there – but he's not in this flat!'

–

Morgan looked down to find the waters lapping at her bare feet. She put her sandals back on and made her way up to the road. The streetlamps cast orange punctuation marks at regular intervals along the pavement. In the distance she could see the neon welcome of the Co-op, but she turned the other way. The road curved away from the shore, the space between taken up by the widening dunes, which swelled and dipped, the sea no longer visible beyond them. Morgan paused, thinking she had caught sight of a vague movement amongst the sand and grasses. The distant roar of a motorbike faded away and in the following silence she could just make out a faint moaning.

If it were an animal in pain she would not have hesitated to run over, to comfort, straighten out a damaged wing, stroke an injured paw. Yet this looked human, even though the keening rising from it was anything but. She moved a little closer to the huddled figure. It was outlined as a darker silhouette against the charcoal sky and was swaying backwards and forwards. Closer still, now, she could make out a black jacket with the collar pulled up high, and black, spiky hair poking out above. The figure shifted slightly and she glimpsed the dull shine of a blade, glistening in his hands.

She had long known there was evil on St Cedd. She had only the faintest suspicion of where it originated and what form it took, but what she did know was that this tormented person would do her no harm. She went closer.

'Who are you?' she asked in a low voice. The swaying stopped; the moaning stopped. The blade was slowly lowered to the sand and the boy turned his head and looked up at her. His black eyes stared into her face. The pain in them pierced her, tearing her between wanting to turn and flee so that she would not have to look at that anguish – and wanting to take him in her arms and rock him until the hurt went away.

Again, she asked him who he was and this time he seemed to understand.

'Alex… my name's Alex.'

'I'm Morgan.'

Then she realised she knew him. She remembered him from school, even though he was a year or two below her. He had stood out – a loner, with stark, pale skin and hair black as a raven. She sat down cross-legged beside him and pulled the shawl tighter round her shoulders. They both looked out towards the sea – invisible but for occasional glimpses of phosphorescence as each wave broke in its unstoppable rhythm. The low sea mist drifted in and covered the pair of them with tiny droplets of dampness.

'What've you done, Alex?'

'Nothing.' He turned to her, his eyes begging for understanding. 'I don't know… I don't know.'

Morgan nodded. There was nothing strange in this to her. They sat on in silence for a long time. The presence of another body beside his seemed to calm him down a little. His sobbing reduced to the occasional sniff, then he said, 'I found it. It wasn't me. I found it.' He clattered the knife onto the pebbles and it skidded away. 'It was by the cat.' He shuddered violently. 'It was horrible… ripped open.'

'A cat?'

'Yeah, another one. There's been quite a few, I've heard. Cats – even one or two dogs – just slashed open in the night. You not heard?'

Morgan stared in front of her, into the blackness.

'First one I've seen myself,' he went on. 'Horrible.'

Morgan started to shiver in the cold night air. She shook herself and sat up straight. 'Come on. You need to go home. Where do you live?'

He wiped his nose. 'At the Dog.'

'Come on then, you. Back to the Dog.' She rose and helped him to stand, put her arm round his waist and guided him over the dunes to the road. Together they walked the deserted streets until they came to the pub, where she watched him as he slipped in through the back door.

Morgan made her way home, but with a new wariness in her step. She found herself glancing down side streets, avoiding the darkest of the shadows and starting at every tiny sound. She knew the feeling of being the only person on the move while the whole of the rest of the world was cocooned in sleep. She was often out at what other people called odd hours. She relished the freedom – being able to open her arms and her face up to the infinite darkness of the sky, to see the stars, to hear the sounds of the night. And tonight, as always, there were plenty of noises. Cats, certainly, out on their nocturnal business, far removed from the lap-sitting and purring that occupied them during the days and evenings; foxes sniffing around after the odd pizza crust that had missed the wheelie bin; small rodents scuffling for a snack in the fallen leaves. She had always loved it – for her it was the best time. But tonight she jumped at vague shadows, turned suddenly to look behind her, feeling that she was not alone – though whether it was man or beast out there she did not know. It was more just a sensation of lingering menace.

The dampness in the air turned to a fine drizzle. She raised her face and relished the soft coolness of it. It wasn't long, however, before the drizzle turned to a steady fall and then a heavy downpour. The wind rose and slashed it into her face. She broke into a run, the ends of her shawl flying out behind her. As she careered into the lane leading to her cottage she flung back her head, spread her arms wide and yelled at the riot of the sky.

She plunged through the door and ran to the fireplace. Kindling and logs were arranged ready; she struck a match with a flourish and set it to the balls of paper underneath. She dragged the soaked shawl off her shoulders as she climbed the narrow, creaking staircase to the bedroom. She would have undressed and put on PJs, but the feeling of another presence, of a watcher, was still with her, so she just pulled on a fleece on top of her other clothes.

Back downstairs, she hung a pan of water on the hook above the fire. She opened the fridge and remembered she should have done some shopping. She hesitated, then reached for the umbrella that stood in the corner by the back door. The wind and rain were as fierce as ever, but Morgan knew the path well to the rickety henhouse down the garden. She opened its door and the four Lincolnshire Buffs blinked at her from their perches. It seemed they too had not been sleeping but were staying on guard, waiting for the safety of the dawn. She felt inside the nesting box until her fingers closed round a warm egg, ran back up the garden and plopped it into the simmering water.

CHAPTER FIVE

THE SHEEP RAISED THEIR HEADS AND STARED AT MAGNUS AS he shoved open the gate with a clang. They had been fed early on by Brenda, but they seemed to prefer the way Magnus doled out the nuts, so they started ambling down the field towards him. He looked them over as they gathered round the trough. They weren't looking too bad, all things considered. He looked around – so many jobs to do – and he'd already lost more than half a day. He strode back to the yard, yanked the trailer out of the old barn and dragged it over to the tractor. Roughly, he forced the coupling together and swore as he caught his hand. The dog, Toby, backed away, whining, then slunk away to lie down in a corner.

Magnus had a few words with Balt then climbed up into the cab. The engine turned over reluctantly but failed to start. He thumped the steering wheel over and over till his fists ached, then buried his face in his hands. The dog shifted a few feet across the dusty yard to follow the sun and fell asleep again. Eventually, Magnus raised himself up, rubbed his face and ran his hands over his head. Enough. He turned the key and the engine started straightaway.

The tractor turned and bumped over the rough concrete out of the yard gate and up the lane to the twelve-acre field. He stopped it near the gate and loaded up the pile of fence posts that were waiting for him there – had been waiting a long time, as the grass and brambles growing up amongst them testified.

Maybe he should look to all his boundaries, get them properly secured, then the night visits might stop and he wouldn't have to be on edge all the time. His mind wouldn't be such a swirling mess of worries. He was sweating heavily now as he loaded up the last of the posts. He slammed up the tailgate of the trailer and rested his forearms on it, sinking his head onto them. *Christ. Too much to think about – always too much.* And as he climbed wearily back into the cab he could hear his mother's distant voice, from years back, crying, 'Louise! Lulu!' And he, though not much more than a toddler, had heard and started to echo her voice. 'Lulu? Lulu?' he would sing.

Lulu had been his name for her; he was so young when she was born that he found it hard to pronounce Louise. The rest of the family had adopted it – even though they were not the sort of people to favour nicknames. But Louise was different. For all of them she was just a memory. She never had time to become real. Now the name filled his mind in a confusion of hazy memories – false or true he did not know; rumour and half-whispered suggestions from women with blank faces standing in corners of rooms.

Up at the field, as he placed the first post in its hole and began to hammer it into the stony ground with the heavy mallet, the name seemed to echo over and over in time to his strokes – Lulu. Lulu. Lulu.

–

Elaine was on the phone to the brewery and she was not happy. 'First you tell me this morning, then you tell me this afternoon for sure, I'm running very low. You people need to get your act together!' She listened impatiently to the excuses on the other end of the line, excuses which seemed to be changing every two minutes. First a sick driver, then the clutch on the lorry going, then a mixed-up order. She gave up, slammed the phone down and walked through to the bar. Dave was still clearing up the last glasses from lunchtime and giving the tables a desultory wipe with a grubby cloth.

'Oh, for goodness' sake!' she exclaimed, and took the cloth from him, went into the kitchen and rinsed it out, then strode back into the bar and started scrubbing furiously at the tables. Dave pulled a face and made himself scarce in the kitchen, loading up the glass washer. Though her teeth were clamped tight with the strain, her head ached and she was tired already, she couldn't help thinking: *Wise lad.* That Dave knew when it was best just to keep quiet and that this was one of those times. A door slammed upstairs and Alex stomped down and joined Dave in the kitchen.

'All right?' she heard Dave ask him.

''Spose. You?'

'Your mum's in a right strop.'

'Huh. Tell me something new.'

'Ha!'

Though she couldn't see him from the bar, Elaine knew that Alex would be opening the fridge, staring into it and taking out orange juice, butter and a lump of cheese, and heading for the breadbin.

'You off out tonight?' Dave went on.

'Maybe. Might just stay in. Catch up on *Stranger Things*.'

'Yeah. Not much to go out for round here. Unless you've got a girlfriend?'

No answer.

Elaine went in and both boys fell silent. Dave closed up the glass washer and set it off. Alex slapped some pickle on his bread and started piling on chunks of cheese. She took a breath to launch into the automatic tirade relating to what sort of time did he think this was to get up; if he was around at proper times he would get proper meals; had he put his dirty clothes into the laundry basket or was she supposed to go round picking them up off his bedroom floor and how was she supposed to do that if she was banned from his bedroom? But she let the breath out slowly. She couldn't be bothered.

'I'm going out,' she announced. 'I'll be back in time for opening up.' They both nodded. She went upstairs and put on some lip gloss and brushed her hair, then left the pub.

It took her a quarter of an hour to reach Suzanne's house. It was a small semi, but in the garden stood the large shed Suzanne used as a studio. Elaine went straight there.

'Anyone in?' she called.

'Hello there.' Suzanne appeared at the door of the shed, wiping her hands on a rag. They had a hug and Elaine stood back and looked at her friend. She was small and neat with short, wavy, dark hair with the ends tinted pink and an elfin face – rather dominated now by a red nose.

'You've got another cold. Aren't you ever going to get proper heating in there?'

'Oh, one day, I expect. Let's go in the house, get some tea on.'

The kitchen was warmed by the big range and Elaine sat down at the scrubbed pine table while Suzanne put the kettle on and laid out mugs and milk in a blue-spotted jug.

'I made some apple flapjacks.' A heaped plate was plonked down. They both munched.

'How's Chloe? Still got that drippy boyfriend?'

Suzanne laughed. 'Yes, he's quite sweet, really. Calls me Mrs Lawrence and says please and thank you. Makes a real change.'

Elaine looked down into her mug. 'I can't see Alex ever going out with a nice girl like Chloe.'

They sipped and munched.

'She's not that nice – I think she's on the pill.'

'Oh. Right. Hmm.'

Elaine sat back and looked around her. Every surface – the pine dresser, the draining board, the worktop – was covered in small oil paintings left to dry. There were still lives of pots, jugs and bottles arranged on drapes and checked tablecloths. There were lemons, figs, apples, on plates or in bowls. Only a few were landscapes: stark, distant views across flat fields and grey marshes. Many of those were painted on Magnus Bostock's farm, up at Slegholm. Suzanne's ex-husband's Dan was the Bostocks' cousin. But what caught Elaine's eye were several, their paint still glistening, that depicted seabirds – soaring, swooping and diving. She stood up to go over to one for a better look.

'These are new, aren't they?'

'Yes. I've got quite excited about those – they've turned out better than I ever thought.'

'You've really caught the movement – particularly this one.' Elaine pointed at a square canvas leaning against the breadbin, which showed a white bird plunging vertically towards the waves.

'What's that then?'

'I'm pretty sure it's a gannet. I was out by the old lighthouse taking some photos, playing around with the light, when I saw it. So I took loads of pictures and then did the painting.' She came over and looked at it – tilted her head. 'I'm quite pleased with it.'

For a while they stood and studied the painting.

Elaine went back to the table and picked up her tea. 'So these'll all be in the exhibition?'

'Not all of them – there won't be space, but I'm taking them all for framing on Friday, then I'll decide. Fancy a trip to London?'

'Love to, Suze. Absolutely love to. But I still haven't done anything about that tatty spare bedroom. And I need to do B&B. I'd taken a booking from some woman from up north who wanted to stay for three weeks. Three weeks – I could so do with that money! I don't want to have to find her somewhere else to go.'

'Holidaymaker?'

'Not sure. Don't think so. Think she said she was studying something, but I can't remember what. Something historical. Indian sort of name… or Pakistani. So there's no way on earth I can leave the pub right now, what with Alex' – she fiddled with the silver chain round her neck – 'and my staffing problems, as you might call them, i.e. Dave the walking dead and Barbara the unsmiling.'

Suzanne started laughing and in the end Elaine did too.

–

The heavy trundle of a lorry disturbed the last of the night as a soft, grey light trickled round the sides of the curtains.

Morgan turned over and stretched. She slowly opened her eyes and blinked away the sleep. Her left arm lay before her with the hand dangling over the edge of the bed. Thin, red tramlines extended from her knuckles to her elbow, ugly and irregular. The pale skin felt tight and stiff.

She pulled back the pile of blankets and stood up. Pushing her hair off her face and rubbing her eyes, she went downstairs to put on the kettle. No milk. There never seemed to be any milk. Carrying the black tea through to the bathroom at the back of the cottage, she shivered. The cold and very old lino was unforgiving to the soles of her feet. She turned on the taps and the water gushed into the deep, narrow bath that had been there since the time when Nan moved in, long before Morgan was born.

She poured some oil, scented with geranium leaves and lemon balm, into the water, climbed in and lay down, wincing as the water hit her cuts.

Some time later she woke up, in a haze, to find the water nearly cold and the phone ringing. The answerphone kicked in.

'Hello, Morgan, it's Auntie Anne. You must be out somewhere. I'm just ringing because Mike's found this very good website that's doing electric blankets at a really good price…'

Morgan had got out of the bath and was dripping and chilly.

She looked out of the window at two sparrows pecking at a crust of bread.

'...and while we're getting them for Rosie and the kids, I can easily get one for you as well...'

The crust was being tossed from one to the other.

'...because I know how damp that cottage can get – and with the winter and all...'

The male sparrow had won the crust and was heading off for the holly tree. The female was not going to give up and set off in pursuit.

'...But I did want to say, Morgan, you know we worry about you out there on your own. Simon's off to uni soon – you could have his room. Then in the holidays...'

Morgan could hear a door slam and a dog barking at the other end of the line.

'Oh, here's Mike back now. He's very willing to come over and have a go at the plumbing. But listen, I'll ring again soon.' The machine beeped.

Back on the ground the smaller sparrow hopped about forlornly, pecking here and there at the grass in the hope of a dropped crumb. Morgan picked up Nan's biscuit tin and opened the back door. At the sound, the bird cocked its head and looked hard at her.

–

Magnus followed PC Wray into the kitchen, where Brenda stood at the sink. She glanced over her shoulder then turned quickly back to scrubbing the metal pan she was holding. The policeman looked like he was used to being ignored. Magnus imagined a lot of people didn't like having uniforms in their house; but she was a victim of this crime too and it was she who had finally agreed to call the police in the early hours of that Wednesday morning.

'It would be good if I could speak to you both this time, Mrs Bostock. I realise you're busy, of course,' said the officer.

‘I’ll just get this done,’ muttered Brenda.

‘And you have an employee. Baltasar… er… Baltasar Visser?’

‘He’s down on the twelve-acre.’

‘It would be really useful if I could speak to you all together.’

Brenda stared at the roasting tin in her hands, then dropped it into the murky waters in the sink. There was a tea towel hanging in front of the range and she took it up, rubbed her big hands on it slowly before moving to a phone on the worktop.

‘Sit down,’ said Magnus. ‘If you want.’ Both Brenda and the policeman were still standing; both continued to stand. Then the policeman pulled out a chair and sat down. He glanced in the cardboard folder he was carrying. ‘Back in June, three of your sheep were found mauled to death and a sheepdog whose name was…’

‘Meg.’

‘…was also found with serious lacerations from which it—’

‘She.’

‘She… subsequently died.’

Magnus nodded. He looked across at Brenda. Her narrow mouth had become even grimmer. She turned to fill the kettle from the tap. ‘You’ll be wanting a cup of tea,’ was all she said.

PC Wray looked like he didn’t want a cup of tea; he looked like he didn’t want to be hanging around waiting for Balt to drive back from some distant field; and he looked like he didn’t want to have to go over, yet again, the details of a crime for which there were no witnesses, no evidence apart from the corpses of the sheep themselves, and no motive.

‘Just a few more details about last Tuesday night’s incident we need to sort out,’ said the policeman.

‘Tuesday’s incident.’

Was it only last Tuesday night he had walked out into that starlit field of slaughter? Incident, accident, act of God, act of the Devil. Whatever they wanted to call it. Would they ever find who was causing all this destruction?

But then the door opened and Baltasar Visser came in – sooner than Magnus thought he would, which was a relief. The farmhand kicked off his boots in the back porch and hung up his jacket. He paused in the doorway, a huge, looming silhouette, that brought a darkness into the room.

The chairs scraped on the old stone floor as Magnus and Baltasar sat at the table. Brenda had her back to them all as she took mugs out of a cupboard.

PC Wray tapped his slim folder of papers. Magnus thought he had probably unearthed it that morning from the Undetected Crimes filing cabinet. 'There are some similarities with the previous time your sheep were attacked.'

'Similarities.' A stark picture came into Magnus's mind of himself standing in the gateway to a field of lush grass, the summer sun already well above the horizon, finches darting in and out of the hedgerow, and the guts and blood of three of his flock laid out before him. He could smell the putrid rawness. Flies were already buzzing round the strings of entrails, hanging off the hedges like misshapen red berries, the heads of the poor beasts ripped from the necks and tossed around as in a mad frenzy.

Gradually he'd realised he could also hear a whimpering coming from behind the water trough. He stepped forward, sick at the thought of how he would find his old friend. Meg had been his companion out on those windswept fields for years. She walked the farm boundaries with him in rain and hail; she sat beside him on the old Massey Ferguson as it lurched and bumped its way across ploughed fields. When she was about to give birth to her pups he had carried her into the kitchen, lain her down by the warm range and sat with her through her labour. And it was he who had shed the most tears when the littlest puppy gave up the struggle and died, later that night.

Wrenching his mind back to the here and now, he looked across at the policeman who was waiting for him to speak.

‘Something came in the night and ripped my sheep to pieces. Both times. So yes, there are similarities.’

PC Wray looked down at his almost non-existent notes and rubbed his forehead. ‘I particularly wanted to ask you about these rumours—’

‘Rumours?’ Brenda stepped forward, the tea towel dangling from her hand, though not much drying-up had been done.

The officer looked at her. ‘Rumours,’ he said firmly, ‘about some large animal that people claim there have been sightings of. A wolf or big cat, maybe a panther or something. Ridiculous, of course, it’s not like there’s a zoo or anything round here it could have escaped from.’ He laughed, perhaps a little too long, then tailed off at their stony expressions, cleared his throat and carried on resolutely. ‘Have you maybe seen such a creature or is this a load of baloney?’

Magnus looked through the window. He took a very deep breath. ‘Panthers?’ he said. ‘Panthers?’

That afternoon Magnus sat at the kitchen table. The knots in the ancient wood were smothered by official papers, bristling with officious letterheads, orders, demands, instructions and questions. Brenda was in the small back room they called the office, working on the computer.

Magnus picked up a couple of sheets of paper at random. Words like “Catchment Sensitive” floated in front of his eyes. He hadn’t got a clue, except to know that the payments were vital. But what with Brexit and the never-ending confusion in politics, he felt he couldn’t keep up. He picked up a leaflet and started to read. Maybe Brenda should be focusing on this instead of fixating on lineage in the stock. She was obsessed with breeding, would spend hours on the computer looking at blood lines in sheep or cows.

She came through and reached for the kettle.

‘You might help me with this,’ muttered Magnus. ‘Can’t make head or tail of these forms.’

She turned and stood, square-on, hands on hips. 'I've said it before and I'll say it again.' She had, and she would. 'Sheep. They're losing us money.'

'You've never liked—'

'Like? Never mind like!' She was shouting now. 'We're sinking here, Magnus. They've got to go!'

'I won't let them. We've had those ewes going back generations, as you well know. We get rid of them over my dead body!'

He stood up and stomped out of the room. Every time they talked about the farm it came to this. Every time. He marched down the hallway, looking for space to clear his head. The sitting room was little used and he might get some peace in there. It was all very well for Brenda to sit hunched over that damn computer with her spreadsheets or whatever and say they needed to do this or needed not to do that. She didn't understand the land like he did. Her idea was: if something didn't work, get rid of it. He stood in front of one of the tall windows. Its wood frame was laden with decades of layers of paint piled on top of each other. The pane of glass he was looking through was one of the originals. It had a slight distortion to it that made the walls, the hedges, the trees and telegraph poles waver, grow fatter then thinner. As he shifted his weight from one foot to the other, the picture changed continuously.

Maybe he was being unfair to Brenda. She had a hard early life, he knew that. Dumped at birth, by, probably, a teenage mother; adopted by a farming couple in Lincolnshire who were distant, not interested in any little achievement of hers. Everything to her was black or white; right or wrong. Which was why last week's phone call had made her so angry.

It was in the evening, and they were both indoors. He was nearest the phone when it rang, so he answered it. 'Hullo?'

'Now then,' said a brash, loud, male voice. 'Would that be Mr Bostock I'm speaking to? Mr Magnus Bostock, brother of Nick?'

Magnus was on his guard straightaway. 'Yes,' he mumbled. 'Who is this?'

'Well, my old son, you don't know me. You don't know me at all, but my name's Patrick Rokesmith.'

Magnus didn't say anything, but it seemed like this Rokesmith character needed no encouragement.

'And I gather you're in charge of quite a large farm – am I right?'

'Well… yes,' replied Magnus.

'With outbuildings – barns and sheds and the like.'

'What's all this about?' asked Magnus. He could sense Brenda, stiff as a statue, in the doorway behind him, listening.

'I do a bit of business with your brother, young Nicholas. Let's just say he helps me shift a few… objects. Let's call them livestock. Thing is, some of these… livestock… need storing for a few days before I can move them on. Storing somewhere quiet and out of the way, with a bit of food and drink available, if you get my meaning.'

And Magnus did get his meaning. This part of the coast was getting notorious for the numbers of illegal immigrants being brought in, usually in small boats in the dead of night.

'And of course I'll pay top dollar if some of your barns could become available,' Rokesmith added.

After he had hung up, Magnus turned to face Brenda. And he knew his face gave away everything that was going on in his mind. They needed the cash desperately; it would be easy money; they had the space. He could even kid himself they would be helping the refugees, though in his heart he knew he would only be helping the people who were fleecing the poor buggers.

Stumbling with the words, he tried to put forward his argument.

Brenda grew more and more angry. 'You would risk everything! The farm, our livelihood, the cows, the good name of Bostock!'

Bostock. She seemed to care – she definitely cared – more about the so-called good name than he did.

'Everything we've worked for, slaved for, you would put at risk just to get some ready cash out of this man. This man we know nothing about. It's not going to happen, Magnus! It's not going to happen.'

Thinking back now, Magnus had never seen her so angry. He turned away from the window. As he left the room he stubbed his toe on something hard and very painful. 'Shit, shit, shit.' He looked down at the culprit. A winged serpent made of heavy bronze, about a foot high, glinted its evil eye at him. They had used it as a doorstop forever, but never before had he hurt himself on it. He kicked it back. 'Bastard thing.'

CHAPTER SIX

'I'LL KILL HIM! GOD HELP ME, I SWEAR I'LL MURDER THAT boy!'

'Whoa, hold on, Elaine. What's happened now? Take a deep breath.' Suzanne could be supremely calming when Elaine needed it most. But this one topped the lot. Alex had really done it now; she was fuming beyond belief.

She found herself squeaking and snorting alternately down the phone until she finally got her voice under control.

'I'd just got that guest bedroom – the one I let out for B&B – really nice, because I'd got that woman coming to stay. Sounded good, staying for a while because of her job, so I washed the curtains; lovely, fresh-smelling bedclothes; even ironed the duvet cover; matching towels in the bathroom; all that crap, when bloody Alex – bloody, bloody Alex—'

'Oh no, what's he done now?'

'Ooh, I could ring his neck! So he brought a couple of friends back after school, which I was quite pleased about really, as he doesn't seem to have many friends, doesn't often talk about anyone.

So I was friendly; let them make snacks, take them upstairs. So then I was busy in the bar – because Barbara was off again with her trouble – and I suppose I saw them going out and coming back in again later, but I didn't take much notice. By the end of the evening I'd assumed they'd gone home and Alex had gone to bed. Half past two in the morning – smoke alarm goes off!'

'Oh no!'

'Yes! So I charge out onto the landing in my dressing gown and there's Alex and his mates in the doorway of the guest room trying to get the fire extinguisher working. Bed's gone up in smoke – bedclothes, pillow, duvet, all ruined. Walls and curtains all stained and stinking of smoke.'

'So you managed to put it out? You didn't need the fire brigade.'

'Yeah, we managed to put it out.' Elaine could hear that her voice wasn't so squeaky now, and she had calmed down a bit. 'But I was so angry, Suze, you should have seen me!'

'So how did they start the fire? Was it on purpose?'

'No, no. They're not quite *that* evil, these kids, just incredibly stupid. So they were smoking—'

'Spliffs?'

'Well, yes. And just kind of fell asleep without putting them out properly. Idiots.'

She fell silent, then Suze's voice came back: 'What you need, girl, is a trip out. Drop everything and come on over.'

Which she did. And within an hour they were driving over the causeway with a plan of treating themselves to lunch out. The old van had other ideas, however, and gave up the ghost, or at least the electrics did. Suzanne managed to steer the blue and white VW camper van to the side of the road. Elaine thumbed through the dog-eared manual, while Suzanne called the roadside rescue people.

'We've several people off sick today,' was the response. 'We might be up to an hour and a half coming out to you.'

So the pair settled down to wait, with a bag of wine gums they found in the glovebox.

'You heard from Dan lately?' asked Elaine.

'Not for ages. Last thing I heard he'd settled down in Hackney with Amanda.'

'That's the twenty-eight-year-old floozy, yeah?'

Suzanne laughed at that. 'Yes, she's the floozy. Actually she looked like a perfectly normal person the one time I saw her. I hope for her sake she can cope with his moods.'

'You're too generous. So he never comes back this way?'

'Sometimes.' Suzanne shoved in another wine gum. 'I think he visits his great-aunt Dorothea up at Laurel Dene. And then there's the cousins, of course, though I don't know how much he has to do with them.'

Elaine nodded, remembering the fight those two had started in the Dog a few days before.

'I will say, in his favour,' went on Suzanne, 'that he was really good to Magnus and – what's her name? – Brenda when they had all their troubles. They can pull together when they really want to, and with that Dorothea going around muttering about "bad blood" they needed all the help they could get.'

Elaine nodded and took the last sweet, then jumped in her seat and spun round to see who it was who could be driving that black Golf so ridiculously fast.

–

The causeway narrowed towards its end and a signpost offering two options came into view. Jasmin Kapoor braked – too sharply, as it turned out – since the untidy pile of maps, files, papers and an iPad on the passenger seat shot forward into a heap on the floor.

'Shit.' She reached across to try to rescue the pile while attempting to read the signpost and steer the car. Then she chose the left-hand turn and headed on towards the village. She arrived at what she assumed was the main street, running parallel to the beach. The earlier sunshine had long since faded away as cloud rolled in off the sea and there was little difference between the granite tarmac of the road, the steel of the water and the only slightly paler grey of the sky. She pulled up outside what she feared was the only pub for some distance and turned off the engine, then pulled down the sun visor and examined the smudged eyeliner and clumped mascara.

Already the city had been drained out of her. Her smooth, light-brown skin, long nose and rich, glossy black hair usually had a dynamic, fresh look to them. No point in doing anything about it now. A powerful hot shower would help a lot. She leant across and looked through the passenger window at the pub. When she'd booked the room at the Dog and Whistle it sounded like a nice, quaint, country pub, built of some warm, honey-coloured stone; maybe with a thatched roof and roses round the door. But the brickwork she was looking at now had been painted white, once upon a time. It was unadorned by leaves or flowers.

She got out of the car and stretched. A deep breath. But there was no softness to the air. She crossed the road to the shingle beach that stretched monotonously to either side. The horizon was a long, black, flat line. A wire fence separated the pavement from the beach. Up against it clung the forensics of seaside village life: crisp packets, cider cans, cigarette ends.

Bloody hell. She'd driven for four and a half hours, leaving behind her the buzz of Manchester. Now she was here, she felt deflated. It was a dismal spot and now a sharp drizzle, driven by the east wind, slapped her in the face. This made her heart sink further. *Huh. So much for the magic. So much for the mythical beasts.*

A friend of hers at the uni, Daniel, a post-doc researcher in the English department who focused on myths and legends, had passed on to her stuff to read about the island. There were stories of people who could turn themselves into wild beasts and stalk the countryside, killing at random. Tales of ghosts who taunted you, pursued you and finally drove you to madness. Sea-dwelling female creatures, like sirens or harpies, that lured ships and boats onto rocks or into the deadly sinking sands. She'd spent a couple of long evenings looking at it, just to humour him, really. It wasn't so easy to laugh now.

An old man in a flat cap walked past with his dog, glanced across, but failed to meet her eye or acknowledge that she was there. He pulled his coat collar up higher round his neck and plodded on. She supposed that, to him, she looked sharp, polished, long-haired and long-legged in her shiny, new, high-heeled ankle boots. She was suddenly aware of the huge silver hoops dangling from her ears and the tiny silver stud in the side of her nose. A seagull shrieked with laughter above her.

So much for the locals. She glanced at her watch and headed for the door of the pub. Totally standard sort of place: dim interior, tankards hanging from the beams. A shaven-headed youth leant on the bar reading the sports pages of the paper. He looked up and folded it away as she came in. She could see him sizing her up, clocking "not from round here". She looked around her at the dark, shiny, sticky tables, mismatched chairs and stools, the fading pictures and photographs on the walls, mainly showing fishermen, or dead fish.

'All right then? How you doing?'

Not really the sort of greeting Jasmin might have liked, but she let it pass.

'Hello. I'll have a lime and lemonade, please.'

He started to make the drink, while in a desultory way asking her the usual questions. Was the weather nice out there? No. Was she new in the area? Yes. Visiting friends? Not exactly. *This is going well,* thought Jasmin of her first interaction with a meaningful person in this godforsaken place. Was she really going to be staying here?

'I need to book in,' she said, sliding onto a stool at the bar. God, she was desperate for that hot shower, otherwise she'd try to find somewhere else – anywhere else.

'Ah.' He turned off the lemonade tap. 'You must be the academic historian down from Manchester looking at family trees or some such?' He laughed – a surprisingly high-pitched giggle. 'I tell you – you wouldn't want to look too closely at some of the families round here. Anyway, I'm afraid your room's cancelled, or rather, it's gone up in smoke last night.'

'What?'

'Yeah.' He finished her drink and handed it over. 'The bed went up in flames what with the landlady's son and his mate having a bit of a party in there, if you get me. She's been trying to ring you this morning. Didn't she get ya?'

She'd turned her phone off for the journey, just in case her mother or sister thought of anything else she ought to have packed for the middle of nowhere.

'I'll try her now – see if she's managed to come up with anything else,' he said, and went out into the hallway off the bar, where a phone hung on the wall.

Crikey, this was all she needed. The idea of that hot shower was fading fast. She found she'd been staring at the beer taps, with their oval- or shield-shaped metal labels that described each brew. Skippers: *Fair enough for an island that looked like going out in boats was one of its main activities.* Cat-Tails, though, that was a weird one. There was a picture of a cat with an arched back and open mouth, as though hissing. Its tail was raised and curved over at the tip, which was split into two. *Freaky. Would you actually want to drink something like that?* And Kerkbuurt Wit. *What the hell? How would you even ask for it?*

She looked at the barman, who was cradling the phone against his chin while he held a grubby tea towel up to the light, maybe searching for a clean patch. He obviously decided to err on the side of hygiene and tossed it into a wicker basket of used towels on the floor behind him.

Then he replaced the phone on the wall and came back. 'Can't get hold of her. Sorry.'

'Is there anywhere else around here that offers accommodation?'

He sucked air through his teeth. 'Well,' he drew out his answer, apparently relishing the prospect of letting her down. ''Fraid not. No hotel or nothing like that. There's a few bed and breakfasts back of the harbour, but they're all shut up for the winter now.'

Silence reigned for a while and he mopped the bar. 'I know about someone who's got a room she might want to let – but it's right out on the marsh and it's only a tiny cottage and I don't think there's much in the way of mod-cons.'

'Wi-Fi?'

'Doubt it.'

'Do you have a phone number?'

'No, but I'll draw you a map.' This he executed on a slightly crumpled napkin, imaginatively inking in dry stone walls, ditches and lone trees, leaving Jasmin with not much hope she could ever find the place.

She took it, folded it and put it in her pocket. 'But first I need to find somewhere called Laurel Dene. It's a nursing home.'

The car park at the front of the Victorian red-brick pile was quiet, so Jasmin sat there for some time sorting through the mixed-up papers. She could hear the echo of Howard's voice as she had backed out of his office on Friday, laden with files and folders. 'Organise, Jasmin, organise! Get it all put on your computer!'

Ha. Easy for him to say, with his team of eager research students ready to slave over hot scanners in libraries. And it was pretty unfair of him to call her disorganised. She had done loads of background research for this project; it was just that this had raised more questions than it answered.

Well, she was here now, and she would start with some simple fact-finding. She twisted in her seat and looked around her. Three weeks had passed since the day Howard had called her. 'Pop into my room if you have a moment.'

So she had put aside the tedious data-inputting that was paying the rent, shut down the websites that promised to find her a fabulous job instantly if she ever got around to finishing her CV and wandered through the lino-lined corridors of the Institute to Howard's book-lined office – to be told that they had got the funding.

Her packing had been meticulous; her sister, Asha, scathing.

'You're taking a huge torch? Why? Don't they have street lighting in this place?' And, 'Wellies? You've bought wellies? You planning on wading through mud to speak to these people?'

Jasmin had shown her the maps, explained about the desolate romance of the marshes. 'You've read Dickens – picture it!'

But her sister just snorted and turned away. 'You're not cut out for the country. If you can't use your iPhone every five minutes you're going to have panic attacks.'

Laurel Dene stood on the gentle slope of a lone hill that, in such a flat, sunken landscape, offered a view in all directions for miles. As Jasmin approached the front door of the house, she paused and turned around. A wide lawn, edged by dull shrubs, swept down the slope; the sea beyond it looked quiet. Far out, on the horizon, the long silhouette of a tanker blotted the pale picture like a squashed fly on a hospital wall. The few trees, to her left and right, all strained in the same direction, as though preparing for a race. She approached the door.

The receptionist led Jasmin to a pair of upright chairs in a corner of a deserted sitting room, close to a wide bay window with a view over a rose garden at the side of the building. Jasmin sat down and stared through the glass. Several of the wispy bushes had a few tatty leaves clinging on.

She looked up, then stood up, as the old lady approached. If she had expected she would be meeting a frail little old lady, Jasmin would have been badly disappointed. Somehow, though, she had never imagined that the widow of the great-grandson of the object of her researches could be anything other than stern, self-composed and unflinching. She saw a woman once tall, proud – what used to be called stately – walking slowly towards her. Her hair was piled up and held by pins and combs, with the inexpert help of one of the carers, Jasmin thought. Her face was powdered with a touch of rouge. Here was a woman proud of herself, of her lineage, her capabilities. Yet she was leaning heavily to one side, the hand holding the stick shaking with the pressure.

They sat. Dorothea Bostock's expression barely changed as Jasmin introduced herself, adding detail to the letter she had already sent.

'The Siege of Cawnpore was a crucial event in the Indian Rebellion.' She glanced at the woman who sat stern and stiff. 'For months, Mrs Bostock, I have been sifting through the records of the army and the East India Company and from the High Commission.' Still no reaction. 'It was never fully understood what happened during the siege – why so many people died – but your husband's great-grandfather's name comes up again and again in the records.' At this there was a slight reaction: an imperceptible lifting of the chin, a narrowing of the nostrils. 'He was obviously a pivotal figure in the events of that year,' Jasmin went on resolutely.

A frail old man was making a break for freedom, with the help of his walking frame, across the immaculate lawn. The two women watched as he was halted in his tracks by uniformed members of staff who caught up with him, seemed to be reasoning with him, then turned him round and pointed him back in the direction of the house.

At last the old lady spoke. Her voice was croaky, which obviously annoyed her. 'Pivotal? He may have been pivotal. I cannot say.' She turned her head to Jasmin and then away again. 'I myself was brought up in India, you know.'

Jasmin didn't know. Was it relevant?

'India is a strange country,' Dorothea Bostock went on. 'Things are done… differently. Even in my youth attitudes were very different. So anything that happened as far back as the middle of the nineteenth century would be worlds away from how things are now.'

Jasmin felt the old lady was getting away from the point but felt it best to let her carry on.

'For myself, my only memories are of the spacious rooms of the company house in Delhi, kept cool against the searing heat by the lazy, giant fans operated by half-asleep punkah-wallahs. Other servants would drift, equally lazily, in and out of the rooms which were kept half in shadow by the shutters on the windows. Or we might be allowed to play under the trees in the manicured gardens which tried yet failed to bring a little of England out to this strange country where dusty roses would struggle to survive.

'My brother and I spent nearly all our time in the nursery, or at least that's how I remember it. It was a wide, light room, with windows on three sides and, in the centre, a rocking horse, beautifully carved, with peeling gold and red paint.

'To go outside would have given my mother a fainting fit. She saw dangers everywhere – real or imagined, it didn't matter – we had to be protected at all costs from what she saw as the horrors of India. These included snakes, sunshine, ornamental pools and above all, the ruffians from the village below.

'The ayah would see to all our needs, the cook would bring us our meals, other servants whose names we didn't even know would wash and press our clothes, bring us our toys, sweep the floors.

'We were taught only to speak to them to give orders. We were taught to hide our feelings in front of others. Frustration, fear, anger, disappointment, self-doubt – all these were to be contained, suppressed. Yet the servants too would hide their feelings. They would not look us in the eye. We didn't know if they cared about us or hated us; but then I don't remember ever giving a moment's thought to what they thought of us.'

She turned and stared into Jasmin's eyes. 'Of my husband's family and their time out there, I know virtually nothing.' She turned away again.

Jasmin studied the impassive, noble profile. She didn't believe this woman knew nothing. 'You may think I'm just a university researcher, but the fact is, I have more personal reasons for pursuing this.' She twisted the silver bracelets on her arm.

By the time Jasmin left Laurel Dene, the pale sun was low in the sky and the tables were being laid for tea.

Less than half an hour later she was away from the care home and driving slowly back towards the village, frowning deeply. She drew up on the outskirts and pulled out the napkin the barman had drawn on. More by luck than judgement she finally found the cottage, where the road gave way to a rough track and then a path leading out into the marshland. Jasmin looked at the house before her. This had to be the place the guy in the pub was talking about.

She knocked on the front door and since there was no reply, wandered round to the back. A girl in a floaty dress, with long, corkscrew hair, was picking green leaves from a row of plants in a little raised bed.

'Nice crop you've got there. Are they lettuces?'

The girl straightened up quickly and looked at Jasmin before replying, 'It's mizuna: grows all year round, good for calcium. Try some?'

Jasmin stepped forward and took the proffered handful. She tasted it tentatively. 'Mmm. Bit like rocket.' It was like eating leather. They both chewed for a moment. 'So, anyway, I've come to St Cedd for a week or two' – she thought back to the stone wall that was Dorothea – 'or maybe a little longer, so I'm going to need somewhere to stay. The chap working in the pub said you might be looking for a lodger. My name's Jasmin.'

Morgan looked down the garden to where two blue tits were squabbling in the apple tree. Then she looked back at the ramshackle cottage with its sagging roof and drooping gutters. 'Yes, I suppose I am. Come in and have a look. I'm Morgan.'

Jasmin found the rickety staircase, the unheated downstairs bathroom and the unmodernised kitchen not very inspiring, but the house had a cosy, friendly feel to it. Once she saw the little spare bedroom with its view out over the fields and marshes and its bright patchwork quilt with matching curtains, she was won over.

'Great, I'll take it.' Yet with instant misgivings she pulled out her phone. Good enough – just about.

–

Magnus dragged himself up from a deep, fuzzy sleep, which had involved a confused dream of swirling greyness and unhappy whispers. Brenda was fast asleep beside him, humped under the duvet. With a thick head he realised what had woken him: the phone was ringing. He sat up and flinched as his feet landed on the cold floorboards.

'Hello? Yes?'

'Sorry to wake you, Mr Bostock. This is Margaret at Laurel Dene.'

'Oh. Yes?'

'I'm afraid we've had to send for an ambulance for your grandmother. We think she's had another stroke. Natalia found her collapsed—'

'Oh. Right. Right. I'll go there.'

'That might be a good idea.'

'Ipswich Hospital, is it?'

As he drove the Toyota through the last of the night, a myriad of confused thoughts and memories flashed through Magnus's mind: Grandma putting him into an uncomfortable overcoat to send him off to Sunday school; her striding along behind him, holding onto the saddle as he tried to learn to ride a bike; the family sitting round the tea table in heavy silence, him staring down at his sardines on toast.

Strangely, as he realised later, he never once thought of Nick – it never occurred to him that he should have rung Nick and told him to get to the hospital.

The tide was well on its way out as he drove the Toyota across the causeway, but it had left a dampness that cast a dull silver sheen on the road surface in the first light of the coming dawn. He could drive fast at this hour – not even the milk lorries were out yet.

Reaching the outskirts of the town he turned onto the ring road, and although he was now on a dual carriageway he slowed down. He was remembering earlier journeys on this stretch of road, looking out for the red A&E signs, Brenda pale and silent in her pain beside him. Three times they had rushed to this hospital, three times they had left it – Brenda drawn, exhausted, deflated; Magnus sad for her, sad for the lost baby, but confused by all the medical explanations that made no sense to him. Why them? Why did this keep happening to them?

The stark white lights of the hospital car park brought him back to the here and now. Car Park A, Car Park B; which one did he want? He parked at random near the main entrance and hurried towards the building.

His grandmother looked smaller. Under the bedclothes she looked almost flat; wires came out on both sides, hooking up to machines that flashed and beeped in the otherwise silent ward. The nurse took him into her office and gently explained the possible effects of the stroke – the partial paralysis, the vision problems, speech problems – and the likelihood of another one occurring.

He sat by Dorothea's bed for some time, watching her and thinking about how things used to be, and how they would be in the future. Finally she stirred. The nurse came and sat her up a bit in the bed and held a plastic beaker of water, like the ones they give to toddlers, to her lips. Some of it dribbled down her chin and Magnus wiped it away. Trembling, she held out her hand to him and he sat and held on to it. Physical contact had never been a common thing in their household, but somehow their roles seemed different now. A sea change had occurred in their relationship that was unlikely to be reversed. And sure, he realised this was a common enough thing to happen between young and old; he knew perfectly well that it happened to a lot of people, possibly most people, that at a certain time in their lives the cared-for became the carer.

For the two of them, though, the relationship was charged with that extra knowledge – that shared understanding – that must not be allowed to escape the boundaries of that special connection. Dorothea stirred again and tried to speak. He leant forward to catch her words.

'Mag… Magnus.' It came out slurred and thick.

'I'm here… I'm here.'

'We… the whole… Louise. No…' She fell silent, her head fell to one side and she seemed to have fallen asleep.

Magnus stroked the dry, bony hand. 'I know, Grandma, I know,' he whispered to the ashen face.

For several hours more Magnus sat at the bedside. Hospital staff came and went. Around midday Brenda came in and made him go down to the café while she sat with Dorothea. He nursed a cup of tea and a ham sandwich and stared into space.

On his way back to the ward he saw Nick, leaning against the doorjamb of the nurses' office and chatting animatedly with a young girl in uniform. Nick fell silent and straightened up when he saw his brother. 'Magnus.'

'What're you doing here?'

'Hey, she's my grandma too, remember. It took long enough for anyone to bother telling me she was here. It wasn't till Brenda rang Stacey—'

Magnus pushed him aside and stepped back into the ward. Nick followed and overtook him and sat down on the chair close to his grandmother's head.

'Hey, Gran,' he said. 'How're you doing? Here's a fine mess to get yourself into, eh? Soon have you back on your feet, though…'

Magnus took up position on the other side of the bed. She turned her head slightly towards him and imperceptibly shook her head. He nodded.

CHAPTER SEVEN

MAGNUS PARKED THE TOYOTA TRUCK IN THE CAR PARK, TURNED off the engine and sat, still holding on to the wheel. Brenda climbed down, clutching her handbag.

'Have you got the present?'

He lifted the bag to show her.

'And the card?'

He raised that too. Brenda stood staring at the granite pillars that flanked the double doors. She stepped forward, heavy-footed, and he followed.

A banner was stretched across the reception area. HAPPY BIRTHDAY, it said, in bold colours; then DOROTHEA, almost as an afterthought in blue and green, as though the red and yellow had run out. The A of Dorothea was drooping.

The manager on duty – Connie, according to the name badge on her comfy chest – bustled forward, a special birthday smile on her face. She wore pink lipstick. Magnus looked at his wife, who never wore lipstick, not even for a party.

'Well, isn't this splendid!' The woman actually clapped her hands together. 'And your grandmother's so much improved. They do like to get them on their feet and back home as quick as possible these days, don't they?' She pointed along the corridor. 'The others are already here, and you've got the Activities Room all to yourselves.'

'Yes,' said Magnus. 'Thank you.'

'I'll bring the tea through in a moment,' called Connie.

'Thank you,' he said again.

The group of people gathered in front of the unlit fireplace made up his entire family. A sorry excuse for a family.

Dorothea, his ninety-year-old grandmother, commanded the centre. She sat stiffly upright in her wheelchair, and nodded to Magnus and Brenda as they approached. 'You're late.'

Brenda said nothing. Magnus had to fill the expectant gap. 'Yes.' He cleared his throat. 'We had trouble starting the truck.' He sensed Brenda's head turn slowly towards him, felt her blank stare on his reddening face. Why didn't he just tell the truth? Say they'd been arguing before they left the farmhouse? He still felt bruised.

The only other guests at the party were his brother, Nick, and Nick's girlfriend – *Stacey.* She was standing beside the wheelchair and had on skinny jeans with ripped knees and a tight, white top with a shiny silver cat pattern on it. He looked at the round swell of her breasts pushing through the thin material and thought how out of place such a bright thing looked in these surroundings.

The last he'd seen of Nick was when they'd argued at the hospital. Now they looked towards each other, but their eyes did not quite meet.

Nick raised a lazy hand to Brenda. 'Hi, Bren.' No one called her that. Stacey looked up from her phone, put it away in her jeans pocket, nodded and tried a half-smile at them both.

'It's all right now, is it?' she asked Magnus.

'Is what?'

The girl, with her pale blue eyes and open, enquiring face, was looking at him. She was just making small talk, but normal, casual conversation was too difficult for him.

He went to put his hands in his jacket pockets, but had trouble finding them. 'Oh… you mean the truck. Yes, yes, it's okay.'

The girl nodded and turned to look out of the window, bored already. His brother had moved out of their grandmother's line of sight and was checking his phone, fixing yet another dodgy deal, probably. Dorothea herself was like a statue, stony and unmoving, her hands folded on her lap. They were wrinkled, with knuckles made thick and knobbly by arthritis, yet still adorned with the heavy gold, ruby and emerald rings she always wore.

A silence fell. He looked around him. The room was large, square and high-ceilinged. The elaborate cornices and ceiling rose had been softened by the layers of emulsion slapped on them over the years. The moulded window frames the Victorians were so keen on were coated in once-brilliant white gloss, thick as the icing on a Christmas cake. And in a style all institutions seemed to have to have, the stretches of wall beneath the dado rail were painted green. The staff had pushed the upright piano back against one wall and dragged a table to the centre of the room, with dining chairs arranged around it. The padded seats of the chairs were upholstered in the same, slightly faded green and purple twirling-vine patterned material as the curtains hanging at the tall windows.

The tea arrived. He supposed the staff in the kitchen spent most of their time producing easily digestible, easily chewed meals, so Magnus was surprised to see smoked salmon and cream cheese sandwiches garnished with dill and slices of roasted vegetable quiche. They had even been offered a choice of teas but had all opted for PG Tips, apart from Dorothea, who had asked for Darjeeling.

'I have it delivered from Macey's,' she said. 'And they keep it in the kitchens for me.'

Christ, thought Magnus. *She's on the ball. She doesn't really think she's in some outpost of the Empire keeping the natives in their place. But that doesn't stop her from talking to the staff as though they are servants.* She would raise her voice slightly and talk in more clipped tones when she spoke to them.

They talked about the weather, the planning dispute about the new supermarket and farm subsidies. Even that was contentious, though.

'They have it handed to them on a plate, they do,' said Nick. But he wasn't talking about all farmers and he wasn't just talking about subsidies, Magnus knew. He felt his face redden; he clenched the napkin on his lap and examined the chequered pattern until he dared look up at the other faces round the table. Brenda's expression was blank as she chewed away at a sandwich. His grandmother was sitting very upright, looking across at Nick with pursed lips. Stacey was tapping Nick on the upper arm and mouthing something at him, but he just sat back in his chair and grinned across at Magnus, daring him to rise to the bait.

It was this moment that the manager chose to fling open the door and march in bearing a large cake, which was decorated with white fondant icing and delicate pink sugar flowers. The flames of the candles streamed back towards her large bosom as she strode forward, bringing in her wake as many members of staff as she had been able to round up. She started a fine, operatic rendition of "Happy Birthday to You" with her followers joining in as best they could, one of them in another language – maybe Latvian or Polish or something.

Magnus was too slow, as always. Nick had jumped up and pulled back his chair. He cleared room on the table for the giant cake. It was placed before Dorothea and the manager stood back, smiling and clasping her hands across her ample stomach. Magnus looked at his grandmother.

'Thank you,' said Dorothea after a while. The retinue withdrew and the family were left staring at the spluttering candles.

–

Nick Bostock was struggling with the boat. The engine was coughing so badly it might die any minute. Maybe a fast run would sort her out. Or maybe not. Either way, all the arrangements had been made for tonight so he had no choice. And where was that Matt? Looking back up the jetty he saw him loping towards the boat. Matt stamped out his cigarette on the slimy boards of the jetty and started to climb aboard.

'Where the hell have you been?' hissed Nick. 'We're late already.'

'No problem, though, yeah? Not as though they're going anywhere!' The lanky man laughed loud and long at his own joke.

'For Christ's sake!' Nick straightened up from the engine housing and peered towards the harbourmaster's office several hundred yards away. 'Get yourself on quick and let's get going.'

They powered off over the sluggish, black waters, heading for the open sea. There was only a thin sliver of a moon, struggling to show itself through the intermittent, low clouds driven swiftly by the winds.

It was a grim journey. They used minimal lights, but Nick still found himself staring out into the vast black, imagining he could see the shape of the coastguard's boat looming. He caught the first sight, some distance ahead off the starboard bow, of the faint, flashing light he'd been looking out for. Then the faint throb of an engine came to him through the thick night air. He slowed down. 'Nearly there, Matt. Get some space cleared, can't you?' he added irritably to the other man, who was lounging with a can of beer at the back of the boat.

A larger boat now loomed out of the darkness and manoeuvred to come to a stop beside them. A large figure loomed up, grasped the rail and looked down on them. He was dressed in a parka, with a scarf wrapped around his face. Reaching across with a hook he managed to pull the two boats alongside each other and steady them in the waves. Then he started waving his arms at a dark mass huddled in the bottom of his boat. The mass tentatively sorted itself into individuals; men and women all dressed in dark clothing, climbed to their feet, some stretching tired limbs, others helping up the slower ones.

'Get a move on. Come on, come on!' the man in the parka growled at them. 'Onto the other boat – quick now!' Nick was leaning over the side, ready to help pull the people over; but there seemed to be a problem. They looked at him then turned away; stood in a close huddle, whispering urgently amongst themselves.

'Come on, Martie, get them over!' shouted Nick. Their voices, plus the noise of the engines, were echoing out into the darkness for maybe miles and he was looking around nervously for any sign of lights. 'What's the matter?'

'Christ knows.' Martie grabbed at the sleeve of the man nearest him, who pulled away sharply and shouted in his face, waving his arms at Nick's boat. The other man looked ready to lash out at him, so Nick vaulted the rail and came between them.

'Steady!' He looked at the agitated man, still shouting in a language Nick couldn't begin to recognise. 'Steady.' And he made that palms-down gesture that policemen used so irritatingly often. 'Come on, mate.'

Now someone new was pushing through the uneasy group. A younger man, his eyes shining white in his dark face, grabbed Nick by the jacket. 'Your boat is no good. It is too small. My people fear it will not stay up. They say they will drown out here in this cold sea.' He was shouting louder now. 'You people… you do not care… you take our money… all we have—'

'Oh, for God's sake.' Nick just wanted to get them on board – to get away from here. There wasn't time for a debate. He pushed the man aside, spotted a child, a boy of maybe six or seven in a purple jacket and, grasping him roughly by the arms, heaved him over the rails onto his own boat. A woman cried out, reached out, and Nick took hold of her as well and pushed her across. Martie and Matt started to follow suit, and soon all the women, the girls, the children and the older men were on board the *Lady*. The two angry men had no choice but to go as well. Martie pushed the boats apart, revved up his engine and veered away.

The journey back to the shore was always the most nerve-wracking bit of all of this for Nick. He and Matt would get it in the neck if they were caught now. And they were like sitting ducks out here on the open water. Matt flicked his lighter to light a roll-up and Nick swung round at the sudden flare which seemed as bright as one of those very lights shot into the sky from a lifeboat.

God, he was jumpy tonight – more so than usual. The *Lady* was massively overloaded, which didn't help. He turned and looked back at the sorry group, huddling, scared and cold. He could see one skinny man rubbing the back of the woman crouched beside him, while she tried to stretch her back out. He saw the rounded belly showing through her layers of clothing. *Christ. What would drive you to make this hideous journey when you were pregnant?*

Despite the chilly night, Nick was sweating heavily by the time they pulled into the cove. He killed the engine, climbed overboard and forged his way through the shallows. He was freezing by the time he got to the top of the dunes. He pulled out a torch and flashed it into the darkness. After a moment, headlights flashed back.

Getting the group out of the boat and into the van was not too hard – they seemed relieved to be away from the water. But they moved so slowly. All right, so they'd been cramped in the bottoms of boats for hours or days and they were probably cold and stiff, but they had to get out of here pronto. The moon would be up soon.

One large, older man was being particularly slow. Matt gave him a bit of a push in the back. 'Come on, mate.'

The man straightened up. He was certainly big. He turned slowly and towered over Nick and Matt. His eyes opened really wide, the whites shining in the torchlight. He slowly raised one arm and pointed at the pair of them. 'May the Devil smite you down for what you do,' he boomed, in a deep bass voice. 'You –

and you – are the scum of the earth, the lowest of the low. You are the worms that feed upon people's souls. Be warned.' And he held up a forefinger and shook it in their faces. 'You may destroy our dignity today, but we will rise up tomorrow and with the angels of righteousness and decency riding on our shoulders we will come for vengeance. And you will never know when it will be. You will always be looking behind you in fear.' And he turned and climbed into the van.

Rokesmith slammed the door on them and as he turned, Nick grabbed him by the jacket. 'There weren't supposed to be kids,' he hissed. 'And one of them's pregnant. I suppose you're charging her double!'

'What if I am?' the bulky man hissed back. 'They should be bloody grateful I didn't just dump them in the water. Now get out of here, dickhead!'

The terrified face of the mother whose boy Nick had snatched away flooded into his mind. He looked away, shaking his head. 'Just give me my money.'

Rokesmith took his time pulling a brown bag out of his pocket. Nick snatched it from him. 'This is the last time – you hear? The last time I'm doing this!' He was shouting now and shaking.

Rokesmith laughed in his face. 'We're all in this together, Bostock. No one pulls out now or they'll really regret it.' They stared hard at each other. Every muscle in Nick's body was shrieking at him. He wanted to let all the tension go by smashing his fists in this bastard's smirking face. Rokesmith really knew how to get people under his thumb so however much you wriggled it was impossible to get out. Finally, Nick turned away, rubbing the back of his neck.

'But these people—'

Rokesmith stepped forward and hissed in his face, 'These people are desperate to come here – they'll pay anything and while they'll do that,' he was smirking now, 'it's our job to oblige them. I don't hear you objecting to taking their cash,' he went on.

Nick started to turn away, then swung back. 'Well then, not enough of it's coming my way. I'm taking huge risks here and this' – he waved the bag in the big man's face – 'half of this goes on fuel for the boat and keeping the damn thing afloat.'

Rokesmith stared steadily into Nick's face, so he turned away and made his way back down to the *Lady* and Matt.

It was almost dawn by the time Nick crept into bed beside Stacey. He was exhausted, but his mind was still racing. She turned over in her sleep and put an arm over him. His worries swung from Rokesmith to her. *Babies. Christ.* He tried to imagine himself and Stacey in a little house somewhere, with roses round the door and a neat little garden with a swing and a slide; upstairs there would be two bedrooms painted in fresh, bright colours – one for them and one for the baby, who would have a little white cot with a mobile bearing tiny aeroplanes twirling gently above it. Planes – or should that be fairies or clouds, maybe?

What was he thinking? What *was* he thinking? He didn't do babies. He didn't do roses round the door. This was *not* going to happen. He pulled himself up in the bed so that he was leaning against the headboard; but this had the effect of Stacey's hand flopping into his lap. *Christ, no.* He pushed the duvet aside and got up, went into the kitchen and poured himself a glass of water.

Outside, the sky was turning pale grey, with faint streaks of yellow above the rooftop opposite. He rubbed his face and ran his hands through his hair, stiff as straw from the saltwater spray. It wasn't just that he was a useless, feckless bugger. Nor even that he liked the idea of freedom and no baggage. No. Bubbling up from the very back of his mind was the memory of his mother's words that day.

Slegholm Farm had not changed a great deal between then and now. It was years and years ago, but the whole episode had spooked him so much he would never forget it.

He and Magnus had been over at the farm, visiting their grandparents. They had spent a lot of time over at Slegholm since their dad had died in that car crash. Lost, as Mum and Grandma and Grandpa called it. But Nick had worked out by then that he wasn't lost at all – he was gone forever.

Little Nick and Magnus and Grandma were sitting in the big dining room, with its dark, looming, heavy furniture, having tea – the sort of tea with a huge, flowery china teapot and matching milk jug and sugar bowl; sandwiches, where you were only allowed to take one at a time; and Battenburg cake. Their mother had arrived too early to take them home and they both whined about it.

Back home she made him and Magnus sit down at the kitchen table and then sat facing them. Had something happened? Had someone come to see her? Had she received a letter? He probably wouldn't have noticed anyway, wrapped up in his own little five-year-old world. He did notice, though, that she was serious and stern, which was usual these days. His memories of her had faded almost to nothing; but if he stopped and closed his eyes to think about her, he had an image of soft, delicate hands doing up buttons, pink cheeks, pale, wavy hair and a sad smile. But that afternoon there was no smile. She sat stiffly, her lips pursed, and looked from one boy to the other. He wasn't to know it then, but already she was ill with the sickness that carried her off only months later.

'Mummy, can we go now?' Nick hadn't liked this.

Magnus pushed him. 'Shut up.'

He remembered that his mother then cleared her throat and leant forward. 'I want you both to listen to this; and to remember it always.' Both boys fidgeted. 'Our family – the Bostocks – are well-known, long-established.'

They both nodded, but they didn't know what she was talking about.

'Your father.' She looked away for a moment. 'Your father was a good man, a simple man. Maybe he was a weak man, but he worked hard to keep life on an even keel. To keep it normal.'

Magnus was looking down, pulling at a loose piece of wool coming out of his jumper. But Nick kept his eyes firmly on her face.

'In his own way he was trying to put things right. Because he knew… certain things… about the other members of his family: his father, his grandfather and those before them.' She clasped her hands together so tightly Nick could see her knuckles go white. Her eyes were huge and staring.

'There's bad blood, boys, bad blood in this family.' She was really frightening them now. 'And it has to stop. It has to stop with you both. There are to be no more sons born to the Bostocks. Do you hear me?' She reached across and grasped their hands – held on to them tightly. 'Do you understand me?'

They both nodded and fled.

CHAPTER EIGHT

THIS TIME THE OLD LADY WAS LOOKING EVEN MORE LIKE AN eagle. Her head, with its high cheekbones and hooked nose, was held high and twitched from side to side as a member of staff wheeled her into the room. *Scanning for her prey*, thought Jasmin. But this time she was prepared. She hadn't come all this way for nothing; she needed information and this old woman had it.

She stood up and nodded at Dorothea. 'Mrs Bostock.'

'Dr Kapoor.'

Well, at least she'd looked closely enough at the letters Jasmin had sent her to notice that she had a PhD. And someone like her would be a stickler for getting the detail right.

'Good of you to see me again.'

They both knew it wasn't goodness that had made Dorothea summon Jasmin – and Jasmin come running. Each needed something from the other.

They sat at a small round table near one of the high windows. The old lady raised her chin. 'I have agreed to see you because I am – what shall I say? – interested to understand your motive in delving into my late husband's family history. I have my grandsons' interests to think of. One cannot have just anyone prying into one's private affairs.'

Patronising old cow, thought Jasmin. *Who the fuck does she think she is with her "delving" and "just anyone"?* She raised her head. She too could do a long neck. Oh yes. 'My research began in a more general way, looking into the power accumulated by the East India Company by the mid-nineteenth century.'

The old woman was at least listening, with apparent civility, so Jasmin ploughed on. 'I became particularly interested in the siege of Cawnpore, partly, I'll admit, because my great-great-grandfather died there.' Should she be blunt – or should she try to skirt round the subject? *Sod it.* 'He was one of the mutineers tortured and brutally killed by the British.'

Dorothea Bostock's head turned away slightly and her nostrils narrowed.

Jasmin carried on. 'A lot is known about these atrocities. It's no secret. But there is also a lot of detail that has never come to light. In particular, hints of especially gross behaviour in some of the letters the British officers wrote home and which are now in the archive at Manchester. And these hints tend to centre around Major Bostock.' She paused. 'It's only fair now for all the truth to be known.' She sat back, looked down at her hands, waiting for denial.

But the old lady branched off on a different tack. 'That sounds like a very solitary pursuit. Shut up in a library all day.'

'I'm fine alone. I've learnt to be self-reliant.'

'I am sure you have. Yet no man – or woman, to paraphrase Donne – is an island.'

'No? I reckon we're all islands to a certain extent. I like to work alone. I'm happy sitting in front of a computer all day, delving into records and archives. The difference is, I suppose, that once I've discovered something I like to share it with people. Knowledge should be shared; it adds to our collective wisdom.'

‘Wisdom? But suppose it adds to the misery in the world? Suppose that knowing about something simply spreads the evil of it? Surely some knowledge needs to be suppressed; needs to die out, even?’

‘But that can’t be.’ Jasmin was not going to let the discussion go in that direction. ‘Can’t be for any one person to decide.’

She fell silent. How much should she pry? She wasn’t much interested in the private life of this ancient relic of imperialism, though she felt a sneaking suspicion she was developing a degree of admiration for the feisty old crow. Bugger it – she needed to know. ‘I suppose… I suppose your husband’s family didn’t keep any documents? It is well known that Major Bostock wrote a lot – letters and so on.’

Mrs Bostock took a deep breath and turned away to look out across the sloping lawn. Again, she twisted the subject. ‘My grandsons are weak – in their different ways.’ Now she faced Jasmin again. ‘My role is to protect them.’

‘What happened to their parents?’

‘They died, when the boys were quite small. My son in a car crash on the M11. A multiple pile-up, as they called it. A dreadful time. And then his wife – not long after – of cancer. My husband and I took the boys in.’

–

Down on the beach, in a deserted cove some distance from the village and from any human habitation, a lone figure was standing on the shoreline. The tide was at its lowest and the silver sand, glisteningly wet, merged gently into the shiny grey of the gently lapping waves.

Morgan stood, wrapped tightly in shawls against the chill of the dawn. A black figure sharply defined against the yellow sky. She was gazing up at the gulls whirling high above a distant ferry. On her arm she carried a basket. Eventually she turned and made her way towards the rocks that formed the edge of the cove. She pulled out a blue patterned scarf and tied it round her hair before bending down to pick the dulse off the rocks. As she pulled each strand away she shook it out to release the bits of shell and small creatures that had become entangled in it. Each piece was carefully laid out on a rock to dry while she searched for more. At times, she would break off a small piece, pop it into her mouth and chew on it.

The sun was well up by the time she had filled her basket. She straightened up and rubbed the small of her back with both hands, then set off for the long walk back to the cottage.

Jasmin was sitting at the kitchen table, her hair rumpled, a cup of very strong coffee in front of her.

'Good grief, what's that – seaweed?' she asked as Morgan set down the basket near the stove. She pushed back her chair and went over to run her fingers through the long strands.

'We'll have it tonight with our supper,' said Morgan.

Jasmin sniffed at it suspiciously. 'It looks very worthy – is it very worthy?'

'Oh yes.' Morgan was unfazed by, or maybe unaware of, the sarcasm. 'It's a very good source of minerals and vitamins – at least as good as other vegetables. It has all the trace elements, plus loads of protein—'

'Yeah, I get the picture: worthy.' Yet Jasmin smiled as she reached down for the mass of papers on the floor beside her.

'So, it's some sort of local history you're researching into?' asked Morgan. She had taken off her shawl and replaced it with a floaty pink scarf. Jasmin watched her pour a beige mixture of seeds, nuts and oats into a bowl.

'Yes, some sort.' She hadn't yet decided how much about her work she should reveal to the locals. Yet although Morgan lived here, so was local, Jasmin had the impression that this girl didn't mix with the villagers – or indeed, with anyone else. She was an odd person: a loner, yet perfectly friendly; apparently vulnerable, yet self-contained; vague and dreamy, yet self-sufficient. *Altogether interesting*, she decided.

'All this… all of this,' she repeated, indicating the pile of papers, 'relates to the scion of a family that has lived on this—'

Morgan was walking away, towards the bookcase that stood at the foot of the stairs. She lifted down a large, tatty, red book and leafed through it. 'Scion,' she read out loud. 'A living shoot or twig of a plant used for grafting to a stock.' She turned and looked at Jasmin with raised eyebrows.

'Well, yes. Botanically, yes. But in human terms, "a child or descendant of a family, especially a rich, famous or important family".'

'Okey-doke. Go on.' Morgan came over and sat down opposite Jasmin, resting her chin in her hands and looking expectant.

'Although it's not so much the scion as the original member of the family himself I'm looking into, which means a wholly different paradigm…' She could see Morgan's eyes going out of focus already, so decided to drop that line of explanation. She downed the last dregs from her cup and stood up abruptly. 'We're going to need a large pot of coffee if I'm going to tell you the whole story. And I don't mean dandelion root coffee or chicory – lovely though it is, I'm sure,' she lied. 'I'm talking coffee that'll make your hair curl.' She looked at Morgan and laughed loudly.

Five minutes later she was set to go. 'The Indian Rebellion, the Indian Mutiny, that is, in 1857 – you've heard of that?'

Morgan smiled and shook her head.

'OK. So.' Jasmin rubbed her head vigorously. 'Right. The Indian soldiers working for the British East India Company revolted. Don't get me started on colonial suppression or we'll be here all day. Anyway, it eventually led to the end of Company rule and the British government taking over running the country. The sepoys – the soldiers – were getting seriously pissed off with the way the Company was treating them. More coffee?'

Morgan shook her head to this as well, but Jasmin topped up her cup and stirred in some sugar.

'Some people believe that the final straw was that these sepoys had to start using a new type of ammunition for their rifles. They were paper cartridges that came pre-greased and the men had to bite them open to release the powder. But this grease contained tallow – animal fat.'

Morgan shuddered.

'Yeah, not very nice, for sure. But you have to bear in mind that if it was pork fat it would be offensive to Muslims and if it was beef fat it would deeply offend the Hindus.'

'That's awful – how could they make them do that?'

'Yes, well that was just one way they were badly treated – there was a whole load of other stuff. But what I've been looking into in particular,' this with a rueful sweep of her arm at the piles around her, 'is one incident that happened during the Rebellion.'

CHAPTER NINE

THE REST OF THE AFTERNOON PASSED, NIGHT FELL, AND JASMIN stood up to stretch, glimpsing a pale face which backed away into the darkness outside the little window. 'You've got a visitor,' she told Morgan. 'Or maybe a stalker.' The girl's head lifted and twisted and she stared, like a startled bird, towards the blackness. The pale face again approached the window.

'Oh, it's all right,' said Morgan. 'It's only Alex. What's he doing here?' She went to the door and coaxed him in, but he stopped short when he saw Jasmin. *He's not best pleased to see me*, she thought. *But then, tough shit, I'm here and I'm staying.* Jasmin and Alex nodded at each other.

'Alex lives upstairs in the pub,' said Morgan. She twirled, raised her arm in the air and the pink scarf floated down from her hand, winding itself, snake-like, round the length of her arm. Jasmin noticed that she didn't even begin to try to explain to this boy what Jasmin was doing on the island.

'How do you get to live here on your own, then?' asked Alex. 'Whose house is this, anyway?'

Jasmin watched him drift round the room. He peered at the drawings tacked up on the walls and stopped to study one fading watercolour that had also caught Jasmin's eye when she first entered the cottage. With his finger he traced the outline of the dead robin in the picture. It looked stiff, its eye a dull stone, the breast washed-out red. Yet its form was beautiful, the shape of it, from beak to tail; the exquisite neatness of the tiny rows of feathers.

He moved on and fiddled with the shells and other little treasures Morgan had scavenged from the beach and lined up on the dresser. She could see Morgan was nervous, unsettled. Probably she was afraid he would stand on the little driftwood sculptures on the floor, sculptures that to Morgan represented mermaids twined around mermen, or sea anemones wrestling with squids; but to him might just look like scraps of old wood. He had big feet. The laces of his trainers trailed muddily over the rug.

'Come and sit down by the fire.'

He turned and looked at Morgan, probably surprised by how high and squeaky her voice was, but then came and flopped down in front of the flames.

'You'll need to warm up.' Her voice was a bit calmer now. She obviously wasn't used to people touching her things. She also sat down, cross-legged, on the rag rug made by her nan, well faded now, but which depicted a ship at sea, in shades of blues and greens. She arranged her floating skirt to cover her legs.

'This was my nan's home,' she told him.

They piled cushions in a semicircle on the rug in front of the fire and made themselves comfortable.

Alex started pulling items out of his scruffy backpack. 'I brought a few things… my mum won't miss them,' he said. The haul included two big bags of Doritos, a nearly full tub of roasted red pepper houmous, a two-litre plastic bottle of Coke, a bag of cashew nuts and a nearly full box of Lindor chocolates.

Jasmin seriously doubted that the landlady of the Dog and Whistle was not going to notice those had gone missing, but, hey, there wasn't a lot of junk food in Morgan's cottage, so she went for the Doritos.

Morgan fetched some plates from the little Welsh dresser. No two were alike and Jasmin imagined they had been picked up singly in charity shops or at car boot sales. Morgan brought glasses, too, but turned her nose up at the boy's offer of Coke. 'It's an evil product of capitalist society,' she announced. 'And it rots your guts.'

Alex shrugged and poured himself some. Then he delved again into the backpack and brought out a dark brown, tall, narrow bottle, with squiggly writing on the label. 'This has been at the back of the cupboard forever,' he said. 'Haven't got a clue what it is. Is that your language?' He held the bottle up to Jasmin.

She looked at it, then looked at him, but decided to let it pass. 'No,' she said. Then, 'But those might be plums in the picture, so maybe it's some sort of plum brandy or liqueur or something.'

Morgan had a collection of little glasses, not much bigger than shot glasses, so Alex filled three with the thick, dark liquid and laid them out on the hearth. They sat looking at them for a while as they ate the Doritos.

'Jasmin's been telling me about all these historical documents she works on,' Morgan told him. 'Terrible things used to happen in India in the eighteen-hundreds.'

'Terrible things used to happen here in the eighteen-hundreds,' replied Alex. 'Terrible things happen here now.' Silence. They all gazed towards the fire, thinking their own thoughts. Alex reached forward, picked up two of the glasses and handed them to the others, then took the third for himself.

'Cheers,' he said, and knocked his back while the others sipped. 'Ha.' He breathed out and Jasmin almost expected to see his breath on fire, like a dragon's. 'Wow.' He topped up his glass.

Morgan was lapping hers in tiny sips, like a cat. 'It's quite nice,' she declared. They munched more Doritos.

‘So all this stuff in India,’ said Alex. ‘Was it real, or just one of those things that gets blown up by them in charge rewriting history?’

‘Oh, it was real enough. At least, the atrocities people did to other people were real enough. But it is sometimes hard to sort out the fact from the fantasy – they often got jumbled up in the written records.’

‘Fantasy?’

‘Well, what we might call urban myths, I suppose. Legends, fairy tales. Strange creatures being conjured up—’

‘Oh. We’ve got plenty of legends about this place,’ said Alex.

‘Were you born here?’

‘Yeah, on the beach.’

‘On the beach?’

‘Well, maybe not exactly on the beach, but my mum and dad were these hippy types.’

Alex opened the chocolate box and spilt some out on the rug in front of them. ‘We’ve always had our share of strange creatures round here, too,’ he said. He turned to Morgan. ‘You know about the Mermaid Rock?’

She shook her head.

‘Out there.’ He flicked his head towards the darkness outside. ‘Off the East Point there’s a jagged rock looks a bit like a mermaid. I heard about this years ago – spooked me for ages afterwards. You know, nightmares and stuff.’ He picked up a chocolate and twisted it between his fingers, staring at it intently, though Jasmin could tell he wasn’t seeing it. ‘There was a night one January when a storm was going on – felt like it would never end. A group of fishermen had come up the coast and got stuck, so they were staying at the Dog. The wind was so strong all the windows were rattling, so I crept downstairs in my pyjamas and hid under the bar and listened to them talking. Of course, it was only an old fisherman’s tale, my mum would call it, but back then I thought it was real.’

‘There’s always a basis—’ began Jasmin.

'No. This was just a silly story. Bunch of blokes, bored, drank too much.' He dropped the chocolate. 'So there was this young girl in the village, used to go down to the shore to collect shells and stuff. One day she was there on her own and some men came along and saw her and got hold of her and raped her – one after the other, right there on the beach.'

Morgan hugged her knees more tightly.

'Christ,' said Jasmin.

'They left her for dead and went off singing and laughing and joking. It was a full moon, high spring tide, and when the water came in it took her body and carried her off out to sea. And the sea was angry. Angry for her. And it turned her into this creature—'

'Who sat on rocks and flashed her tits and lured sailors to their deaths…' Jasmin was enjoying this. She was shocked by the black look from Alex.

'Don't you laugh at our stories. It might just be a stupid fairy story, but it's our stupid fairy story.' He uncrossed his legs and stretched out, leaning on his elbow.

'Oh, I'm sure she wasn't—' Morgan jumped in.

He rolled on his back. 'It's okay.'

'And then there's St Osyth,' went on Morgan. Jasmin could see the girl was eager to keep them both happy, like a little puppy running back and forth between its warring owners, so she reached out for the bottle and poured them all another tot. She raised her glass. 'Here's to St Osyth,' Jasmin declared. 'I'm sure he was a fine chap.'

Alex looked up at her with a bit of a smile and clinked his glass against hers. 'Yes. Gawd bless her old bones.'

'Ah.'

'Go on then, Morgan.' He pushed her glass towards her. 'Spill the beans on old Osyth.'

The girl smiled but didn't immediately launch into her story. Jasmin wondered how often she had a sustained conversation with another human being.

'She was real. She was definitely real. Her father was a king. Her mother a queen, daughter of a king—'

'Posh, then?'

'Shh.'

'She was brought up in a convent. Must've been quiet, calm. Then – I don't know how old she was – she was forced to marry a prince. Sighere, he was called. King of the East Saxons. Forced to marry him. Forced to… forced to bear him a son. One day her husband went into the forest to hunt. He shot down a beautiful silver stag. Perhaps the stag had to die for her freedom, 'cos she escaped while he was out hunting, ran to a nunnery. Eventually, she built her own nunnery and became the Abbess. But then the Danes came, from over the water.' She swung an arm wide to indicate the wide expanse of unknown, out there. 'They destroyed the lovely building and they cut off her head.'

'Wow.'

'But she was brave and she was bold.' Morgan sat up straighter. 'She picked up her head and walked towards the church. Angels came down,' she raised her arms and fluttered her fingers, 'and guided her. But there she fell.'

Jasmin had a flash of the woman's head rolling down a gravel path.

'And a fountain sprang up.'

'Does it gush blood?' asked Alex.

'No. Pure water.'

Jasmin stood up and stretched. 'Making me hungry, all this,' she said. She went into the kitchen, where she was pretty sure she had seen the makings of cheese on toast, and started slicing and grating.

'These old stories like their severed heads and limbs, don't they?' she could hear Alex say. 'All part of that scary, Roman Catholic, you will rot in hell suffering perpetual torment stuff they used to go for. Hieronymus Bosch and all that.' He stared into the fire; watched the flames licking at a log whose bark was curling, bent backwards unnaturally upon itself as its native moisture was stripped and ripped away. 'A thousand different ways you can be tortured by demons in hell. Love it.'

Jasmin, pausing at the door from the kitchen where she was about to ask them how many slices they wanted, glanced at Morgan; the girl's round eyes were fixed on Alex.

'But I've always thought.' He looked up now, to see if they were listening; yet when he realised they were both watching him, he instantly went back to being gauche and tongue-tied. 'Doesn't matter,' he murmured.

'No, go on,' urged Morgan.

Alex looked back at the fire and picked with his fingers at the loops in the rug. 'What I've always thought is what's most scary isn't the blood and gore at all, it's what you can't see, can't hear, but you know it's there – and it's evil and destructive, and gets inside your head and drives you mad. And I think this island's worse for that than some other places. There've been smugglers round here for centuries. Well… still are, tell the truth. And way back they used to go in the, like, taverns and places and they'd tell all these scary ghost stories just to keep the locals away from the bits of coastline where they would bring in their contraband, or the barns where they would stash what they'd stole.' He bent forward further over his crossed legs, his fingers working at the rug. 'But there was one I heard that stuck in my head, clear as day.

'This time it was a lock-in at the Dog. It was when my dad was still around.' He looked up at the two of them. 'He was a musician… sort of. But he used to have friends who played in bands up from London sometimes. This one night there was quite a few of them and they played their guitars – bit of singing and stuff in the back room. Some of the old boys, the regulars, weren't very keen.'

Jasmin could picture that. Old men hunched over their pints in the corners, grumbling.

'I was loving it, though. Course I was. Finally the singing stopped and I went back to bed, but I couldn't sleep – so excited, what with the real-life musicians and singers and stuff.'

For a split second, Jasmin saw his staring eyes soften with the memory. She came back in with the piled-high plate of cheese on toast, cut into triangles, and a jar of pickle. They all breathed in deeply the warm, tangy aroma.

'Then I realised I could still hear voices from below,' Alex went on. 'So I crept back to my spot on the stairs and listened. There was this one old boy, Monty they called him, retired sailor, dead by now, I guess. He didn't look like your typical sailor – no white beard and pipe – but he did have these watery, pale blue eyes that gazed into the distance. So he had everyone gathered round him, and he was telling this story. I suppose it was to show off to the Londoners. Or scare them off. Give them the willies when it was time for them to leave and they found themselves walking out into the dark, the real dark you don't get in London. And I've never told it to no one since. But it's always stuck in my head.'

He sat up straight, lifted the bottle with the curly writing, then put it down again.

'You won't know this,' he said to Jasmin. 'But people here have always relied on this coast – this sea – to make their living. Yes, there are farmers and all the usual jobs, but it's the sea where the real money comes from. And people have always got greedy. Years ago, there were smugglers. Well, like I said, there's smugglers now, but back then it was bigger. Much bigger.

'Over on the east of the island,' he went on, 'there's a beach called Cormorant's Landing. Not many people go there. You'll know it, though.' He glanced at Morgan. 'I'll bet you've been there – for your bird-watching and seaweed-collecting and the like.' Morgan nodded. He turned back to Jasmin. 'It's just rough shingle – nothing to attract the holiday-makers. And there's a cliff, with trees right up to its edge. Those stiff trees that lean away from the wind, with fingers reaching as though they're clutching for something to grasp on to. The cliff's not high, maybe twenty foot – but it's wearing away all the time and bits crumble and fall down, so that scares some people off. And anyway,' he was looking down at his hands that were fiddling with the cashew bowl, spinning it this way and that, 'it's weirdly bleak there. The sea is brown, always brown, even under a blue sky. And there's rocks just under the surface. The ones that make the water move in strange whirlpools and flow through fast channels, so that if you look down from the cliff there seem to be these dark, sleek, huge sea monsters weaving in towards the shore from out at sea.

'So Monty started telling his story and I'll never forget it – never forget a single detail.'

Jasmin and Morgan looked at each other. *Alex was a goth, but more than that he was pretty much a ghoul*, thought Jasmin, *so for something to unnerve him it must be pretty gruesome.* 'Go on then,' she said. 'Tell us.'

He stretched out again and looked into the fire. 'Okay.'

'My great-aunt Ruthie, says Monty, lived in the farm at the tip of the peninsular with her mum and dad. She was about twenty when this happened and worked in the fish sheds. There wasn't much on offer for young women in those days.

'Down the coast, in one of the workers' cottages, there lived old Mrs Dee. She was a fisherman's widow who had three sons who had all moved off the island. One summer, when she was very old and frail and close to death, her youngest son, John, returned to look after her. And he was a thin man, permanently hunched over as if scouring the ground ahead of him for something unexpected. He looked older than his years and the lines on his face were deep, his eyes sunken and staring. But he cared for his mother in a gentle way, he cooked hot meals for her and helped her to wash.

'Ruthie watched him and saw that he seemed to be a good man, very different from the rough, loud farmworkers and fishermen who were the only other men she knew. At first, he would barely meet her eye or speak, but after a while they took to sitting together on the porch of Ruthie's parents' house in the evenings. John Dee told her he had been to sea. He left St Cedd when he was seventeen and travelled the world in merchant ships, learning to become a ship's carpenter. He told her of the exotic places he had seen; yet she felt melancholy in all his stories as though some shadow was cast over everything he saw, turning the exotic colours to shades of grey.

'Ruthie fell in love with him and so they married. After old Mrs Dee died they moved into the cottage and John was a loving and attentive husband, though still quiet and reserved. And more – he suffered terrible night terrors, waking convinced that someone was grabbing at his legs. He avoided the coast path overlooking Cormorant's Landing where the water was always brown and the current was swift and dangerous.

'On the day they moved into the cottage Ruthie went into the bedroom that was John's as a young man. She saw that the mirror had a hole, with jagged, crazed cracks radiating from it. She put her finger in the hole and felt the smooth outline of something round and hard lodged in it. She asked John about it when he came into the room and he stood beside her, staring into the mirror. He told her it was a musket ball, shot there by him when he was young and drunk and foolish. Facing back into the mirror Ruthie realised it was like a hole in the face of the person reflected in the mirror.

'She found herself disliking intensely a bronze statue that John insisted must be allowed to remain on the mantelpiece in the kitchen and must not be touched. It stood about a foot high. It had a flat base with a sphere on top; and standing on this ball, clutching with sharp talons, was an evil creature. It was not exactly a dragon – more like a snake, a cobra, but with outstretched wings that had sharp, serrated edges. The head was elongated, the eyes malevolent, and it had two huge, curving fangs with points sharp as needles. One day, Ruthie picked it up and found, when she turned it upside down, that roughly scratched on its base, with a sharp point, was the name "Bostock". Below that, in a more wobbly hand, the word "*Sarpsipahi*". John treated the blessed thing with an unholy reverence, which she could not understand, when he should probably have sold it if they were going to have any money or peace.

'His moods, his nerves did not improve. Trying to find out what was afflicting her man, Ruthie asked questions of people living on that side of the island and learnt about the villagers' smuggling and wrecking past. Back in those days all that land towards the sea was salt marshes. Unstable, dangerous. Anyway, John Dee wanted to get rich, Ruthie was told, wanted to out-do his brothers and everyone who scraped a living from fishing and stuff.

'And back then there were wreckers. There'd been wreckers for centuries, and this particular thing happened in the middle of the eighteen-hundreds, when people still used sailing ships. The wreckers would put out the fire in the lighthouse, then light their own beacon on the Cormorant's Landing cliff, so the ships would misjudge the coast and hit the rocks. Though no one said they knew of John's involvement, some people remembered he disappeared straight after one major shipwreck.

'Now they were living together, Ruthie realised that night after night John left the cottage and wandered along the clifftop, staring out to sea. One wild night Ruthie followed him. She found him standing on the cliff edge, waving his arms in front of his head as though to ward off some brutal, invisible attack, shouting out and weeping at the same time. He was soaked through and chilled to the bone. Ruthie managed to lead him back to the cottage, took off his soaking clothes, wrapped him in a blanket in front of the fire and demanded he explain. Like a child, he capitulated. Sobbing at first, he told her. He put into stammering words those vivid pictures that had filled his mind and haunted him since that stormy night all those years ago. He told her it was the first time he had been allowed to join the wreckers – he had just turned seventeen. They said he was too young, too soft. But this was rumoured to be a big ship, bound for Hull and carrying goods back from India; from wealthy British traders or military men. He followed the others on to the beach. The moon was hidden behind the low clouds and the cold mist – the haar – was coming in off the sea, stinging his eyes and making them stream so he could barely see. He described the angry waves, how the ship crashed onto the rocks and broke its back.

'All the cargo – crates and barrels – started being washed ashore. But of course the crew of the ship also began to swim towards the beach – those that could. The leader of the wreckers told the others to let them be. It's too dark for them to see our faces, he said. They won't want to tangle with us, they'll just run off into the darkness.

'John was right down one end of the beach. He strained his eyes to watch the ship go down. It was frighteningly fast, he thought, how it went from being a safe haven, transporting you home, to a smashed pile of matchwood that bursts it sides and lets the sea rush in to take you.

'John Dee's voice sank to a deep, cracking whisper. Ruthie held the cup of brandy to his lips, then he carried on. As he stared at the sinking ship, he said, something grasped his leg. It held on tight, painfully, and he couldn't shake it off. He looked down and he saw these two young boys, cabin boys maybe, who'd made it to the land and were crawling out onto the shingle. One of them had John Dee by the ankle and looked up at him with a naked plea for help on his face, gasping for breath. The other was clutching some piece of treasure he had salvaged. It gleamed in his hand in the darkness. John Dee just panicked. He grabbed up a piece of wood, heavy, with big nails sticking out of it. And he beat them to death. Over and over he crashed down this club onto them and he was screaming and crying at the same time, because he didn't want them running off and reporting him, or he'd be hanged; but they were only young boys, maybe gone to sea for the first time, and they were going to have mothers at home weeping into their aprons for them. So he beat them and beat them as they lay there. He saw the nails in the wood driving holes in their faces and their skulls and their hands as they tried to shield themselves; the way the bone splintered, the blood gushed and the sea darkened. He smelt and tasted the metal and salt in the mix of blood and seawater that spurted up into his face.

'After he told his story, John grasped Ruthie by the shoulders. He begged her not to leave him. He had always known, he said, that she could not stay with him if she heard the truth. Ruthie could not speak at first. She turned away.

'All that night she was awake, sitting in a kitchen chair staring at the dying embers in the grate. She was trying to push aside the horrific pictures that now filled her mind. She had to determine whether or not she could forgive him. All through the next day she went through her daily tasks as in a half-dream, weighing up what she knew about this odd little man she has grown to love, recalling the tender way he treated his mother before she died, how he came back to this island that he must have hated and feared with a vengeance just so that he could care for her when she needed him most. And she thought about his constant gentleness towards her, Ruthie. The attentive way he cared for her; his sadness that he would never have enough money to buy her jewels or beautiful clothes or a handsome house with tall windows. Things she never cared about. Things which, if she had them, she would exchange at the drop of a hat for a good, loving man.

'All the next day John Dee hid himself away in his workshop. As she went about her chores Ruthie heard the occasional sound of him sawing and hammering. He was still there when she went to bed; but she respected his privacy, so left him alone. She had, by then, concluded he was a good man and worth saving. She would tell him in the morning.

'In the dark, still hours of the night, she woke to an empty bed and saw, through the window, a flickering light. The wrecker's beacon had been lit. Downstairs, as she looked wildly around the kitchen for any sign of her husband, her eye was caught by an absence – a blank space on the mantelpiece where that infernal bronze snake statue always stood. Now it was gone. She gathered her shawl about her and ran out into the night, calling his name.

'Ruthie knew where he must be: on the beach. She ran through the darkness to the cliff and looked down at the figure on the shingle below, lit by the flickering fire. He was standing close to the crashing waves. The wind blew in gusts, so she could only hear the noises he was making in bursts that strengthened then faded then rose again. The noise was not like a human, but nor was it like any animal or bird. It made the hairs rise up on Ruthie's neck and a chill, like drops of freezing water, ran down her back. With all his strength, he was casting the statue into the surf, trying to return it; but it kept drifting back and back and back.

'"John! Stop!"

'He turned to look up at her, tried to wave her away. Yet she would not leave. She slithered and slid down the cliff but stopped short of going too close because he looked so wild, possessed, unfocused.

'"I'm trying to give them what they want," he cried out, sobbing.

'She moved closer. "They don't want the stupid statue," she said. "They want you."

'He stopped, his body sagged and he looked hard at her. He said, "I know."

'The look on his face terrified her. This was no longer her John. She snatched the statue from his hands, backed away, then turned and ran, scrabbling along the shingle to a large rock. She grasped the statue by its base; she smashed and smashed it again and again on the boulder, though it scarcely seemed to dent.

'As she paused to catch her breath, she caught the sound of something coming into the bay. Something huge forging its way through the waves. A ship that she couldn't see, though she strained her eyes into the swirling blackness. And now there was the sound of something breaking apart, wood crashing and splintering on rocks – even though there was nothing there. Now she could hear people screaming and splashing and crying out. It was as though he had summoned the ship back from the land of the dead.

'She dropped the statue, crying out John's name. There was no ship, there were no bodies, flotsam or anything. But she saw John fall to his knees and she saw – she swore she could see – long grey arms, bony arms, rising up from the water's edge, stretching out their hands for him. Thin, scrawny fingers reached out like tentacles. And faces. Two horrible faces, formed out of the shallow waves, ever-changing, ever-screaming. The hands reached out of the surf for him, clutching at his throat and pulling him down.

'She stumbled back to him and pulled him free, managing to drag his body out of the waves and onto the shingle. She heaved him over, only to see she had no need to save him from drowning because he was already dead; his skull was splintered, holes in his face and his hands. Deep holes, as though nails had been driven into his head and body, with unstoppable fury. The worst of all was his eyes. Wide, wide open, they stared, unseeing yet with a look of utter horror that made her blood turn to ice.'

Alex's voice faded into silence, like the soft hissing of the tide pulling at the shingle on the beach, then ceasing. For a long time, none of them moved. Then Alex reached forward and picked up the last triangle of toasted cheese. The crunch as he bit into it was unnaturally loud.

'And what happened to the snake statue?' asked Jasmin, though she feared she knew the answer.

'Dunno,' said Alex. 'Maybe still on the island, maybe long gone.'

CHAPTER TEN

'What time does the pub open?' Jasmin had had enough coffee and felt in need of a lift that didn't involve caffeine. After their late night, her morning had been slow. She was finding it hard to concentrate.

'I don't know – I never go there. They stare,' Morgan replied.

Jasmin laughed harshly. 'They'll really have something to stare at when I walk in. C'mon, let's go.' She stood up decisively, suspecting that this was the way to goad her young landlady into action. 'Get your coat.'

The road into the village was so puddly that they had to negotiate a path between families of ducks who had made it their new home.

'God, this place is so… flat.' Jasmin gazed around her at the formless landscape.

'But you can see really far. Don't you like that? Don't you like the way you can watch the birds coming in from when they look like tiny, tiny dots in the distance? Don't you love the way the trees all lean in the same direction, as though the wind once blew so hard that they just bowed under its strength and never felt they had the right to stand straight again?'

Jasmin turned to stare at the girl so hard that she all but trod on a duck that was struggling to keep up with the others.

'Oops.'

Luckily Morgan didn't seem to have noticed – she was too taken up with gazing into the sky.

'Yeah, whatever,' she added, but that went unnoticed as well.

The Dog and Whistle looked less than hospitable in the cold light of day, without the sparkle of the fairy lights that had been put up for Christmas three years ago and which nobody had bothered taking down since. Morgan hung back as Jasmin pushed hard at one of the narrow, varnished double doors. When it finally yielded to her grunting persuasion, they found themselves in the brightly lit bar, with the eyes of all those within turning to fix on them. Looking neither left nor right, she strode across to where a woman with a great deal of hair and a disturbingly cross expression was polishing glasses with dangerous vigour. The woman plastered a smile on her face, looking with interest at her mismatched pair of customers.

'Hello, ladies. What can I get you?'

'Hi. Er, I'd like a large white wine.'

'Of course. Sauvignon Blanc or Chardonnay?'

'Right, er, I'll have the Sauvignon. Morgan?' She glanced back at her companion standing behind her, only to find her looking down at her feet. The landlady folded her arms and leant heavily on the bar, a grim, twisted smile on her face.

'Now, are you sure she's old enough?'

Jasmin looked from one to the other; raised an eyebrow at Morgan.

The girl half-lifted her head, her hair covering most of her face. She didn't quite manage to meet the unwavering eye of the landlady, whose focus shifted back to Jasmin.

'Only as I recall she was only a year or so above my boy Alex at school – and he's only sixteen.'

'I'll have an apple juice, please,' muttered Morgan, sounding more eight than eighteen.

'Good choice!' Jasmin rubbed her hands together heartily, wondering what was going on between these two. *Village life, eh?* How could she ever have thought it might be dull? The woman moved away to serve the drinks and Jasmin leant on the bar to study the clientele. A trio of what looked like fishermen were sitting at a table in one corner. They were looking her way and smiling. *Well, leering or smirking might be more appropriate descriptions*, she thought, but she'd give them the benefit of the doubt. This once.

As far as possible away from them sat a morose-looking couple – definitely been married for years, as they sat sipping their halves in silence. She turned to smile encouragement at the subdued Morgan who was still suffering from her put-down, then she noticed beyond her a figure standing in the shadows just inside the door leading out of the back of the bar. It was a pale youth with spiky hair who was staring, hollow-eyed, with a bleak intensity, at Morgan. Jasmin elbowed her. 'Look, there's what's-his-name. Alex.'

The girl turned and looked at the boy.

'Go on, go and talk to him. The mother's busy – she's not going to know.' Which was true enough, since a large, loud group had just come barging through the door.

A slightly warm glass of wine later, Jasmin and Morgan met in the car park to walk back to the cottage. For a while they walked in silence, full of their own thoughts.

'It's good of you to put me up, Morgan,' said Jasmin. 'I don't think I'd get much peace and quiet staying there. I get the feeling there's comings and goings at all hours.'

'Oh, you're welcome. I'm pleased to have…' Morgan's voice tailed off.

'Hey! Let's go for a drive,' said Jasmin. 'You can show me some of the countryside.' She strode forward; turned to encourage the girl, who was still drifting along, staring at the puddles. 'C'mon. C'mon! You can tell me the names of the mountains and the lakes.' The girl looked up and shook her head; but a smile was starting. 'You can point out the best places to go clubbing and skiing, and where you'll build your massive country estate when some hunky rich guy comes along and sweeps you off your feet.' Morgan was laughing now.

–

She couldn't put her feet on that carpet. How could she put her feet on that carpet when her shoes, once the colour of sunset, were now sludgy brown and dripping with mud and ducky-doo? She held the door of the car, swung it backwards and forwards, and didn't know what to do.

'Don't worry about it, just get in,' said Jasmin, doing just that; so Morgan got in and lined her feet up neatly on the black carpet. Jasmin drove up the short lane that led from Nan's cottage to the road. 'Left or right?'

Morgan thought about that. Either way would take them round the island. Jasmin was looking at her, waiting for an answer. 'Left,' she said, and Jasmin swung the steering wheel and roared off to the right – so that was probably left. Anyway, away from the village, which was good. Through her hair, she took a sideways look at Jasmin. She was scarily cool. Her skin was rich, and her hair was black and thick, and she dared to wear black all over, and Morgan would bet no one dared call Jasmin weird.

They drove along the coast road for a bit then came to the point where it veered inland, between fields.

'Ooh, a change of scenery,' said Jasmin. 'How interesting.'

Morgan stared at the flat, dull green fields, then looked back at the silver jewellery flashing in Jasmin's left ear. There was a stud, then below that a wide ring with tiny spots marked into it in two parallel lines, and below that a big, dangly earring with long, thin, silver rods hanging. They looked sharp, cool. They spun and reflected the light as Jasmin turned her head.

'Oh God, I'm sorry,' she said. 'I didn't mean to be rude about your home. Have you always lived on this island?'

Wow. This goddess was actually apologising to her. Actually seemed to want to know.

'No,' she replied. 'No. I was born in Ipswich.'

'And your family – they still live there?'

Morgan watched a crow swoop down heavily and land on a gatepost. 'I don't really have any. Well, only Auntie Anne. My mum's sister. But she's always ringing and saying she's worried. Always worried.' And she didn't want people worrying over her. 'Most of the time I've lived with them, just over the causeway on the mainland, and I went to school there. But their house is very busy. Very noisy.'

'And your mum?'

Morgan felt the squirming in her stomach that always came when anyone said "mum". They were passing a field of cows. One or two of them looked up and stared for a moment as the shiny car flashed past, then carried on eating as though it had never been. *Perhaps they thought they'd imagined it*, thought Morgan. She wondered if they dreamed about their day. 'They take the calves away from the cows before they're ready,' she said. 'They cry out to each other. And the sheep – you can hear them baa-ing for their lambs, but they just shut them off with great, clanking metal gates.' She had long ago stopped trying to remember whether her mother had cried out for her. She knew that would just bring up an empty hole in her memory.

From the corner of her eye she saw the silver flash as Jasmin glanced across. After a while she asked, 'So what's your connection with this place – and the cottage?'

Morgan found herself smiling now. She liked the cottage. She liked her chickens. 'It was my nan's. And after she died they said I could go and live there for a while, if I liked. So I did – and I do.'

‘Good God, what’s this?’ Jasmin braked hard as they came round a bend and were confronted with a bright blue giant archway, with St Cedd Holiday Park written across it in a sort of jolly, mock-children’s handwriting, in peeling, faded pink paint. ‘That’s hideous! Shall we go in?’

‘No, no, I don’t think we’re allowed—’ Morgan started to say, but already Jasmin had swung the wheel and driven in. She pulled over, opened the door and stepped out of the car.

Morgan looked around, then slowly followed. Her nan had always said these people were “dodgy, not to be mixed with”, and she found herself breathing fast. She grasped a fistful of her hair. But looking around, the few people she saw looked perfectly normal. Two young women, in thick puffer jackets, strolled past, one of them pushing a buggy containing a well-wrapped-up toddler. There was a long, low building, divided up into shops, each with a white plastic heading: Convenience Store, Tattooist, Toilets, Off-Licence, Laundrette, Office. The office was unlit.

Jasmin strode forward, her hands thrust in the pockets of her leather jacket, looking around her boldly. Morgan scuttled to keep up; she didn’t want to be left on her own in this place of white rectangles and concrete, endless concrete. The white, plastic-clad boxes stretched further than she could see to either side and in front of her.

Jasmin turned and waited for her to catch up. ‘Why would anyone want to have a caravan holiday here, in the middle of January?’ She turned round, spread her arms wide and laughed. ‘Why?’

Morgan found herself smiling at the woman’s boldness. ‘I think some people live here? Maybe.’

They walked on between the rows of identical caravans, some with tiny picket fences restraining dead-looking shrubs, no leaves or berries. The few people they passed ignored them. The road ended with the sea, dim and murmuring now it was low tide. There were no dunes here, just a low wall and, beyond it, a concrete walkway then a pebble beach. To one side stood a pub, built of the same purple-red bricks as the buildings by the entrance. The Jolly Smuggler. Picnic benches were ranged outside and three men were sitting at one, drinking pints out of plastic glasses and smoking. They all stared at the women. Morgan felt herself squirming and turned away; but Jasmin managed to ignore them completely, looking straight through them like they weren't there. She was brilliant. Morgan would love to do that.

Back in the car they carried on east. A lighthouse poked up from a flat headland and Morgan suddenly remembered. 'This is the place!' She pointed, excited.

'What place?'

'The place where Alex's shipwreck happened – where the man was driven mad by the thing!'

Jasmin started nodding, so Morgan knew she understood her. 'Let's take a look, yeah?' She turned the car into a little road, which ended in a field. Walking to the edge of the field they looked down onto coarse sand dunes twenty feet below. A sign warned them not to swim here and there were ominously large pipes leading into the water.

'Come on – we have to walk on the beach,' said Jasmin, and they found a place to scramble down. The dunes were dotted with prickly sea holly and marron grass. There were no living creatures. Morgan knew that if she were a bird, she would not want to land here. Jasmin was already down by the water. Morgan caught up with her and crouched down onto the sand, which was surprisingly fine nearer the water's edge. It had a soft feel as it ran through her fingers and she heard the gentle, regular lapping of the waves. Yet to her mind, they became angry, crashing and hissing. The words of Alex's story flooded back into her mind. The clashing noises grew louder and louder, hurting her skull.

She shut her eyes tight, put her hands over her ears. She could see those long, grey, bony arms, stretching out their hands; thin, scrawny fingers reaching out like tentacles.

‘My God, are you all right?’ Jasmin’s voice was echoing, coming to her from a huge distance.

Then she was holding her shoulder and Morgan found herself coming back. ‘Yes.’ Her voice was so weak; she tried to make it stronger. ‘I’m all right.’ She looked up at Jasmin and saw the alarm in the woman’s expression. ‘I’m fine. It just happens sometimes. I go to… other places.’ Jasmin helped her stand up and Morgan loved her more because she didn’t start bombarding her with questions – the why and what and how that people seemed to need to ask, if they saw her “going away”, as she thought of it.

They walked slowly back to the car. On they went, round the coast road. ‘So what’s in the middle of the island?’ asked Jasmin. ‘Just fields?’

‘Fields, yes,’ said Morgan. She watched a flock of fieldfares having a busy time eating the berries on a hawthorn hedge. ‘Birds, cows, sheep. It’s dangerous for the sheep, though.’

‘Ha! Can’t believe a sheep would have much to worry about – not until they see the mint sauce, anyway.’

Morgan decided not to mention the killings. She really didn’t want to frighten away this new person who had come into her life. Jasmin was like some exotic eastern goddess descending to live amongst the mortals.

The road took them round to the junction with the causeway. Jasmin pulled over. ‘So… this is the only way off? Back to civilisation?’ She peered at the thin ribbon of road snaking off towards the mainland. The light was obscure and conveyed a feeling of gathering storm that comes with late winter afternoons. ‘It looks wet – does the sea come this high?’

‘Oh yes. The causeway gets covered twice a day when the tide’s in.’

‘So really no escape?’

Morgan looked across at her, but she didn’t seem fazed by the idea of being trapped. ‘Do you go out a lot? Back home? Do you go clubbing?’

Jasmin looked at her and laughed. 'Yeah, sometimes. My sister drags me out, mainly.'

Morgan had to ask: 'Do you have a boyfriend?' but it came out in a more flaky voice than the casual one she had planned.

Jasmin looked away, then looked back. 'Let's say I'm between men at the moment. So, no. No one special.'

As they drove on, a faint, yellow light in the west shone on the pale ribbon of beach, intersected at times by black wooden breakwaters. Jasmin slowed as they passed the entrance to the harbour. 'Boats, then?'

'Yes!' Morgan laughed out loud. 'Lots of boats.'

Then on towards the village. Morgan felt an urge to slip down in the seat so no one would spot her, because she never liked being looked at. And yet part of her wanted them to see her in the company of someone who knew the world, who wasn't narrow and petty like they were. She sat up straight and looked around her. They had come to a halt just before the pub, where a huge lorry was having trouble turning round. A group of men stood around it, all calling out different advice to the driver. They were stocky men; some of them, despite the cold, with rolled-up shirtsleeves. Morgan had a sudden flash of a painting she had seen once of farmworkers with grotesque, leery faces. *Ha!* She really, really had to get that picture out of her head.

Now a different figure appeared: a tall man with dirty, fair hair. Different from the others. He might have looked like a nice guy if it weren't for the expression on his face. He was furious.

–

Nick Bostock forced his way through a crowd of morons trying to turn a brewery lorry. *That bastard Rokesmith. Total fucking bastard.* Dragged Nick into his filthy work; got him so deep in he couldn't get out or Rokesmith would shop him – or worse. Possibly much worse. He'd seen how Rokesmith had treated any of those poor bastards who tried to argue with him. They'd travelled thousands of miles; they had no money, spoke little English. They were all scared. They got off the boats cold, usually wet, hungry, thirsty, sleep-deprived and terrified for their children.

And now Rokesmith had left him seriously out of pocket. In front of those estate agents Nick had had to make a big joke of the splashing Rokesmith had given them. So as soon as they'd docked he had to take them all to the pub and buy them drinks to win them round. Which he'd done. And now he would probably have to do even more runs for Rokesmith just to get some money, even though he'd sworn he'd never work for him again.

The day had started well. Nick was in buoyant mood as he readied the *Star* for the afternoon's fishing, which would earn him some decent cash. Estate agents from Chelmsford. A team-building exercise, apparently. He'd run trips like this before and had a good laugh to himself afterwards when they'd disembarked at the dockside, and turned their backs on each other, never looking back. Mostly men, if not entirely, he'd bet his life on it. Women wouldn't waste their time pretending to like the people they worked with, he reckoned. This lot were full of enthusiasm and climbed stiffly onto the boat. Those who knew each other were chatting, ignoring the rest.

There was a great deal of commotion and confusion as Nick got the rods sorted, lifejackets fitted and seats allocated. Today every line seemed to turn to a tangle in his hands. There was a bit of a problem with the manager of the firm, who turned out to be so big that no lifejacket would do up round his stomach. As Nick was yanking on the straps he had a sudden vision of those whalebone corsets that posh women wore in costume dramas. The maid would have her knee in the girl's back. The girl would be fainting and swooning and going, 'Tighter, tighter, Maud,' or whatever she might be called. He wished he could stick his knee in the gut of this hulk, but it probably wouldn't help him do the lifejacket up – the bloke would probably just puke on him.

Then Nick had to move them all round as the *Star* was listing dodgily to port once the man sat himself down. There was some seating inside the wheelhouse, but Nick didn't want people in there, stretching their legs out just where he needed to put his feet.

Finally, they headed out for open water and Nick was busy helping those who knew nothing about bait, or casting, to get started, while he guided the boat to one of the better spots to be sure of some decent codling catches.

The water was flat, opaque and unresponsive. Before too long the beers had come out. Nick turned down the offer of one; someone had to stay sober, and besides, his head was still stuffed with all his problems.

'I *said* – is there any chance of catching any sea bass around here?' An abrasive voice cut through Nick's thoughts and jerked him back to reality. 'My wife's very partial to a bit of sea bass.'

'Yeah, yeah – could well be some bass.' Nick nodded. Might as well encourage them. 'Once we're a bit further out.' He knew there were no bass. They wouldn't be playing along on a day like this. But these men had paid their money so it was his job to keep their spirits up.

Two o'clock, and the estate agents had a few decent-sized catches amongst them. He had got them all believing they were fine fishermen. And they were much merrier, as a result, in part, of the beers to which Nick was trying to turn a blind eye. They'd picked up some roker, codling and whiting, and all of them had a catch. He took a moment to rest his hands on the roof of the wheelhouse and look into the distance. Heavy, dense clouds, their ragged bases merging with the sea, were beginning to build up above the horizon. He thought his fishermen had definitely had their money's worth. It was time to pack up and head for shore.

He stowed the landing nets then sat down alongside the men to try to get them to learn how to put away their rods without ending up with a massive spider's web of tangled line. Tedious stuff but it had to be done. He leant back to watch them and have a moment's rest and was shocked nearly out of his skin.

A speedboat which he had half-noticed in the distance had suddenly picked up speed and was heading straight for them.

'Shit.'

'What's up, Cap'n?' asked one of the fishermen in a bad attempt at a pirate accent.

Nick grunted. 'Think I might know that boat – that's all. Come on, you lot, let's get a move on.' And he snatched a rod from one of the more inept of the group and started reeling the line in as fast as he could. He glanced edgily towards the approaching speedboat. If anything, it was coming even faster – and was heading straight at them. The *Star* was a carthorse of a boat; she was designed to cruise at around fourteen knots. What was coming at them was a racehorse, and one ridden by a mad psychopath of a jockey.

Just short of collision point, he must have flung the wheel over, as the boat spun to its right. The resulting wash came broadside at the *Star*. Throwing the rod back into the hands of its owner, Nick launched himself between and over the outstretched legs and feet into the wheelhouse and pressed the start button. The engine spluttered but would not fire up. The wave hit them. The men who had seen it coming were clinging on to the sides of the boat. Those with their back to the wave were flung forwards and found themselves sprawling on the deck.

Nick stared through the window at the oncoming boat, sure now about the identity of the bulky figure standing upright at the wheel. Come on, *come on*. Still the engine failed him. The speedboat, a sleek beast, was now circling the *Star*, its engine whining at a mad, hysterical pitch as its driver drove it to its limits. The waves he was creating were making the *Star* bob uncontrollably on the water like a cork.

Nick looked at the useless controls and the panicking fishermen trying to get back into their seats, but he couldn't move

– and anyway, what would he do? He had to cling on to the frame of the wheelhouse door just to stay on his feet.

'What you doing, you mad fucker?' he shouted.

Patrick Rokesmith was like a shark toying with his prey. 'Not so cocky now, are you, Bostock? Eh? Your little townies crapping themselves?'

The fishermen were looking alarmed and confused, but some were also angry. 'Get away, you fucking madman,' shouted one. Rokesmith continued to spin around them. The rods were piling up in a tangled confusion. The overweight manager obviously thought it was time to take charge. He stood up and waved his arms angrily towards Rokesmith, but as the speedboat was moving so fast and the *Star* was still powerless and motionless, it meant he had to turn round fast to keep his eyes on him.

'Pack it in now – we're calling the police,' he shouted. But his feet were becoming increasingly tangled in the lines and ropes around his feet. There was one moment of stillness as he looked down, realised he was shackled; his employees – the senior negotiators, the junior negotiators – stared at the man's ankles, yet in that split second no one could move. He fell to the deck with a mighty crash, and thrashed about among the feet like some massive, blubbery fish dragged up from the depths.

The roaring of the speedboat's engines changed to a deeper tone as the man controlling it slowed it down, swung it round and started to drive away. Over his shoulder he called out, 'You'll do as you're fucking told, Bostock!'

'I'll fucking kill you, Rokesmith!' Nick roared after the rapidly disappearing boat. 'I've fucking had enough! You're a dead man!'

CHAPTER ELEVEN

The next day was Saturday, and Elaine and Suzanne were bowling along the road out of the village in the camper van, quite early in the morning, hoping to hit the shops in Ipswich before they got too busy. They were held up, however, by a roadblock on a straight stretch of the road. There were two police cars, a police van and two sleek, dark cars all parked on their side of the road, while striped tape and some canvas sheeting closed off a whole area where the trees bunched thickly right up to the road. An officer stepped out and held up his hand.

'Sorry, ladies. Been a bit of an incident here. Was either of you on this road last night at all?'

They both shook their heads.

'What's happened?' asked Elaine, craning her neck to try to peer past the marked-off area.

'Serious incident.'

They sat for a while, picturing the multi-storey car park filling up; the last of the January sales items being cleared off the shelves.

'And what's all this about, anyway?' asked Suzanne, hammering the steering wheel in frustration. She suddenly twisted in her seat, cranked down the window and shouted, 'Hey! Ben! Over here!'

Elaine bent forward and saw her friend was shouting to a uniformed policeman who was helping control the traffic.

'It's Ben,' she said to Elaine. 'Max's cousin. I've known him since he was a kid.' She beckoned him over. 'What's going on, Ben? We're not going to be here for hours, are we?'

The policeman came over, looked up the road, and down the road, then leant on the van's wing-mirror.

'Hello there, Suze.' He nodded at Elaine. 'Could be. Major Incident Team's in there. I'd say find another way round.' He shrugged. 'But you know there isn't one.'

'So.' Suzanne leant forward, nodding, looking serious but inviting shared confidence. 'What can you tell us?'

By the time they were free of the traffic jam they knew about as much as the police did, and everything that had come up on Twitter – and Elaine's head was reeling with fact, fiction and wild imaginings.

It seemed that Patrick Rokesmith spent the later part of yesterday wheeling and dealing. He had much to do if he was going to keep the business up and running. His contacts overseas would not wait if he was no longer able to take possession of the goods on the nights they were coming in. They'd simply find someone else to take his place – and to take the money.

It had taken a lot of phone calls, said Ben, a lot of bullying and a certain amount of shouting down the phone – and at the phone – before he felt he was getting somewhere and could call it a day. He'd stayed on his boat, tucked out of the way in a small, quiet bay where he could get a decent signal, so he fired up the engine and took her along to the harbour at St Cedd. It was well after nightfall and he must have reckoned if Nick Bostock had stirred up any trouble it would have died down by now.

He would have steered his boat into a quiet mooring in a corner of the harbour, secured it and walked along the harbour wall towards the road. What he probably needed then was a stiff drink.

He couldn't go to the Dog – too many pals of Nick Bostock were likely to be in there; but if he cut through the woods he could make it to The Smugglers well before closing time and get a few whiskies under his belt. Maybe it was even time to celebrate; word had already got round about how the townies crashed into the water, shrieking and panicking like a load of girls.

There wasn't much of a decent path through the woods, but he must have known his way well enough to work out the general direction. Rokesmith was not, however, a fit man: nutrition for him meant chips with his steak and ale pie, while regular exercise was raising his fists at people who wouldn't back down. After five or ten minutes he was probably breathing heavily, because there was evidence that he had sat down on the trunk of a fallen tree and smoked a cigarette. The half-moon, last night, was largely obscured by the clouds which swept across the sky, making the shadows deeper, then not so deep, then deeper again. All this might have caused a shape-shifting that gave Rokesmith the impression of people or creatures peeking out from behind tree trunks, then disappearing again. But it wouldn't have fazed him. He wasn't one to be scared by a few shadows.

On again, then. He wasn't so far from the road. Perhaps he began to picture the glasses lined up on the bar. He was not the sort of man who could pass unnoticed through an area of woodland. His big feet left prints everywhere; there was a wide trail where he had crushed leaves and twigs underfoot; small branches were snapped by his broad shoulders.

His toe must have caught under some hidden obstacle – a root or a fallen branch – and he stumbled forward. There were signs he had fallen onto his hands and knees, then scrambled to his feet. His first reaction was probably to look around him to make sure no one had seen him looking like a tit – but of course there was not a soul in sight.

From here onwards, the trail became more confused. Rokesmith seemed to be more cautious, more aware of his surroundings. His footsteps were shorter, lighter, as though he were staring into the deep shadows as he ploughed on, glancing from left to right, glaring at every twitch of a leaf, every tiny rustle in the undergrowth. Then, suddenly, the strides become much longer, the footprints deeper. He was running – and running fast for such a big, unfit man. He had almost reached the road.

At this point, Ben Wray stopped his story and pointed to a spot by the side of the road at the head of the queue of cars, where a cluster of police gathered, along with – and Elaine knew this from all the TV drama she watched on catch-up in the afternoons – a forensic team.

'He was scrabbling up that bank – had started to force his way through a broken wire fence. And then they grabbed him.'

'They?' Elaine knew her eyes must be as round and huge as Suze's.

'Or him… or it,' said Ben Wray. 'It left a trail, apparently,' he went on. 'But not footprints, just a sort of smooth, dragging path. It must have grabbed him by the legs, dragged him back down into the darkness of the trees. They can tell that from the mud all over his front and the cuts and mud on his hands. Then it slashed him.'

'Slashed him?'

'Yup, that's right,' and Wray let go of the wing mirror and straightened up, as though to walk away.

'Ben!' said Suzanne. 'You can't just leave it there – tell us about the slashing!'

'I shouldn't really talk about it,' he replied.

Bit late for that, thought Elaine, though it was no great surprise in this place that people felt the urge to talk. She bent across towards him. 'With a knife?'

He leant in the window. 'More like a claw… a huge claw… with huge… I dunno… talons.'

He went back to his job of placating drivers of the dozens of vehicles that had built up in the queue. Eventually they reached the roadblock, passed through it and stopped again at the causeway, as Elaine's phone rang. It was someone ringing from the pub, so she answered it.

'Hello… yes? Everything all right down there?' she asked, thinking it was early in the day for even the most inept of barmen to be unable to change a barrel or to have run out of change.

'Yeah… Elaine… it's Dave. Yeah… look… I was just wondering if you want me to open up as normal this morning.'

'Of course I do. Why shouldn't you?'

'Well, it's just that the police have been going round all the businesses and shops and pubs and the like, saying everyone should keep their doors closed. On account of some axe murderer or something… least that's what Josie says…'

'Axe murderer?' She turned and saw Suze gawping at her, mouthing the words "axe murderer", round-eyed.

'Well, maybe not… maybe it wasn't that.'

'Dave! You can't go around—'

'Yeah… sorry. Anyway… so shall I open up at normal time?'

'Yes, definitely. I'll see you this afternoon.' She jabbed at "End call", stuffed the phone in her bag and slammed the van door.

Bouncing round in her seat towards the still-goggling Suzanne, she said, 'Get that engine started and let's get out of here – if I have to spend another minute in this gossip-ridden, parochial, tiny-minded, incestuous little shit-hole I'll go mad.'

Suzanne pulled away and they headed over the causeway. The waves were shrinking away from the road, yet again having succeeded in their twice-daily quest to surge over the edges and lick at the tarmac. The women chatted a bit about the new gallery in Lincoln that sounded keen to show some of Suzanne's landscapes; and Elaine at last found herself relaxing and beginning to enjoy her day off.

Her phone rang: the pub again. What now?

'Hey Elaine, guess what's the big news around here?'

'Go on then, Dave, put me out of my misery.' She turned towards Suzanne and cast her eyes upwards. 'What's the gossip machine saying now?'

She listened for some time, nodding occasionally into the phone and staring ahead at the road. When she'd finished the call she shoved her phone away in her bag and pulled the collar of her jacket more closely round her neck.

'Actually, this is a bit scary,' she said, turning towards Suzanne. 'Apparently they really do think it was murder and they really are warning people to be careful.'

Suzanne forced the gear stick of the ancient van into third gear as they approached the junction at the end of the causeway, trying to ignore the grinding noises. She sighed.

'Oh dear. That's going to set off a whole train of people going: "I don't know what the world's coming to"; "This place has really gone downhill"; "Wouldn't have happened in my day"; "Immigration"; "Youth of today"…' She glanced across at Elaine, who was staring stonily through the windscreen. 'Look,' she added, 'I'll bet this has all been hyped up. It's not going to be as bad as it sounds.'

She's good like that, thought Elaine. Suze had no idea why she felt the need to reassure Elaine that no one had been murdered. Except that she knew her friend worried about things and had a lot of stressful stuff to put up with, what with the pub – and Alex.

Within an hour, though, they were both laughing over cappuccinos in the Cabra Verde in Ipswich. The café was buzzing with chattering shoppers and steaming from the warmth rising off discarded coats in the over-heated place. Elaine had taken back a top to White Stuff and changed it for something she liked better. On the strength of that she had treated herself to a pair of boots she could justify buying because they were reduced by fifteen per cent. On a market stall they'd found a tee shirt she hoped Alex might like.

Suzanne had bought the latest *Artists and Illustrators*. She was happy with that. As they were walking back towards the market her phone rang. Unknown.

'Hello?'

She stood still and Elaine turned round and walked back to her.

'Oh… Stacey… hi.' She glanced at Elaine, shrugged and gestured to a bench where they could sit for a moment. 'That's all right. What's up? How are you – and Nick?'

She listened for a short time, then: 'What's happened?' There seemed to be a long explanation, then Suzanne said, 'Don't worry. Go back to the flat and I'll be with you in less than an hour.'

Suzanne explained it all to Elaine as they headed back to the van. 'That was Nick's Stacey.'

Elaine nodded.

'Nothing about him would surprise me. He's always been a troublemaker. Not that I see much of him, and I think I've only met Stacey about twice. But now he's in real trouble.'

'Oh yeah?'

'The police came. He got really angry and said they had it in for him and there was a bit of a fight – and then they took him away. Honestly, Elaine, her voice was cracking. I must say I felt my heart going out to her. Everyone called her skanky, chavvy and worse when Nick first appeared with her. She said she rang the police station, but they wouldn't tell her anything and she doesn't know what to do, or whether she needs to find him a brief, or even what they think he's done! I mean, it could be anything, but they said it had to do with a really serious crime.'

And when they stopped at the Co-op to pick up a newspaper, they found several people who were all too ready to talk about it.

'I heard it was a drug deal gone wrong – gang warfare,' one fragile-looking, white-haired lady leaning heavily on her shopping trolley was saying, with a tremor of excitement in her voice.

'My Bill reckons it was someone fell asleep at the wheel, got concussed, wandered off and died of hypothermia,' announced another customer.

There were general mutterings, then: 'They said he was torn apart by wild animals,' chimed in the boy fresh back from his paper deliveries.

All the customers and Mrs MacLaren behind the till turned to stare at him.

'Away with you, you wee scaremonger,' declared Mrs MacLaren sternly. 'No one has said any such thing – that just came from your wild imagination.'

The boy shrugged. 'Well, he might have been. You don't know he wasn't.' There was no possible reply to that.

Elaine waved Suzanne goodbye, then turned and stepped into the pub. There was a big lunchtime crowd and a definite buzz in the air. People sat in small groups, heads close, deep in conversation. *Surmising* was the word that came into Elaine's head. As soon as Dave saw her he burst into excited gabbling, which Elaine cut dead with a hand in his face.

'Is there any more news?'

'Yes! Well, no, not exactly—'

'Thought not. I'll be upstairs.' And she walked away, leaving him opening and shutting his mouth like a stranded fish.

Once upstairs, she took her new top out of its bag and held it up to shake the folds out of it. It was dark blue with a pattern of tiny white birds in flight and the low, scooped neckline that she liked. The only thing she didn't like so much was the size 16 label; so she cut it out. The new boots then came out of their box. She admired them, then held one to her face and took a long, deep breath. *Ah… new leather.* Reluctantly, she put them down on her bed and walked across the landing to Alex's room.

She sighed, opened the door wide and stepped in. Another

long, deep breath, but this time her nose was assaulted with teenage boy smell, making her hasten across the room to open the curtains and struggle with the window catch.

'Have you had something to eat? I could make pancakes,' she said to the shape under the duvet. News of people dying untimely deaths put things into proportion, sometimes. There were worse things than lying in bed for half the day with earphones stuffed in your ears.

'Shut the window – it's freezing.'

She did so, and after a moment a thin, white arm, followed by a shoulder and head, came out from under the bedclothes.

'Er, yeah. Pancakes. Yeah.' The croaky voice paused. 'You been out?'

'Yes, into Ipswich with Suze. We went to the market, had coffee and stuff.' Elaine almost stooped to pick up random dark garments from the floor, then stopped herself.

'I got you something from that stall you like – the one run by the vampire, or zombie or goth or whatever he is.' She went back to her room and returned, holding out a black tee shirt to Alex. 'Here – take it.'

The thin arm reached out again.

Elaine peered, then grabbed hold of the wrist and pulled it towards her. 'What's all this? What's happened?' She was staring, shocked, at the long, thin, parallel scratches. They stood up in angry red wheals, disfiguring the pale flesh.

He pulled back, turning away. 'It's nothing. Just… just a cat.'

'A cat? What cat? Jaggers wouldn't do that!'

'Not Jaggers. Look… forget it… okay? Christ!' and he thumped back onto the mattress, pulling the duvet over his head. This was normally Elaine's cue to stomp off, slam the door and spend the next half hour fuming over yet another break-down in communication with her son. But today, with all that might have gone on in the village the previous night still in the back of her mind, she was too anxious to let it go. She folded her arms and stared at the lump in the bed.

'I've just about had enough of this, Alex. You don't speak, you barely eat, you hardly ever go out, except at odd hours of the night. It's got to stop, Alex.' Reaching out tentatively, she plucked at the covers. 'Can't you tell me, love, tell me about what you've been doing? Maybe I can help—'

'*No!*' He sat up and twisted round violently. 'No! You can't help – you can't do anything!' And to her utter dismay he flung himself away from her and sobbed like a toddler.

Down in the bar, later on, the evening rush was underway. The phone rang behind the bar and Elaine put down the glass-cloth to answer it.

'It's only me,' came Suzanne's voice. 'I thought you might want to hear the latest.'

'Huh. I've been hearing nothing but the latest. Every time a new person comes in I have to listen to some new theory that someone heard from someone's auntie, whose next-door neighbour got it from some van driver.'

'Ha ha!'

'So it seems we've been invaded by Martians and a huge invisible dome has descended over the island. But it also seems a load of zombies have arisen and are wiping out random people.'

'Well, that sounds reasonable,' said Suzanne. 'I'll go with that. However, more to the point, I've just heard from Stacey again. Apparently they've let Nick go.'

'Well, that's good.'

'I suppose. Like I said before, though, whenever there's trouble he always seems to have a hand in it somehow.'

'Nice for Stacey to have him home, though.'

'Yes, of course. Though she told me she's pregnant and I'm gathering it's not all sweetness and light in that department either.'

'Shame.'

'Yes, it is a shame.'

'Well, I'd better get back to the punters and listen to the latest drivel.'

'Okay, see you soon.'

CHAPTER TWELVE

Nick was back in the flat. He'd had a shower and a can of beer and was trying to put behind him the unpleasant time he'd had at the police station. *Talk about being guilty until proved innocent.* One minute they were all shouting in his face, the next minute he was all alone in a dim, colourless, cold, damp cell, with no idea of how long he would be there.

True, it wasn't the first night Nick had spent in a police cell, and probably not the first time he'd been wrongly accused of some crime, but he had never known such intensity of questioning, nor such a buzz of focused, meaningful activity in a police station. He'd had his clothes taken away as soon as they got him into the building and he'd stood naked and shivering, not understanding what crime he might be accused of.

A grim-faced detective inspector had demanded to know every detail of his activities the day before, and especially the night before. Out of habit, Nick had been evasive, trying to think through the implications of his answers before making them, not eager to reveal everything he did or everyone he spoke to, even when the interactions had seemed harmless.

'Tell me about this business with Patrick Rokesmith.'

'Business?' Nick's mind whirled while he tried to keep his face bland. *The boat people? Who had blabbed? Kev? Matt?* He had to stay cool – he couldn't guess how much the police knew. In the silly white onesie they'd given him to wear he felt vulnerable, like some sort of albino rabbit surrounded by a pack of wolves. And yet… and yet… they didn't seem to be asking him about the *Star* or what he'd been doing with her. As the shouting in his face, the thumping on the table and the stomping around the room continued, he realised they were more concerned about what he'd been doing last night, where he'd been and when he'd last seen Rokesmith.

'You were heard threatening to kill him!' roared the inspector, his face about two inches away from Nick's.

'What?'

'What? What? Is that all you ever say?'

And so it went on.

'Why did you resist arrest?'

'Force of habit. How long are you keeping me here? Don't you have to arrest me, or something?'

'Believe me, lad, you don't want to be arrested for this one. And we'll keep you here until we've checked this so-called alibi of yours.'

Eventually they had, and grudgingly let him go. On the steps of the police station the evening light glowed gently in his face in contrast to the harsh glare of the interview room. Stacey sat behind the wheel of the old green Polo, staring at nothing. When had he last seen her look happy? When had they last had fun? He crossed the road, opened the passenger door and got in. She barely glanced at him, looking down at her fingers which were twisting each other nervously. No shouting, no accusations, no reproachful stare; he in turn didn't try to put his arms round her or tell her to stop being a wet blanket or for God's sake to get off his case. They had driven home slowly and in silence.

Stacey was now offering him a second chilled beer, but he shook his head. Then he stood up and went towards the kitchen. 'What about you? Fancy one of your fruit teas?' He rummaged through the rows of little paper packets. 'What about raspberry leaf? That good for pregnancy?' He dared to glance round.

Her chin raised, she was looking at him hard. 'Pregnancy's not an illness, you know.'

He put down the teabag and moved towards her. 'Yeah. No, I know. And I ought to tell you…' Nick put his hands to his head and rubbed his hair briskly. 'I ought to tell you…' he said again, then put his face in his hands and started sobbing.

It took a while before he was able to speak again properly. 'Patrick Rokesmith's dead. Patrick Rokesmith's dead.' He raised his head from Stacey's lap and looked at her face. *Such a sweet face.* He sat up and pulled her towards him, resting her head on his shoulder and stroking her hair.

'Oh, Stace, you wouldn't believe what a mess I'd got into. But he was evil, that man, evil. And now he's dead I should be pleased. I should be fucking delighted. But—'

'But you didn't cause his death, so stop beating yourself up about it.'

'It's not that. I just… I dunno… everything's spun out of control… it's like I'm in this whirlpool and any minute now I'm going to be sucked down the drain. Hold on to me, Stace, hold on to me.' He twisted her hair round his hand, binding himself to her. 'Please stay with me, Stace. Don't leave me on my own.'

'But it's not only me, is it? What about the baby? You're the one who leaves me – I've never left you. Are you planning to stick around – or just come and go as the fancy takes you? Look at me, Nick. Look at me and tell me you want this baby.' She pushed him. 'Eh, eh?'

'It's not that I don't want a baby. And we can manage—'

'Huh! Yeah, you always say that. But it's not the money I'm talking about. Or even the responsibility – I've never expected that from you, I know you don't do responsibility. No, there's something else – some problem you have with the whole idea of babies.'

He pulled away, hiding his face in his hands. She waited.

'It's my family.'

'Yeah, well some of them have always been a bit odd, for sure.' She grasped his shoulder. 'But maybe now – with your involvement with Rokesmith out of the way and with the baby coming – now would be a good time to, you know, reconcile with them. Maybe you could get on with your brother a bit better—'

'You're joking! That miserable loser? Total wanker.'

'Yeah, well, he might be, but he's still your brother. And then there's your gran – you don't seem to be able to talk to her much. It might be a good time now to go and tell her about the baby. She'll be really pleased about that, won't she? She must look forward to being a great-granny – they all do. Hey, she might even want to buy us a cot or a buggy or start knitting—'

'Knitting? Are you crazy?' He had leapt to his feet with an anger that made Stacey jump back and put her hand to her mouth. 'Oh, God, Stace. How can I explain?' He looked down at her pale, upturned, face and so wanted to smooth out the worry lines along her brow, to kiss the downturned corners of her mouth until they smiled and dimpled again. He turned away. 'Believe me, Stace, she really, really doesn't want to be a great-granny.'

–

On a crisp, cold morning, three days later, Magnus Bostock visited his grandmother. She wasn't so well this morning, he was told, so he went up to her room and sat in the winged armchair beside her bed. Her hand was frail and wobbly as she lifted the teacup to her lips.

How much should he tell her about what had been going on on the island? She wasn't stupid. She had a television and radio;

there were newspapers in the lounge; and of course the staff were chattering and gossiping all the time – probably adding their own lurid imaginings. He would talk about the farm.

'Silage is holding up not too bad.'

'And lambing?' Her voice was croaky but there seemed to be a genuine interest in the watery blue eyes.

The question threw him. Did she even remember the attacks on the sheep? 'Quite soon,' he finally said. 'Might be a bit down on numbers this year,' was all he could think to add.

She surprised him by saying, 'Yes, Brenda was saying that. You have fewer sheep now. She seemed to think it was a good thing.'

'Brenda? She's been up here?' Brenda and his grandmother were worlds apart. When he'd first brought her home, the meeting between the two was stiff and awkward. Afterwards, Grandma had said little, apart from, 'Brenda? An interesting name. Though I always thought it was a little… below stairs… don't you think?'

'She came yesterday.' For a brief moment the old lady looked uncertain. 'Yes, it was yesterday.'

'Oh.'

'She was inquiring about this woman who has arrived; this university researcher.'

'Oh, right.'

'Yes. Brenda came and asked – she seemed concerned.'

'Concerned?' *Why would Brenda be concerned about university stuff?* She never researched anything except livestock prices and grain prices. Though he supposed she was a bit obsessive about breeding lines, particularly in cattle.

'Of course, I didn't tell her anything,' the old lady went on.

Of course? Why of course? His grandma was always so stiff about family history. If this researcher woman wanted to find out about life in India and the army back in the day, then good luck to her.

'She herself is – what is one supposed to call it these days? – mixed race,' she went on.

What did that have to do with anything?

'Anyway,' she added, her voice a bit stronger now as she folded her hands in her lap, a sure sign that the discussion was over and there was to be no argument, 'I shall keep our family's business to myself.'

–

In Nan's Cottage, as she now found herself calling it, Jasmin's eyes were burning and gritty, her head swirling with information overload, her laptop red-hot and the pile of papers now covered the whole table and half the floor. She stretched, wandered into the kitchen and opened the fridge; then shut it again before going into the bathroom to take out her contact lenses.

It was already deep dusk outside, but she realised she was desperate for fresh air to clear her head. No problem – that's what torches were invented for and she had one in her suitcase upstairs. *Hah!* She had the last laugh on her sister for once.

She started off down the lane, then decided to go on a roundabout route over the fields. For once, she was wearing the right shoes. Following the line of a hedge she went up a gentle slope over stone-strewn pitted soil. Not her usual idea of fun, but her limbs were stiff, her mind was stale and she really needed this. Ahead of her a breeze was coming off the sea, carrying with it a damp, briny scent. At the top of the ridge the field gave way to dunes and she could look down now on the blackness of the sea. Small waves were lazily breaking on the shore, occasionally flashing with the silver of phosphorescence.

She surprised herself by how calm it made her feel – the distant, rhythmic swoosh of the waves, the dampness on the breeze easing her tired eyes. Maybe the countryside was manageable – in small doses. She stretched her arms to relieve her aching shoulders. The chill of the evening was getting to her now, but she wasn't yet ready to go back indoors so decided to walk further.

The ridge along the top of the dunes had less loose sand, so she opted to follow that. While she strode along she let her mind drift over the few people she had met since arriving on St Cedd. In the main, they were what she had expected and been warned of by Professor Walker-Phillips back at the university. Dorothea Bostock, though, now she was intriguing. Stiff upper lip, old-school – all that sort of stuff you might expect of one of those matriarchal types. Yet she was even more hostile than Jasmin had feared. Okay, so you couldn't expect someone to pour out their life history and everything they knew about their late husband's ancestors to a perfect stranger the first time she met her; but Dorothea had known she was coming and knew she was conducting research, so it wasn't like it was a total surprise. Yes, she had a long haul ahead of her trying to get information out of the forbidding Dorothea.

And Morgan – she was something else altogether. She was not of this world of farmworkers and fishermen and out-of-work men who hung around, and hard-faced women with their sleeves rolled up. In fact, she was hardly of the world at all. What was she doing here?

She paused and looked out towards the sea again. There was nothing but blackness out there now, dotted with the occasional twinkling of a light – white, red-yellow – that she supposed came from boats or buoys. Further out, far to her left, came the rhythmic, searching beam from the lighthouse. They had passed it on their drive, but she had barely noticed it. Maybe because they weren't painted with red and white stripes, these days. Were they ever – or was that just in kids' storybooks? Katie Morag on her Scottish Island – didn't she have a stripy lighthouse?

It was time to start heading back. Pulling out the torch, she switched it on and cast the light around her. There looked like a path, although a bit rough and stony, heading back inland, so she set off along it.

The sound of the waves rapidly diminished as she left the shore behind and she found the stillness of the night beginning to bear down oppressively on her. She quickened her pace as the path descended rapidly through a copse of trees. Here the blackness was profound on either side. She took her eyes off the path for a moment to flick the torchlight among the trees and instantly felt her foot drop into a hole. Her ankle twisted with a wrench that made her feel sick and she fell to the ground, the torch rolling away from her.

'Shit!' Bloody rabbits, or voles or weasels or whatever stupid animal would dig its hole right where people needed to walk. She eased her foot out of the hole and rubbed her ankle, then scrabbled for the torch. Sitting among the damp fallen leaves which smelt strongly of mushrooms and fungi and rotting things she would not want to name, her first reaction was to reach for her phone; but she did not have it with her. And whom would she call? She thought she had seen a phone at Morgan's house, but she hadn't bothered to ask for the number.

She flexed her foot and decided that she would just have to get up and keep walking. She found she was panting – from the shock as much as the pain. *All right, give yourself a minute, then get up and get moving.* At the first house she came to she would beg for a lift back to the cottage. She was summoning up the energy to try standing up when a noise from the trees to her right made her stop. Was it a rustling – like a little animal moving around? Not exactly. It was a deeper, more resonant noise.

Oh for God's sake. Animal, human or some country bumpkin-cum-swamp monster – she wasn't going to let it spook her. Time to get back to civilisation. She found walking wasn't too bad as long as she didn't put much weight on the injured ankle. Keeping the torch beam firmly on the path directly ahead of her she made some progress. An owl hooted way off in the distance and another one answered it. But then closer – much closer – there was movement. Something was walking – stalking – along a line parallel to hers.

She swung the torch round and flickered the beam amongst the trees. Nothing. The noises stopped. A few steps more – again the movement mirroring hers, a nightmare version of Grandmother's

Footsteps. Further periods of standing, listening; moving on, no doubting that a presence was shadowing her. After staring long and hard amongst the trunks of the trees for a fourth, fifth or sixth time, she resolutely redirected the torch ahead of her and staggered on.

A crashing noise now, straight ahead, brought her up short. She leant against the trunk of a tree and eased her ankle, feeling it already swelling inside her boot. While she stood still the sound stopped. Silence. Nothing to hear, nothing to see; but there was a sensation, which it took her a while to understand. The hairs on the back of her neck were slowly rising to stand on end. Bizarre. Each individual hair was straining from its follicle and the prickling sensation ran all the way down her back. The stillness bore down on her, compressing her chest, tightening her limbs, constricting her chest. She must move on.

Gingerly she took a few more steps – and it was the lack of any movement now that was the worst thing. Where was it? What was it doing? What was it? And now a howl – an inhuman, echoing roar – echoed around her. It filled the air, not seeming to come from any direction, yet from all. Jasmin screamed out loud, but she could not hear her own voice, swallowed up as it was by the hugeness of the endless roar around her. She found she was running blindly, the torch still in her hand but waving madly as her arms and legs pumped the night air. Twigs and branches snatched at her face; her injured ankle was sending burning stabs of pain up her leg. The noise still filled the air, but as it faded it seemed to suck all the oxygen out of the atmosphere. Her scream faded and turned into heavy panting and a sort of rasping, rhythmic moaning. But she couldn't control it. Getting away was all. Getting back to the light.

CHAPTER THIRTEEN

John Wiggins tottered through the door into the main bar and sat down on a stool. Elaine looked up from checking tonic supplies.

'Evening, John,' she said. 'You taken up jogging?'

He was breathing heavily, which didn't look healthy in a man his age. 'Weird thing,' he said. 'Weird thing.'

She poured his drink and leant on the bar to listen.

'I'd lost the dog. Bloody stupid thing,' he said. 'Just out on our usual evening stroll,' he added. Elaine knew this would be from his bungalow in Brougham Avenue. Their route hadn't varied in the twelve years since the little border terrier had been given to him by his grinning grandchildren on his sixtieth birthday. Down to the corner of the avenue, left into Western Road, all the way along to the Co-op, left into Laurel Crescent, then back home for a cup of tea and a Hobnob.

Maggie was getting on a bit these days – but then so was he. He needed to walk with a stick and he was getting a bit deaf – but then so was she. He kept calling her, his voice gruff in the damp mist coming off the sea. Where the hell had she got to? Outside the Co-op he paused, not knowing what to do. She would never have gone beyond here, yet she had been running ahead of him and not returned.

'So I called her,' said John. 'Maggie! Maggie, I calls.' He went on to tell Elaine how he limped on along the road. The gaps between the streetlights were greater here, the patches of almost total darkness longer. His weak eyesight caught, he thought, a flash of brown fur across the road, disappearing up the narrow path into Friar's Wood. He hadn't been down that path for years. It led towards the sea through a few hundred yards of unkempt trees, shrubs and brambles. No developer had found it worth his while to do anything here – in fact not many people even knew who owned it. All they did know was that it was a rough tangle of paths, dotted with discarded, rusting beer and Coke cans, and disintegrating crisp packets blown in on the stark winds from the North Sea, which swirled over the shoreline before heading off inland.

The trouble with Maggie was she was a feisty little bitch and if she'd seen something she wanted to chase – a rabbit or cat or whatever – she'd crank up her arthritic legs and really go for it. John crossed the road and stopped at the place where he thought he'd seen her. He peered down the path. All was black and damp. Then faintly he heard growling.

'Maggie?'

The growl came again, rose higher and weaker, then turned into a whimper. Then a crashing noise in the undergrowth and Maggie burst through, going flat out, her little legs a churning blur. Her ears were flat back, her eyes round and unfocused. She didn't even stop when she reached John but bolted straight past him and into the road. A screech of brakes and angry shouts almost made John's heart stop.

'Hey, you! Keep your mad dog on a lead, can't ya!' The driver of the Ford Focus had leapt out of his seat and charged round to the front of his car.

John limped forward as fast as he could and the two of them rounded the bumper to see Maggie sitting on the far kerb, panting and wild-eyed.

'You were lucky there, mate. Bloody lucky,' said the driver. He patted John on the shoulder and drove away, leaving him to scoop up the little dog in his arms.

'And I don't mind telling you, Elaine,' said John Wiggins, 'there were tears streaming down my cheeks all over my poor little Maggie.'

–

Dawn. Morgan shivered and pulled her scarf round her chin to ward off the chill. A low mist covered the field before her, tingeing the grass with silver. Behind her, an untidy line of trees marked the edge of Friar's Wood. If she had turned around she could have seen nothing in the wood – the darkness still clung to the bare trunks, the densely knitted branches and the thick, dark layer of decaying leaves on the ground, reluctant to let the early-morning light penetrate.

She was looking for Jasmin; though why a townie like her would come to such a place she didn't know. Morgan just strongly felt that she had – which made little sense, even to herself. Nor was she sure she ought to be out looking for her. Morgan had little sense of what the duties of a landlady were, or of how a lodger ought to behave. She didn't know if she should expect Jasmin to come home every night. She didn't know if she was allowed to worry if Jasmin wasn't there.

She glanced round once but could see nothing and hear nothing apart from the slight creaking of the trees, despite the stillness of the day, and a faint rustle of the leaf mould shifting. Then her focus was back on the distant skyline ahead of her. And before too long her patience was rewarded as a few tiny dots appeared, then dozens, then scores. The flock of starlings wheeled black against the pale grey of the sky. They circled the field, seeming to note the huddle of sheep in the corner where the edge of the wood met the lane, and the one dark figure of Morgan, tall and straight, now raising her arms. They swept low then within moments soared upwards, circling again above the field.

The bored sheep paused in their chewing to stare momentarily and wonder. But then a sound, or a smell, or perhaps some slight movement within the darkness of the wood was making them edgy. They shifted their feet, raised their heads to look around them. Those nearest the woods bleated faintly and backed off, their nervousness spreading to the others, who moved stiffly further up the field onto more open ground.

The birds, meanwhile, had finished their circuit and were coming in to land. They spread themselves along the bottom edge of the field, pecking at the damp earth and chattering amongst themselves. Perhaps whatever touched the nerves of the sheep did not affect the birds. Perhaps they were aware, but knew the threat was not aimed at them or that they had the speed and agility to get away if a predator struck. Morgan ignored them and focused on the sheep, looking from them to the woods. She started to move forward, in the direction of the wood, but her feet were dragging and she found she had to force them – one in front of the other, one in front of the other.

The woods began with shrubs, growing denser and more prickly and hostile as she forged her way through. These gave way to small trees – holly and birch – but further in the trees became bigger, denser, more overpowering. The gloom and the eerie stillness were stifling and once she was completely out of sight of the field Morgan paused. She gazed up into the canopy, stretched out her arms, palm upwards, and slowly turned on the spot, her head thrown back. The green mass above her, with the white, early-morning light filtering through, formed a kaleidoscope that spun dizzyingly above her. Gradually, she slowed and came to a stop; and the realisation came over her that no birds were singing

– there was no movement at all in the branches. This was the time of morning when the birds should be at their most active – waking up, chattering and gossiping, setting off in search of breakfast. She looked down now, then all around her. A trail of broken branches and crushed leaves and undergrowth, smeared with mud, led off in one direction. Reluctantly, she followed this path of destruction.

Where the trees were most dense, the light least penetrating, she came upon what at first she just thought was a discarded boot. But the boot was joined to a leg, a body, arms and a head. She did not rush forward to check for breathing – try to find a pulse. She simply stood, almost dispassionately observing the scene before her. Yet two seconds later and she was on her knees beside the still form.

'Jasmin. Jasmin!'

Now she was slapping at the face then rubbing the frozen hands. For a long time there was no response – then the tiniest moan and the slightest movement of the head.

'Jasmin. Jasmin… it's me. Open your eyes, Jasmin. Come on… please.'

And the eyelids fluttered, just a little, and then the brown eyes were looking up. They looked towards her, yet were totally unfocused, staring without seeing.

'How did you get here? What happened? How long have you been here? You're freezing.'

She continued to rub the cold, limp hands, then pulled off her scarf and tried to wrap it round the woman's neck. But Jasmin's neck was so stiff when Morgan tried to lift her head, that she had to just lay it round her head and neck as best she could. Jasmin's pale, parched lips moved a little and Morgan leant over her face.

'What? What is it?'

Nothing. Jasmin seemed unable to speak; she was still staring blindly upwards, her face stiff, her eyes dead – or the eyes of someone who had passed through death and was staring deeply into the horrors beyond.

Chilled by this sight, Morgan sat back on her heels and looked around. Had it gone – whatever it was that had so scared or attacked Jasmin? She smelt the air, she listened to the near-silence; she listened beyond the minute shifting of the leaves in the upper branches where a slight breeze now stirred them, for any trace of the presence of anything unusual – anything hostile.

'I'm sorry,' she said. 'I'm sorry I didn't even notice you hadn't come home. I'm not used to having to look out for anyone else, you see. You do see, don't you?' But she was talking to herself. Right – it was time they got out of here. What did people do in such circumstances? Running for help – finding a phone – was not her first thought, but it slowly occurred to her that, yes, she would have to find people who could carry Jasmin out of the woods – she certainly couldn't do it herself.

She leant forward again to kiss Jasmin gently on the forehead, then reluctantly stood up and began to head, speeding up with every step, towards the road and people who could help.

–

Business was slow in the Dog and Whistle. Elaine turned to Dave, who was having an animated conversation with an equally droopy, lanky youth at the end of the bar.

'Dave – you'll be all right for a bit, won't you? Barbara will be along. Her shift starts in half an hour. Only I've arranged with Alex that we're going to sit down and have supper together – and I don't want him to change his mind.'

'Yeah, that's fine, Elaine. I can run things here – no probs.'

She doubted that, but what damage could he do in half an hour? *Apart from driving away all their regulars by boring them to death, smashing all the optics when he waved his arms around and giving everyone salmonella with his sloppy glass-washing*, she thought, disconsolately.

'Excellent. Well, I'll be upstairs if you need me.'

Once up there, she stirred the Bolognese sauce and snapped the spaghetti into the pan. Reaching down two plates from the cupboard she put them on the table, then took them off again, found a checked tablecloth in a drawer and flapped it out over the table before replacing the plates and putting out cutlery. As she grated Parmesan she called out to Alex that dinner was ready. After a pause, she heard his light footsteps approaching. She found she had been holding her breath, and let it out in a long sigh.

Alex did not look her in the face as he took his seat and stuck his fork into the steaming pile on his plate. She started to eat too, and waited.

After a long while: 'Tasty,' he mumbled.

'Good.'

More chewing, more silence. Then: 'You know that girl I see sometimes – Morgan?'

'Oh, that pale, skinny wraith who drifts around like a lost puppy, you mean?'

He clattered his fork onto his plate and flung himself back in the chair. She could have bitten her tongue: *Stupid thing to say, just when he'd started talking at last.*

'Sorry. Go on.'

He stared at her, then finally shrugged and started to eat again. 'Yeah, her. Anyway, I was, like, worried, see.' A long pause. 'I had this stupid idea she might have had something to do with this guy dying. Stupid – I mean, she never would.'

Elaine didn't dare to speak – simply nodded.

'She never would. It's just that she's disappeared. Suddenly completely vanished. I've been searching for her everywhere, but there's no one at her cottage. She wouldn't have gone away; she's got nowhere to go – she told me.'

'Oh my goodness!' Elaine tried to sound concerned, but did she actually care? No, but she had to remind herself that Alex obviously did – a lot.

'Yeah, it's really scary. So that's where I was the other night. I went into the woods to see if I could find her.'

'What – in the woods in the middle of the night?'

'She often used to wander around in the woods or on the beach at night. I've… it's magical… or creepy… or both. But it's a whole other world. You wouldn't understand…' He waved his fork dismissively in the air. 'There's things…'

Strange, disturbed girl, thought Elaine, but said nothing, just nodding again.

'Anyway, she wasn't there,' he added.

'So why did you think she might have anything to do with that man's death?'

Alex stared down gloomily into his nearly empty plate. 'I suppose it's because she's so different.' He got up and fetched a Coke from the fridge, then sat down again. 'She's just… not like other people. She can get herself to places other people can't, does weird things, says weird things.'

Elaine was out of her depth so decided to change the subject. 'And is that how you got those scratches on your arm – out in the woods?' She realised she was clutching her fork tightly; the handle digging into the table. She did not want to discover – to have it said out loud – that her child was self-harming; that her Alex would slash his own flesh open because the pain inside was so bad. But the alternative, that someone else had hurt him, was just as excruciating. He started scratching at the cuts. Why wouldn't he answer?

'You don't have to tell me. Of course, you don't have to tell me anything.' Under the table her right hand was balled so tight her fingernails were digging into the palm. Above the table, she tried for a calm, sympathetic expression, though it was probably coming out as a twisted grimace. It didn't matter; he wasn't looking. He was looking at his plate or staring at the can of Coke – anywhere but at her. But he was still sitting here, and for that she thanked God and tried to breathe steadily.

Finally: 'It was dead spooky.' His voice was not much more than a whisper. 'I was in this dip, where the trees are really close and it was almost pitch black. Then there was this rushing noise all of a sudden and something rose up and lashed out at me. Christ, Mum, I've never been so freaked.'

She wanted to reach across – hug him, stroke him – but of course she didn't. But that her boy, her little boy, had been alone in some woods in the middle of the night with some horrific creature that had killed a man – killed a man! – made her blood run cold.

'I just ran.' He gave a weak smile. 'I'll bet you've never seen me move so fast.'

Elaine laughed, which she had to curtail quickly before it turned into something massive, hysterical and uncontrollable. She picked up her plate and walked with supreme steadiness towards the sink. 'Well, I'm glad you can run fast when you have to. And I'm sure that girl, Morgan, will turn up. I expect we'll find she didn't have anything to do with this horrible business.'

CHAPTER FOURTEEN

Nick Bostock had been to the chandlers in Felixstowe. Once he was back on St Cedd he found himself easing off the accelerator, reluctant to go home, reluctant to get back to work. He wanted a smoke. He pulled out his tobacco but there was hardly anything left in it. *Sod it.* Where could he get some?

He was approaching the turnoff to the caravan park. They had a shop. He swung the wheel, turned through the entrance, with its bright blue archway, and drew up outside the convenience store. He bought the tobacco and some Rizlas, then stood outside the shop to roll the cigarette. As he lit it, a small dark child's face peeked at him round the edge of the nearest caravan, then vanished. Then she was back, and another face appeared above hers. Nick stared. It was the little boy in the purple jacket. One of those – Somalians, were they? – that he'd brought in with Rokesmith.

What the hell? They aren't supposed to be here. He walked towards the point where he'd seen the children vanish and stared along the row of identical caravans. A flash of purple disappeared round the edge of a van and he followed it. A flash more purple as the child was pulled through the door of a caravan, and the door was firmly slammed shut.

Nick stamped out his rollie and started forward, then stopped. None of his business. And yet he really wanted to know what they were still doing here. They shouldn't be anywhere near here. They should have gone to London or somewhere and be asking for asylum. What had that bastard Rokesmith been up to? Well, he sure couldn't help them now.

His curiosity got the better of him and he strode up to the door of the caravan and thumped on it. After a few seconds it was flung open and Nick found himself face to face with the big man who had come in on the boat – the man whose booming voice had said the Devil would smite him down. But he didn't look like he had righteousness on his side now. He looked sunken and haunted. He grasped hold of Nick's arm and dragged him through the narrow door. Nick could see a huddle of scared faces staring at him from the living area of the van.

The man had him by the shoulders. 'You. You must help us. We are desperate. That man, Rocksmit…'

'Rokesmith?'

'Yes, Rokesmith. He bring us here in the dark. He force us into this,' he waved his arms around then grabbed Nick again, 'this place. He says we stay inside. There are twelve of us in this one – too many. He brings us food and drink, but then he stops coming. We do not know where we are. We dare not go.'

Nick stopped trying to shrug him off. All the pride and pomposity had shrivelled out of the man. The fire in his eyes had died and been replaced by hopelessness. Nick guessed that the nasty geezer who owned the site – Langeveldt, was it? – would make money out of these people or use them for his own ends, but he wouldn't be good for them. People round here hated him enough already – if they thought he was exploiting children there'd be hell to pay.

But what did he care? And what did they think he could do? He didn't know the right people. He had no idea what usually happened to these immigrants after he'd done his bit and landed them on shore. He'd never given it a thought. He looked again at the scared, hungry faces, the round, pleading eyes. He snatched out his wallet.

'Here.' He pulled out the notes and shoved them into the man's hand.

'Thank you. I thank you.'

The man was looking ridiculously grateful, but he probably had no idea how little forty or fifty quid would buy them. Nick had a sudden thought of Stacey's auntie in Lincoln. She'd been talking once, over roast chicken at Stacey's mum's, about how she volunteered with the Citizens' Advice Bureau. He pulled out his phone. Searched for it, and it came up, though "bureau" was a stupid word to write. *Christ's sake – why?*

'Do you have paper? A pen?' he asked the man. There was rapid conversation and a kid brought them to him. Nick wrote down the number and thrust it at the man. 'Ring this number,' he said. 'They'll tell you what you need to do.' He pointed. 'There's a phone box up by the shops.' He scrabbled in his pockets and pulled out all the coins; piled them into the man's hands. 'Take this – you'll need it for the phone.'

He jumped back down the steps of the caravan, turned and looked back. 'Sorry, mate. Sorry. That's all I can do.'

The man's eyes shone with tears as he nodded gravely. 'You have done much, my son,' he said. 'May God bless you.'

–

Lunch at Slegholm was parsnip and bean soup with doorsteps of bread. Magnus Bostock and Brenda were sitting at the kitchen table finishing it when the Dutch boy, as they still called him between themselves, Baltasar Visser, came in.

'Will you take some soup, Balt?' Magnus pointed his spoon at the steaming pot.

But the big Dutchman looked in no mood for food. He was clutching his hat tightly, moving agitatedly. They stared at him.

'What's wrong, Balt?' asked Magnus.

A list of confused words poured from the big man's mouth. The seated pair heard "lorries", "saws", "destruction" and something that sounded like "pits of hell".

Magnus rose and went to the door. 'Show me.' He glanced back at Brenda, still sitting at the kitchen table. Her face was like stone.

The two men strode through the yard and up the lane, then through the twelve-acre field. As they approached the low brow of the hill, the harsh whining of the chainsaws reached them. And when the source of the noise came into full view the two men stopped, stared across at what was, indeed, a hideous scene. What had been a dense copse of beech, poplar, oak, birch, ash and sycamore was rapidly collapsing into so much firewood. A huge team of men in pink or orange hi-viz gear and helmets were dangling from ropes in the trees that remained, cutting out the tops, shouting to warn the men below before each sawn-off section came crashing down. Others on the ground had already started cutting the felled trunks into sections, before grabbing machinery lifted them onto long low-loaders to trundle them away.

'Terrible. Terrible,' muttered the Dutch man. Magnus stared at the destruction laid out before him like one of the circles of hell. Could they do this? Did they have permission? He suspected he already knew the answer. That Langeveldt family were too wily to blatantly break the law.

'But where the birds to nest?' Baltasar's voice was squeaky with desperation. 'Where will my little goldcrest live? She who is so shy. No tree for the nuthatch. No tree for treecreeper to creep up? No bark for my woodpecker to peck into?' He was almost crying. Magnus put a steadying hand on the large, trembling shoulder.

'No longer I listen out for the whistle of the dusky warbler.' He turned to Magnus. 'She came once, you know.' Magnus nodded. He didn't know. 'She has whistle – carry across fields.' He raised his arm, his hand open and flat and moved it sideways to indicate the extent this bird's voice carried across the landscape. 'She very rare.'

They stood in silence for a few more minutes until neither could bear to see any more, so they turned and trudged back towards the farmhouse.

–

The driveway up to Laurel Dene was oppressed by heavy, dull-green leaved trees. As Nick drove between them, heading towards the house, big drips fell onto the roof of the old Polo, sounding to him like drums from some distant part of the jungle sending out a message of doom. The torrential rain, which had instantly blocked drains and brought fears of flash-flooding to those in the more low-lying houses, had now all but stopped, though the air was still full of the threat of more storms.

He parked the car in the small visitors' car park and headed up the steps to the front door. This building had once housed the landed gentry, who had farmed, hunted, shot, and held parties and balls; but now it was home to the fading gentry to whom these hunting or dancing parties were distant, vague memories, or even simply figments of their imagination. The grandeur of the building with its art deco flooring and chandeliers did not meld well with the smells of antiseptic and cleaning fluids, the bright orange emergency-pull cords which dangled at handy intervals and the rows of Zimmer frames lined up in the entrance hall. Nick had to explain who he was to the receptionist and then made his way along the corridors to his grandmother's room.

Dorothea preferred, in the main, not to sit in the communal lounge or the sun-room with the other "guests", as she called them. Her stroke had left her weak and uncommunicative; yet Nick had a strong feeling that the sharp mind was as quick as ever. The acerbic wit would have been, as well, if only she could have summoned words more readily to her lips. She turned her head slightly as Nick opened the door, then resumed gazing out of the window into the shrub-laden grounds.

'Here – here's some grapes and satsumas. Stacey thought you might not be getting enough fresh fruit.'

At the name "Stacey" Dorothea's nostrils narrowed and her lips puckered slightly. Fair enough – Nick knew she would never like Stacey, or anything else that had been in his life since he was about fourteen years old: leaving school early, smoking, drinking, staying out all night. Just about everything he'd ever done had won him the puckered lips from Grandma.

But Stacey was the reason he was here. As he stood staring down at the iron-grey curls on his grandmother's head, Nick knew, even more strongly than ever, that Stacey was the one good thing in his life; the only person he'd ever loved – loved properly in the sense of wanting to protect her from all the horrible things in life – the evil people, the grim surroundings, the wearing misery of never having enough money. Poor Stacey had never had it good, yet she deserved it. She'd been good to him; she'd given him another chance over and over. Now he was going to sort things out for good so that they could start again and put this place and these people behind him.

'We're having a baby,' he blurted out.

A proper reaction at last. Her chin jerked up; her shoulders stiffened. Slowly, Dorothea turned her head and looked up at Nick, looking at him, then seeming to look through him as her thoughts went back to somewhere in the distant past. She had so shut in on herself since the stroke that Nick feared he would never get the truth out of her.

'Are you pleased?' His voice was high with a mixture of tension and sarcasm. Of course she wasn't pleased, and it was as though this was the perfectly normal reaction to have. How far had this family removed itself from the range of normal behaviour? It was so entrenched now that they had this difference from other families that he found it altogether predictable that the knowledge that she was to become a great-grandmother made Dorothea clamp her lips together. She stared now into the middle distance as though she were staring into the abyss.

He turned away and strode across the room – found he was clenching his fists and had an urge to smash one of them into the ornately gilt-framed mirror that stood on his grandmother's dressing table – one of the few pieces that she had brought with her from the family home. But instead he stuffed his hands into the pockets of his jeans.

'You know… you know…' Her voice was croaky from lack of use and blurred as a legacy of her stroke. She shook her head and looked down at her hands, her fingers twisting a tissue; but whether she had stopped through frustration at not being able to summon up the words she needed or because her lips were sealed through long habit, Nick did not know. He was surprised, then, when she suddenly and clearly said, 'That Indian woman came to see me. To ask about the family history.' Nick stared. 'I would not speak with her.'

Indian woman? Did she mean that one who'd come into the Dog the other day with that freaky girl who lived up on the dunes?

'Perhaps the time has come when certain people…' She turned her head slowly to gaze out of the window while Nick continued to stand in the middle of the room. The time had come all right. The time had come and gone long ago in his opinion.

'Certain people?'

Her head snapped back round to look at him. 'Not you!' she hissed, with a vehemence that made him take a step back. 'Not your father's son!'

Oh, for Christ sake! What? This again?

'Fetch that woman.' Dorothea waved a hand imperiously. 'Fetch her now.'

For God's sake. Didn't he have enough to do without traipsing round the county trying to find some stranger?

Dorothea's voice was failing now. 'Fetch her. Bring her here.' His grandmother's voice was fading away and her chin nodding onto her chest, but he thought he heard her mumble, 'And I'll tell her… tell her.'

CHAPTER FIFTEEN

THE GEARBOX OF THE OLD POLO GRATED HORRIBLY AS NICK swung the car onto the causeway. It wouldn't keep going for much longer, but he didn't know how he was going to afford a new one. He had been so wired since – well, really since the moment of being arrested, though maybe for a lot longer than that – that he hadn't had time to think, to think properly. He had barely showered and shaved and changed his clothes, let alone got around to checking his bank account.

A sudden and conclusive bang brought the car to a halt while a plume of industrial-looking dark smoke curled up from the bonnet.

'Bugger!' Nick thumped the steering wheel, flung his head back and stared for a moment at the grey and tatty roof-lining, then started beating the steering wheel with his fists. 'Hopeless, fucking useless piece of shit! Bastard car – I bloody hate you!' When his hands started to hurt too much he stopped and slumped forward over the wheel, pressing his forehead into the backs of his hands, breathing hard. He knew the tide was coming in rapidly and he needed to get over the causeway, but he couldn't give a shit.

A while later – maybe a long while – he was roused by the cheerful hooting of a horn and raised his head slowly to see his cousin's ex-wife Suzanne in her camper van pulling up alongside him.

She leant forward and called through the window, 'Given up the ghost, has it? Need some help?'

Help. Yes, help would be nice right now. Help to crawl under a nice, warm duvet and have someone stroke his hair and sing quiet lullabies to him and tell him he was the best boy in the world and they would always look after him. *Sod that.* He opened the door and climbed out as Suzanne manoeuvred the van to park in front of him. He was so tired. A sloshing noise around his feet made him look down and realise that the tide was rising; this was not the best time to break down on the causeway.

He looked up again to find Suzanne gazing at him with some concern. He hardly needed to say a word – just grabbed his jacket from the car and climbed into the passenger seat of the van.

'Not that this old bus is much better,' she said. 'But she's a great old girl. There comes a point when you've been together so long you're like an old married couple. I wouldn't dream of ditching her for a newer model just because she's a bit cranky.'

'Yeah.'

They were silent for a while as the van forged through the water sloshing across the causeway.

'And this seawater doesn't help. It's a disaster for the chassis – so corrosive. I'm forever having to get welding done. But I expect you have the same problems with your car – or Stacey's car, is it?'

'Er, yeah.'

'Of course I always try to make it back over the causeway at low tide.' She laughed, a bit nervously, as Nick continued to stare, stone-faced, out of the window. 'You really don't want to get stuck on the mainland when a storm gets up.'

'Huh!' The bitterness of his tone and the desolation in his face seemed to shock Suzanne. 'Yeah,' he said. 'And you *really* don't want to get stuck on the island and not be able to get off. Not ever.'

Silence for a while.

'So where can I drop you off?'

'Don't really matter. Where you going?'

'Actually, I think I might pop into the pub for a minute and see how Elaine's getting on. She's been having a bit of trouble with her boy Alex.' She paused, seemed unsure how much to say – not that Nick was listening much anyway. He found that he had been staring into the middle distance, like a drunk waking up to find himself in a strange landscape, since she picked him up. But she seemed to think the continued silence a bit unnerving and wanted to fill it with any old chatter. 'Alex… well, Alex is a bit difficult. He's always been… different… but lately he's been acting so weird it's scary. My Chloe's in the same year at school…'

She stopped there. Nick wasn't interested.

Suzanne had barely stopped the van in the parking space at the pub when Nick jumped out and headed towards the door. She hurried in after him. Seeing Elaine look up from behind the bar, Suzanne waved her hand over Nick's shoulder to warn her that he was in no mood for any sort of jovial greeting.

Elaine took the hint – and the tactful route – and simply smiled.

'That woman – that Indian woman. Researcher or whatever she is. Where's she staying?' he blurted out.

Elaine took a deep breath and carefully placed the laminated menu that she had been wiping clean down on the bar. It was none of her business to look out for that woman; but Nick Bostock looked like he wasn't planning a nice, quiet chat. What was his beef with her? However, it was indeed none of her business.

'I believe that she is, or at least was, staying out at that little cottage off the Marshedge road. With that young girl Morgan.

Though I must admit,' she added,' I haven't seen either of them for a while.'

Nick turned and strode back towards the door. As it swung back shut after his abrupt exit, Elaine turned to Suzanne and said, 'That's a man on a mission, then?'

–

The cottage looked deserted as Nick approached it. He knocked on the front door, then peered through one of the low windows but could see no movement in the dim interior. He went round the back, without much hope of finding any sign of life, so was surprised to see the girl. She was crouching on the ground, her arms wrapped tightly round her legs. He might not even have noticed her amongst the overgrown herbs if he hadn't heard the keening noise she was making. It sounded like a trapped or wounded animal.

'Er… you all right?' Bloody stupid question. He'd never seen anyone looking so lost, so desperate. She turned her head and looked up at him, but he thought she could probably barely see him, her eyes were so swollen and full of tears, with her tatty curls rat-tailing down in front of her face. She struggled to stand up, as stiff as though she'd been there for hours – days, even. Nick stepped forward to take her arm and help her, feeling her shudder under his touch.

In the kitchen she seemed to pull herself together, though she hung her head and would not look him in the eye. Perhaps he shouldn't go in too heavy-handed. He felt clumsy, saw the difference in size between her thin, pale forearm, that looked as though it had no room for muscle, and his fisherman's arm. He pulled out a chair and sat down so that he wasn't towering over her.

'Just… you know… if there's anything I can do to help.' What a crass phrase.

When he was little, people came to the house after his parents died and said that to their grandmother: 'If there's anything I can do, just let me know.' And they would be met by that dignified lifting of the chin and the folding of the hands and the clipped, robotic response: 'No, I can manage.'

This girl, too, did not seem to be able to come up with any practical suggestions. Not because she was proud or haughty or protective in a steely way of her and her family's privacy, like his grandma was, but rather because she seemed to have nothing. She seemed to be hardly aware of her own existence, which gave her an almost transparent look. She appeared not to have a clue what to do with herself, standing in the middle of the room glancing from Nick to the floor to the walls. And she barely had any possessions: the room was minimally furnished with no ornaments, and she herself wore no jewellery, no make-up, just a plain, drab green jumper and long skirt. So when he noticed the drawings pinned to the wooden panelling along one wall they stood out incongruously, bringing colour and life into the room. He walked a bit closer to have a good look at them. Each one was tiny and depicted a bird – sometimes it was perched in a tree, sometimes on the ground, pecking at the earth or with its beak half-buried in the mud of the marsh. Others were on the wing, flying or swooping. The detail was extraordinary; every aspect of feathers, claws and shining eyes was beautifully executed.

He looked back at the sad girl. 'Why don't you sit down, eh? Let's have a cup of tea. I'll put the kettle on, yeah?'

At this she turned and looked at the cold stove. Then she looked at the dresser where a red, shiny new kettle stood waiting. 'Jasmin went into Colchester to buy that,' she said. 'Jasmin… Jasmin.' She crumpled and Nick managed to get round the table and catch her before she hit the floor.

Oh, Christ. Should he call Stacey? She'd be a lot better at this sort of thing than he was. He sat the girl in a chair, turned and grabbed the kettle and filled it at the sink, found the mugs and the teabags, milk and sugar. It wasn't the best cup of tea in the world, but he needed it for sure, even more than she did, maybe.

At last, he dared try to ask. 'The woman… er, Jasmin, some, like, university person… I heard she was living here… well, lodging.'

The girl raised her head from her mug.

'So… it's just that I need to talk to her. It's quite urgent. It's a family thing. My old grandma—'

'I think she's dead.'

'What? Who?' Confusion now.

'She was so cold. So cold.'

–

The tide was way, way out. The sun was sinking, casting a shiny glow of candied orange peel across the water and the expanse of exposed mudflats. Morgan wandered barefoot across the cold mud, which squidged up between her toes. She was looking for gutweed. Its bright green fronds were easy to spot in the shallow pools left by the receding water.

She still felt a bit light-headed every time she bent over. That man, he'd looked a bit scary when he appeared in the garden out of nowhere. And he seemed so big in the cottage, filling the space, moving – he never stopped moving. But he had tried to be kind, in his own way. He had found a blanket and wrapped it round her and made sure she was all right before he left.

She came to a clump of gutweed and gathered it up, squeezed out the excess saltwater, and placed it carefully into her basket. Morgan knew the restorative powers of this stuff that looked like intestines. It was all about signature. Jasmin would eat it; it would build her up. Otherwise, Morgan was helpless. She would take it to the hospital and give it to the staff on Jasmin's ward – those very nice women in their neat uniforms who would let her sit for ages by Jasmin's bed, watching her chest rise and fall, mesmerised by the steady, muted beeping of all the machines to which she was attached. They would take the food from her, explain that Jasmin wasn't up to eating yet, but would make sure she would eat some of it as soon as she could; then withdraw to the corner of the ward to whisper together as they glanced at her.

As the basket filled, and the golden glow faded on the horizon, she became more aware of the mud seeping between her toes. She placed the basket carefully on the ground and looked up to the sky. As the sun sank, she spotted a small, dark-brown speckled bird, a pipit, lifting and dipping as it investigated the shoreline. It rose and dropped, rose and dropped, revelling in the agility of youth. Morgan watched it, found herself staring so that the bird became all. It filled a circle in the centre of her vision and everything else faded to grey shadows. She became light; she felt herself raise her arms; her head go back. It would take her in, this graceful beauty – take her within itself and they would fly together, as she had often done before. She was ready. She was ready. But with the innocence of youth the pipit failed to notice the dark shape high above, the shining eye judging speeds, distances, angles, all honed by that basic desire to hunt, to catch, to eat. Morgan saw it.

The peregrine made a last final adjustment to its position then launched itself into the high-speed stoop which would end in it catching its prey on the wing. The pipit caught the merest glimpse, the suggestion of plunging speed, like an arrow destined for its heart, that gave it a split second to take action. It dived off to one side, heading for the low refuge of rocks, knowing the peregrine would not dare to plunge so low. It landed; Morgan fell, her heart beating fast.

First thing the next morning, Morgan launched herself into the ward, ignoring the tutting of the nurses and the stares of other visitors who might have wondered why this pale young woman would imagine there would be any hurry to visit someone in a coma who had all the time in the world, or perhaps all the time in eternity.

'Jasmin.' Her voice was hoarse and weak, but deadly serious. 'Jasmin, you've got to wake up. It's so hard… everything's so scary. I can't manage anymore.'

The nurses had to prise her fingers off the unconscious woman's shoulders.

'Please, please – I have to tell her something. She needs to know—'

'Come on now, dear – this isn't helping. We don't know if she can hear you.' The nurse was studying the screens and bleeps with concern, while trying to pull Morgan away. 'We don't want to upset her, now. I'll get you a cup of tea. You sit here quietly.' She pushed Morgan gently down into the burgundy coloured, plastic-upholstered chair near the high bed. 'Then you can hold her hand. See.' She took hold of Jasmin's limp hand, the one that didn't have plastic clips and tubes stuffed into the back of it, and pressed Morgan's two hands over it.

Morgan's breathing gradually slowed and quieted. She studied Jasmin's hand: the brown skin, wrinkled only around the knuckles; the lines on the palm, those which crossed, those which stopped short; the nails filed into neat ovals, not the nails of someone who would by choice grub around in the decomposed leaf litter found on a forest floor. A vivid picture returned to Morgan of Jasmin as she had found her, flat and apparently lifeless; and of the track, the track through the leaves and damp soil, leading away from her.

And now, many days on, still no certainty that Jasmin would ever come back. Morgan had forgotten the gutweed, though when she finally made the long trek home she would probably go and retrieve the basket. Yet Jasmin could not eat. Would she ever eat again? Or talk again? Or be able to tell anyone what had happened to her? Morgan was aware that police had, at first, come regularly to the hospital to see if Jasmin was yet awake.

Her family, too, had turned up in force. A noisy, chattering sister, or a grandmother, or an aunt or an awkward, distressed father or grandfather seemed to be in the room nearly all the time. Morgan had to time her visits carefully, often had to wait for some time in a corridor before they would go away. Today, however, the nice nurse – the one about the same age as her – popped into the room to say Jasmin's relatives weren't coming today; they'd all had to go back up north to sort out some other family problem.

Just being able to sit here in the quiet and stroke Jasmin's hand was enough for Morgan. Just to sit here for the rest of her life would be fine for her. She would hold Jasmin's hand and stroke her arm; and when Jasmin was finally ready, she would wake up and her clear brown eyes would find Morgan's and she would gaze at her new friend with love and eternal gratitude and a deep understanding of her world.

So when a croaky voice broke into her daydreaming she almost didn't want to hear it; it was disturbing the calmness, being in the moment – here and now – that she so appreciated.

Jasmin groaned and blinked, looked at the ceiling, looked at Morgan. She seemed to be trying to speak. Her face creased in a frown of failed remembering. Then she took a deep breath and closed her eyes again; yet not for long. Even as Morgan wondered if she had imagined the sound, the movement, Jasmin opened her eyes wide and started struggling to sit up.

'What the hell's going on?' She snatched her hand away from Morgan's. 'Shit! My head…' She stared at Morgan. 'What happened to me? And what are you doing here?'

A flurry of pale blue uniforms meant that Morgan didn't have the chance to answer, and she and her shattered daydream were pushed firmly out of the way and into the corridor while machines were wheeled around and doctors summoned.

When they let Morgan back in, Jasmin said her head was thumping. They told her it would pass. Morgan sat down and Jasmin, now propped up, with bedclothes freshly straightened, looked straight at her. 'They told me you've been here for days – just sitting here. Why?'

Morgan shrank back in the chair. 'Your family have been…' she started to say, mouse-like.

'My family? Oh no. I'll never hear the last of this from my grandmother.' She affected a strong Indian accent. 'You shouldn't go out after dark. Were you meeting a strange man? What have I told you about strange men?'

And she started laughing and fell back on the pillows. Morgan laughed nervously too.

Morgan spent most of the next day hiding in hospital corridors, chewing at her nails and twisting her hair round her fingers till her head hurt. She had taken the bus to the hospital first thing, only to find that Jasmin had been moved to a bed in a four-bay room. Staff in various uniforms, other patients, their visitors and, oh dear, what seemed like hundreds of Jasmin's relatives flowed in and out of the room. Morgan hovered outside the door, hoping for a break in the human traffic, until one of the nurses took her by the elbow and took her down the corridor to show her the way to the League of Friends café.

'Try again later,' she advised.

'But really,' Jasmin asked. 'What has been going on?'

It was evening. Already it was dark outside; the evening meal had been served, the room smelt of cauliflower; all Jasmin's family had left and the other patients had settled down with headphones or magazines.

'I came out looking for you. I was in the woods… no, I was on the beach…'

Jasmin leant across as far as the tubes would allow. 'Yes. I know. I know. I want to talk to you about that. This… changing… this… difference… that you have. I'd been reading up a bit about this sort of stuff before I came here – relating to somebody else.

And I believe you can control it. You don't have to just give in to it. Unless you want to, I suppose.'

'I want to.'

'But it's not always a good thing. Don't you ever get scared?'

Morgan thought back to the dark shape of the peregrine in its deadly stoop. 'I want it.'

Jasmin sighed and flopped back on the pillow. Why was she bothering about this ditzy girl who actually preferred to be in a world of her own? However weird that world might be. And what did she know, anyway? 'I think,' she said. She needed to be careful here – it wasn't really any of her business. 'I think that these times you have of… being elsewhere… are maybe more in your head than real. That it's actually neurological. That you have a—'

'Condition?'

'Maybe it would be better—'

'They say I have a condition. Some… lobe… something. I know I'm a bit different from… people. That's why I spend time with the birds. No one understands the way I can change. I know that.'

'Right.' Jasmin decided to leave it at that. She should be thinking about herself. It was just that there was this strange blankness when she tried to think back to the sequence of events of the last few days. She could picture herself sitting in Morgan's kitchen. Some vague idea of a sunset – or looking out over those dreary marshlands? Yet she could not grasp hold of a memory of watching herself moving around. It was not particularly distressing… just, nothing there.

CHAPTER SIXTEEN

'I've come to see Mrs Bostock,' said Jasmin. The duty manager turned from her desk in the little office and looked at Jasmin for a moment before replying. Jasmin was aware that she was thin, paler than she used to be. It was as though everyone was taking time to judge her, to think critical thoughts.

'Oh, yes,' said the manager. 'I'll point you the way to her room. She did mention she was having a visitor. And does Magnus know you're coming?' She spoke brightly now.

'Oh, I'm sure he does.' Jasmin was not at all sure – but then it wasn't him she'd come to see. She'd come to find out what the grandmother was prepared to tell her; whether, in fact, her whole trip to the area was going to be worthwhile after all. She had lost two weeks of her life in hospital getting over the attack by whatever foul creature this island had set on her. It was time now to focus on her main reason – her only reason – for coming here, which was her research. Then she could get back to the department and get on with the writing up.

The difference in the old woman was like a slap in the face. Jasmin wondered whether she would even be able to speak. She sat, propped up by embroidered cushions, in a wheelchair. They had dressed her in a lavender-coloured cardigan, soft and feminine and totally incongruous. The lines in her face had multiplied, the grey cheeks were sunken and her head, bent forward towards her chest, was nodding slightly, as though she was in agreement with a tiny, insistent voice inside it.

Yet there was still elegance and authority in the movement of her bony hand to indicate to Jasmin that she might sit; still a challenging look in the shiny eye. Her voice, though, had lost all its power and Jasmin found herself leaning forward so as not to miss anything.

'You want to know about my husband's family.' It was a croak more than a statement.

'It would be very helpful to fill in—'

The hand lifted, this time as a full stop. Jasmin let out a long breath. If she said anything that would make the old lady clam up again she would kick herself.

'Open that drawer – the one on the right.'

Jasmin looked across at the heavy walnut bureau, a piece of furniture that she imagined had trailed around after the old lady for decades. It was carved with elaborate swirling designs that represented clinging vine stems and their leaves, and as she drew nearer she noticed a dry smell of camphor, linseed oil – the scents of an ocean voyage. The drawer juddered as she tried to pull it out, reluctant to give up its secrets – or just plain awkward, maybe.

'The Bostocks destroyed many documents over the years,' the voice was fading to a rasping whisper, all force gone, 'but what is left should be seen.'

Jasmin lifted out an ageing, brown box file, worn smooth and soft by the touch of many hands. She took it to the little armchair by the window and untied the ribbons that held it shut. Inside were a few sepia photographs with curling edges, showing two people standing stiffly in the photographer's studio setting, their faces faded almost to nothing. They were tall men and wore elaborate military officers' uniforms, complete with swords, plumed helmets and highly polished boots. Their faces held no expression. In the background stood a grand, pale building, with narrow windows and battlements on the flat roof. Barren hills rose up in the distance. She carried the photo over to Dorothea.

'My late husband's grandfather, James Bostock, and his aide-de-camp.' The old woman said these last words with an affected French accent, which reminded Jasmin sharply that she was dealing here with the relics of the imperial way of thinking. This woman would have entrenched ideas about what would have been right and what would have been wrong and was not going to start changing her ideas now, at her age. She must be careful what she said.

'This was taken, I believe, in Cawnpore. It was the time of the Mutiny. 1857.' The croaking voice paused and the hooded eyes focused on Jasmin, the head nodding slightly. 'You'll know all about that, of course.'

Jasmin did – of course – it was her period, an important part of her PhD, but she had a real feeling that it wasn't her academic knowledge the old woman was referring to. The pointed chin jutted forward, the black eyes bright now and suddenly intense. Jasmin caught the faint scent of mothballs rising up from the lavender cardigan.

'Why are you here?' the old woman croaked, with surprising malice.

'I explained—'

'No!' Sharp now, bright as a button. 'Why are *you* here? You're Indian. Why did you come here?'

'I'm not Indian. I've never even been to India. I was born in Lancashire.' She felt her teeth clenching. She must not alienate this woman now.

'But there is Indian blood within you, however diluted it may be.'

Jasmin screwed up her mouth and studied her hands. *For God's sake, here we go.* No, she didn't know anything about that goddess with lots of arms. No, she didn't know how to grind a thousand spices and spend half a day producing a great vat of fragrant curry. No, she'd never ridden an elephant.

She drew back from the craggy face and busied herself with her notebook. She couldn't risk saying the wrong thing so settled for nodding. She'd had this before, this idea that she was bound to carry within her the intrinsic knowledge of all that her forebears had done. It was not a sympathetic look she was getting from the old woman, not an apology down the generations from oppressor to victim. It was almost like a harsher condemnation of a peoples who should not have got in the way of what was right.

'That is of no importance,' was all she could say.

'But perhaps it is.' The intense, craggy face was horrible. 'Why are you here?' On the word "you" a crooked finger with knobbly knuckles stabbed towards her. And again on the word "here". 'Why are you delving into that place – that time?'

Jasmin found herself squirming in her seat, as though hauled up in front of the headteacher. She hadn't planned on saying this out loud to any members of this family. It would just complicate things. However: 'An ancestor of mine was killed at Cawnpore. He was a soldier. Sepoys, they called them.'

The old lady stared at her; gradually her eyes went misty and out of focus as though she no longer saw Jasmin at all, but was in another time, another place.

'I realise I'll never find out what happened to him,' Jasmin added. 'There just isn't enough documentation. But I want to know what happened there – and I want to hear it in the words of people who were there.'

Dorothea Bostock's head started nodding slightly, then the eyes came back into focus and Jasmin found that the black beads were once more boring into her face. The woman was still nodding as though stacking up information in her mind. But then, as if that knowledge amounted to an intolerable conclusion, she fell back in her chair as though punched in the stomach. She sucked air in through her teeth, with a hissing, grating noise. Her eyes opened wide and the skin on her face seemed to be forced back, stretched over her bones – a foretaste of the death mask. Jasmin was alarmed. She leant forward, reached out, but Dorothea lifted her hands in front of her, whether it was in defence or to indicate that she was all right Jasmin was not sure, so she sat back, sat quietly hoping that the rasping breathing would calm down. She was all ready to dash for help from the staff, but she did not want to lose this moment.

Eventually the breathing eased and the old woman pushed herself a little more upright. Her voice, when it came, was a hoarse whisper, all force spent. 'When I am gone,' she said, 'when I am gone, you can see it all. Take it all away. There was a… a logbook…'

Jasmin had to hold herself back from grabbing the woman by the shoulders and shouting at her to say more. She crushed her lips together and nodded. But she had questions. 'Did Major Bostock ever come back to St Cedd?'

Dorothea Bostock's eyelids started to droop, but Jasmin ploughed on. 'What belongings of his came back here?'

The dry lips moved; the voice was tiny. 'Evil embodied in the Sarpsipahi – is it gone now? Is it lost?'

The what? Sarpsipahi? Jasmin persevered. 'Are there any documents that explain his part in the massacre?'

'Little Louise was proof.'

Who the hell's Louise?

'This must be the end. It must.'

Oh, for God's sake. The old woman was rambling now. She might as well leave. But the whispering continued.

'James Bostock never returned to England.'

Jasmin had to lean in to hear the last words Dorothea said before falling asleep.

'Some of his effects were returned. Returned to his widow at Slegholm. Now go. You must go.'

–

Nick Bostock had both his boats tied up in the harbour. The *Star* was in a better state, just about, so he was focusing on getting her cleaned out and spruced up so she wouldn't look like the sad old tub she was becoming. He scrubbed furiously with a sandpaper block at the peeling handrails. An east wind blasted at his hands and face. Pity it couldn't strip off the decayed varnish the way it felt like it was stripping the skin off him. He threw the sand block down and swore at the wind. A couple of fishermen looked up from where they were trying to secure a nearby boat. They said a few words to each other then carried on tying knots. Were they still on about Rokesmith and what they knew, or thought they knew, about his dealings with him? Or were they muttering in sympathy – fellow boatmen bemoaning the dependence on the weather? He didn't know. He no longer knew what anyone was thinking – least of all Stacey. She barely spoke. She should be pleased. She should be relieved he'd finally got himself free of Rokesmith and all that stuff. But then he supposed she never really knew what Rokesmith's business was all about and how deep Nick had got into it, so she wasn't going to fully appreciate how lucky they were to be out of it.

He heard a dog bark and looked up from where he had been staring at the flecks of chipped flakes of old varnish and other detritus around his feet. An old man was walking along the road at the top of the car park, holding the hand of a little boy. The boy, in his bright red jacket and navy backpack, was skipping along beside the old man, swinging his arm and looking up at him, then ahead, then at the dog, snuffling around beside them, then back at the old man – probably his grandad – Nick thought. He looked excited, very happy about the school day ahead of him. A sudden vision of that Somalian boy in his tatty purple jacket, shaking all over with cold and probably hunger and definitely fear at being stuck in a tiny, overcrowded boat on dark, choppy waters. What had happened to him? And to his grandmother? Suddenly, Nick desperately wanted them to be all right, to think of them in a nice cosy little flat somewhere, in a kitchen filled with the smells of abundant, warm food, maybe looking forward to his day at school.

He grabbed up a rubbish bag and started stuffing the sodden scraps of paper, dog-ends and broken bits of fishing tackle into it from the bottom of the boat. Day-trip fishermen made such a mess; they just didn't care. He stood still and looked around him. Did he care? Everywhere he saw peeling paint, exposed, chipped woodwork and greasy, fraying ropes. And the *Lady* was in an even worse state. All very well not to mourn the loss of Rokesmith, but he was certainly missing the money. If he could borrow a bit, just to tide him over, get the boats smartened up, smarten up the office – well, the hut in the dunes they called an office – then he and Stacey would be fine. They could move to a better place, somewhere decent enough for a baby.

No point trying to get anything out of Magnus, the skinflint. He tossed aside the black sack and sat down to roll a cigarette. The farm couldn't be doing too badly. Magnus seemed to be doing well with the livestock, even if bunches of them did keep dropping dead. And that house, that grim, grey, windswept hulk, must be worth a bit. And there was only Magnus and the tight-lipped Brenda living there, with that farmhand guy they called "the Dutch boy" living in the cottage. God. Fancy calling him a boy; he was about fifty, older than them. They were so out of it, those two. Born middle-aged, both of them.

It started to rain more heavily now. He pulled the zip of his waterproof up to his neck and put his tools away in the wheelhouse, jumped ashore and made sure the boat was tightly tied to its moorings. He walked into the car park and dropped the bag of rubbish into one of the bins by the harbourmaster's office. That was enough clearing up for one day. More than enough.

On his way home he found himself walking faster, with more resolve. He would take charge, he would force Magnus to lend him some money, he would get his business legit and make it work, he would tell Stacey he loved her. Had he ever actually said it in the cold light of day?

He almost ran up the stairs to the flat and was shouting out "Hi" before he noticed the silence and the tidiness. He stood still in the dead room. No lights were on despite the heavy gloom, and all the plates and bowls, knives, forks and spoons in the kitchen were washed up and put away. No crumbs on the breadboard, no teabags in the sink. In the bedroom, the bed was made, the pillows and the duvet smooth and straight, rigid, uninviting. Everything gone – all her stuff, even the magazines that would lie around on the chair in the bedroom, the make-up that always cluttered up the bathroom, the shower gel and shampoo. All that remained was a bottle of contact lens solution, on the edge of the basin. He picked it up. It felt empty. He put it back down.

Nick drifted back into the living room and stood, staring at the arm of the sofa where he spilt his beer once and they hadn't been able to get the stain out completely. She'd laughed, then said, 'Sod it, we'll get rich and have a new sofa every week!' Now it was simply a prop on a bleak stage, left behind when all the actors had gone home.

–

The pub cellar stank. Probably it should be cleared out completely and given a good scrub. Elaine knocked on each of the barrels. The dull, mournful, metallic clunk resonated round the room and bounced sluggishly off the dank walls. She climbed back up, emerging into the light where Phil, the brewery delivery driver, was waiting.

'It'll do,' she told him. 'Could do with a sort out down there, but that'll have to wait. I just haven't got the time.'

'That's not like you, my duck.' The large Phil was relentlessly cheerful. He never seemed to stop almost dancing, shifting his weight from one foot to the other. 'Where's the usual smiling Elaine gone to today then?'

She had never found him more irritating. 'Sometimes, Phil… sometimes…' but she couldn't think of how to finish, so she didn't bother.

Once she'd finished with the delivery she still had half an hour, so she made herself a frothy coffee and flicked through the TV channels, settling on one showing jolly couples buying holiday homes. *Huh – dream on.*

She heard Dave come crashing through the back door and sighed, put down her mug and stood up. 'Morning, my duck,' she shouted through. A grunted greeting came back. 'You get started, Dave, I've got to get changed.' And she went upstairs to change out of the dusty tracky bottoms and tee shirt and slap on a bit of make-up.

It was a dull, blustery day. She stopped for a moment to look out of the bedroom window. She was used to this now. The flat landscape, the endless fields stretching away towards the marshes, the long beaches, then the sea. The sparse poplars that bordered the fields all leant in one direction. They had given up trying to stand upright against the continuous onslaught of the chilly winds that never really went away.

Elaine smoothed down her skirt, pushed back her hair and headed for the stairs. A few customers were already in the bar and Dave had the coffee machine steaming away. The coatracks were filling up with damp waterproof jackets. Gordon Meller, who worked at the land agents in Colchester, was on a stool at the bar with his hands round a hot drink. He raised his eyebrows and put on a wry smile when Elaine came through from the back. 'Morning. Another good one.' He nodded towards the gloom through the window.

'Oh, I don't know, my love.' She was back to her bright, professional persona. 'Looks a bit brighter already. I daresay we'll have blue sky by lunchtime.'

The big man in his uncomfortable-looking suit looked doubtful and took a long swig from his cup. 'Maybe today. But I've just seen the forecast. There's a big storm on its way – gusts up to a hundred miles an hour, they said. Serious risk of flooding. Environment Agency's probably going on red alert.'

This was mixed news for Elaine. With the boats all stuck in harbour and the few holidaymakers not able to get out or go on the beaches, there would be more custom for the pub. She'd better check the freezer. But the downside was that cabin fever would set in, tempers would get frayed and by late in the evening drunken arguments might lead to flying fists, which might in turn lead to someone calling out the police, which was never good.

The day moved on, one hour after the other, much like any other. The difference today was that nearly everyone who came in had further news about the deterioration of the weather. The storm, poised now over the white north of Scandinavia, would be on them soon after nightfall. They were saying it might be as bad as the one in 1953. Of course there weren't many people around who remembered the flooding back then, but you could still buy a book of the photographs in the Post Office. It showed a herd of cows crushing together on a tiny hillock of dry land surrounded by a vast sea of floodwater. It showed people – old people, children – climbing out of bedroom windows and jumping into little rowing boats waiting below to catch them. It showed cars – old, upright black Austins and Morrises – stranded in the middles of what would have been roads but were now raging rivers, the waters lapping up to window level. And it showed the devastation afterwards: people's broken furniture lying twisted and broken, dead sheep and cows lying in fields after the waters had drained away.

An almighty crash made heads jerk up and turn. The door of the pub had been snatched out of the hands of a boy who was on his way in, and smashed back against the wall. His parents, embarrassed, closed the door carefully and ushered the child towards a table in the corner.

CHAPTER SEVENTEEN

Magnus Bostock was in the large sitting room of Slegholm Farm listening to the weather forecast. He also listened to the storm warnings. The room was gloomy. The dark furniture had sat there since his grandparents' day, and he and Brenda had never seen any need to replace it. There were two square armchairs of almost black leather, creased at the arms by decades of tweeded or wool-clad arms rubbing along them. A large Kashmiri rug, which once would have shone with jewel colours depicting a hunting scene, covered the centre of the floor on top of a cheap, beige, fitted carpet. The log fire was laid but not lit.

A glass-fronted, carved mahogany bookcase stood against the wall behind the door. It contained books once owned by Magnus's grandfather, but Magnus had not even glanced inside them for years. As a small child he had been forbidden to touch them; as a grown man he had no interest. Fine dust had seeped in. What would happen to them after he and Brenda were dead and buried, he had no idea. They had accepted – or at least he had and he supposed Brenda had – they never talked about it anymore, that there wouldn't be any children now. Baby girls never made it to full term. And all the babies had been girls.

He shook his head to clear the dark clouds. The weatherman had talked his way down the country and now reached their area. Winds of up to seventy miles an hour, gusting to a hundred. He forced himself to his feet. Time to get out there and make ready.

He and Baltasar worked steadily, hammering loose boards in place on the big barn and outbuildings, checking over the animals and stowing away loose wooden boards and pieces of corrugated metal sheeting. Brenda was tacking down the felting on the hen shed, where it had come loose at the corners.

By the time they retreated to the kitchen to make the tea, the winds were already high, driving the low clouds fast across the sky.

'You'd better get off home, Balt,' said Magnus, when their mugs were emptied and the biscuits all gone from the plate. 'Rain's going to come soon.'

'Sure.' The big Dutchman gathered up his jacket, scarf and cap. 'See you at sparrow's fart.'

Magnus, for the hundredth time, regretted teaching that phrase to Balt. He watched Brenda as she put a full casserole dish into the bottom oven of the range. 'You got something in for your dinner?' he asked.

'I'll be fine,' said Balt. 'I have a steak and kidney pie at the cottage.' He stood at the door, pulling on his boots. 'I like steak and kidney pie.' He raised a hand in farewell and left, pulling the door tight shut behind him as the rising wind tried to swirl through it.

Brenda slammed the oven door and turned to her husband. 'You don't have to worry about him.' Through the window she watched the hunched figure of the big man striding away.

All through the night the wind gathered strength. It came in over the North Sea, whipping up the black waters into angry, choppy peaks. It blew low over the shingles, stirring them into a low-voiced, conspiratorial song. The few shrubs and trees in its path bowed low, as they always did. Once it reached buildings it rattled the windows, forcing its way in through any tiny crack. It slid under roof tiles and slates and worried them loose. It slammed against fences.

Magnus stood at the bedroom window. He worried about his livestock. He worried about the state of the farm buildings. He worried about his wife, who had crept out of bed some time ago – was it minutes or hours; he had no idea. She had made him hot chocolate which he drank while he watched the news, then he had gone to bed and slept heavily. He had a vague idea he had heard her come to bed and then in the middle of the night had heard her get up again. He mumbled a question and she had said something about checking the henhouses.

It did not occur to him to go out and look for her. She would just ask him why he had come out; say that she could manage perfectly well; tell him to stop fussing. He went back to bed.

He woke with the dawn.

–

Elaine woke up needing the loo. She rolled over and looked to see what the time was, but the bedside clock was blank. She reached for the lamp to turn it on; but nothing. Power cut. It happened. She lay in the darkness. Total, very relaxing silence, which must be something to do with the power being out. No low-level hums, no creeping glow of streetlamps. However, she needed to get up and go to the bathroom, so she pushed aside the duvet, found the little torch in the bedside cabinet drawer and fumbled her way out onto the landing.

Alex's door was slightly open. It was normally tight shut, so she put her hand on the knob, tentatively pushed the door wider and put her head in. 'Alex?' Nothing. 'Alex? You there, love?' Obviously not. A wave of sadness washed over Elaine. She felt she had lost him, and not just in the sense that all teenagers distance themselves from their parents, turn against their values and despise their actions and motives simply because. No, she felt he had moved on into another world, that there were thoughts in his head that she would not begin to understand even if he could explain them in words. That this new world he lived in was like a shadowy, parallel place where people apparently lived their lives and behaved like everyone else but were beyond a barrier like a grey gauze curtain that she could feel him through, see him through, but never truly reach him. And she feared she would never get him back onto the side of the light.

She went into the bathroom and balanced the torch on the basin. Her reflection in the mirror showed bags under her eyes, lines at the side of her mouth that didn't use to be there and sallow skin that didn't see enough of the light of day. Back in her bedroom she went to the window to look out on the unnatural blackness of a world without artificial lighting. Anything could be out there. The row of conifers that marked the end of the pub garden were swaying in the strong wind.

—

Nick Bostock was woken by the sound of water pouring out of a blocked gutter and splashing hard on the pavement below. His head was throbbing fit to burst, his tongue was thick and furry, his throat like he'd swallowed barbed wire. He pushed himself up from the floor where he seemed to have landed after rolling off the sofa. The light in the bathroom was harsh. He peed, then stood, clinging on to the washbasin and looked in the mirror. *Christ.* His hands hurt as he turned on the tap and he stared at them. The left hand was caked in dried blood, which was ground into his fingernails and coated his knuckles and was matted into the hairs on the back of his hand. He washed most of it off and tried to see where it had come from, but there was no wound.

He found some paracetamol in the cupboard, went through to the kitchen where, with shaky hands, he poured himself a glass of water, then went into the living room. His discarded boots lay in the middle of the floor and he saw that they were thickly coated in a slimy, reddish mud, still damp.

He went over to the window. No person or animal was out and about tonight. Any right-minded creature was hunkering down in the warm and dry. The drains in the street were already blocked with the last of the fallen leaves that hadn't been swept away, along with urban detritus. The gutters were flooding. An empty, abandoned beer can, caught up by a violent gust of wind, bounced down the middle of the road, battered and beaten by the elements. Suddenly there was darkness. The streetlights had gone out and the lights in the flat had gone out. A fox cried out.

–

Morgan pulled the duvet tighter round her head. She didn't mind rain. She often danced in the rain and loved to feel the softness of it on her face, to hear the gentle patter of raindrops falling on piles of leaves. This was different, though. This rain had a force and a purpose behind it and was driven by pure evil. Its sole purpose was to destroy, to obliterate, to smash and drown everything it could reach. And it was doing well at reaching everywhere. Its angry tongues lapped at the edges of the ill-fitting window frames. Its icy fingers pushed under the front door.

And the wind was angry – it was trying to rip the roof off the cottage, tearing at the tiles with each more furious gust, blasting itself up against the glass in the windows, every further onslaught bringing a greater risk of the glass shattering. And once it got inside, she thought, there would be no saving her. The angry wind would swirl around, sucking up everything in the cottage, including her, into a great bundle, drag it outside and up away into the blackness of the sky.

And now there was a great cry, a howl or wail – not human, not animal – that tore the sky in two and filled the air. Morgan launched herself out of the bed, still clutching her pillow, and ran through into Jasmin's room. She found her standing at the window, staring into the blackness.

'What on God's earth was that?' asked Jasmin. She didn't turn round. The two stared at each other's faces reflected in the glass – pale, spectral.

'I didn't know you wore glasses.' When Morgan spoke she found her voice was shaky and feeble.

Jasmin turned round now. She was wearing a baggy, pale-pink tee shirt and black-framed glasses; a mixture of sternness and softness that threw Morgan. Yet again she realised this woman came from a world she knew nothing about. Jasmin took the glasses off and looked at them, then across at the piles of papers strewn on the bed.

'I wear contacts during the day.' She turned back to the window. 'But what was that? Some animal?'

The thoughts started to swirl in Morgan's mind. The thoughts that made her put her hands to her head and turn round and round to try to make them stop swirling. The questions that would bubble up and she couldn't answer. The things she couldn't say. *Don't frighten her off. Don't frighten her off.* 'It won't come here,' she finally said.

Jasmin was staring at her. 'What won't?'

'The thing that's out there. The thing that attacked—'

'Attacked? Attacked what? Attacked me? But they think that was some drunk – some druggie. That's what they said.'

Morgan stared at her feet; she didn't dare look at Jasmin.

'What?' asked Jasmin, harshly.

In a tiny voice, Morgan said, 'It may not have been human.' She looked up. She knew she looked desperate, but she couldn't help it. 'But it won't come here. We're all right inside. I've only seen it outside. In the dark.'

Jasmin had moved across to her, put her hands on Morgan's arms as though to ground her. Morgan could feel the chill of her hands through the thick cotton of Nan's nightie that she had taken to wearing. She found Jasmin staring hard into her face.

'Morgan. What are you talking about?'

'It's so cold. My feet are cold.' She couldn't meet Jasmin's eye. 'Can I get into your bed?'

'What?' Jasmin turned now and looked at the crumpled bedclothes and the papers and cardboard folders spread all over them. 'Morgan, I don't think—'

'No. I'm sorry.' Morgan felt stupid, wretched. She had said the wrong thing. Jasmin had turned away and was rubbing her face. Now she turned back and put an encouraging smile on her face. 'Look, we're both cold. It's a spooky night. What about some hot chocolate, fill the hot water bottles and you can tell me all about it?'

Oh, what a good plan, thought Morgan, and she got busy. They ended up, under Jasmin's instructions, with Morgan back in her own bed, warm and nursing a mug of chocolate, and Jasmin, wrapped up in fleeces and thick socks, sitting by her in the old wicker chair.

'I've seen it,' she told Jasmin. 'Soon after the first killings. There was a dog – a stray dog – that had been hanging around. It wasn't a nice dog. I wanted to stroke it, but it tried to bite me. This was back when the leaves were just starting to turn colour, when the birds were busy chatting, getting ready to leave.'

Yes, thought Jasmin. *Some people call it autumn.* Then she mentally slapped her wrist for being so cynical.

'People had been talking about this dog,' Morgan went on. 'People who worked on farms and with animals. They were saying it had attacked sheep and even calves. They were muttering that something should be done.'

She took a sip from her mug. 'So one night, I was walking through a field – I knew there was a family of foxes living on the edge of the woods – and I could see this dog rooting around. I didn't like that.' She looked earnestly at Jasmin. 'It might have found the cubs. They were still very young. I just stood there. I didn't feel very brave. Then I saw the dog was backing off, with its tail down, and making this weird, high, whining noise. Then I saw what was spooking it. Oh, Jasmin.' She reached out with her hand, then withdrew it and clasped the mug again. 'It was so big, and dark. Just a massive thing, I dunno how to describe it. The dog was cowering in front of it. Then this… creature… raised up its front feet and it was like it had one claw – just the one – with a shiny curved edge and vicious point. And it slashed down on the dog, again and again. It ripped it to shreds.' She was staring ahead now, reliving it, her eyes huge and round. 'I just ran, Jasmin. Ran.'

CHAPTER EIGHTEEN

It was dustbin day on St Cedd, so Elaine was out in the early darkness to open wide the gate to the yard so that the lorry could reverse in towards the bins. God knew if they would turn up. She was exhausted and everything around her looked exhausted. Scraps of newspaper and plastic wrapping lay flattened and sodden up against the fences and hedges where they had been driven and abandoned. More than half the car park was drowned by large puddles of dirty pink water, where the rain had stirred up the rough clay.

She stepped onto the pavement. Large twigs and even small branches were scattered along the road. Mud and detritus filled the gutters. It looked like a battlefield the morning after.

She went into the kitchen and started to fill the kettle before realising that was no good, so filled a pan with water and put it on the gas. They'd better get the power on again soon – there was a freezer full of food that would start going off. She wouldn't be able to pull a pint or make coffees and the heating wasn't going to come on, either. Oh God, this was all she needed.

But by eight o'clock she had the fire lit in the public bar, a paraffin heater on in the kitchen and storm lanterns dotted around the place. *Not exactly cosy, more like a port in a storm*, she thought – one of the string of clichés that her father used to use all the time when she was growing up, and which always stuck in her head. *A port in a storm. Batten down the hatches. Working all the hours God sends. Make do and mend. Battle on.*

She had started to listen to the radio on her phone, but then thought she ought to save its battery, so had found, stuffed away in a cupboard, an old transistor radio that still worked. Finally, the news came on on Heart. Worst storm in years; families flooded out; people stranded; thousands without electricity; lorry overturned on the causeway. That was all she needed. A high-sided lorry had blown over on the causeway, the only link between St Cedd and the mainland, and was completely blocking the road. There was no knowing how soon it could be moved. *Great.* She wrapped her heavy coat around her and sat staring into the fire.

By the middle of the morning the whole village was stirring – people emerging from their homes like hibernating creatures emerging from their winter hideaways to blink in the daylight and make sure the world was still there. And yet it wasn't spring; just a false lull. The Dog had become a hub; the place people automatically gravitated towards in search of hot drinks, warmth and, above all, news. Many people had rung friends on the mainland to find out how widespread the damage was. But as usual the council was moving sluggishly, or so a lot of people were saying.

An elderly man and his even more frail sister, who lived in one of the houses behind the High Street and never normally came to the pub, had taken up residence in the corner beside the fire in the snug.

'Reminds me of '53,' the man grumbled to anyone who would listen. 'They abandoned us then and they're going to abandon us now.'

‘That’s a load of rubbish,’ Elaine heard a woman reply. She couldn’t see round the corner from where she was busy at the bar, but then she didn’t recognise most of the people in the pub now.

‘They did what they could. It was early days, then. And that was different, anyway. That was a combination of the tide, a storm surge and strong winds. The sea defences just couldn’t cope – they’ve done a lot of work on them since.’

‘That’s as may be,’ said the first speaker. ‘But we’ve got the highest spring tides still to come. There’ll be worse than this. And anyway, when they gonna get that lorry cleared away, then? Me and the missus, we’ve got doctors’ appointments tomorrow morning.’

The phone rang, behind the bar, but Elaine didn’t have time to answer it, being torn between helping Dave serve in the bar and hunting out more sausages from the freezer for Mark and Angie, the grungies, who were still churning out breakfasts. It rang again, and this time she reached it.

‘I realise you’re run off your feet.’ The calm tones of Suzanne came down the line. ‘But I was wondering if you know what’s going on?’

‘Well, we’re cut off – haven’t you heard?’

‘Oh, yes, I know about the lorry, it’s been on the news, lots of pictures of highways department people and firemen standing around it stroking their chins. No, there’s something else now. The police helicopter’s been hovering over the house, and now the air ambulance has come.’

‘Oh my God. Ask Chloe, can you, if she knows where Alex is?’

‘Chloe’s not here. She’s in Colchester. There’s a girl in her class, Grace, who had a big party for her birthday, and they’ve all gone over there and stayed the night. Alex might be there as well. Did he say?’

‘He still doesn’t say anything,’ Elaine replied grimly.

‘No. No. Look, don’t worry, Elaine, I’ll go outside now and see if I can find out what’s going on.’

‘You’re a star. But be careful.’

'Will do. Bye then.'

Elaine went into her living room, closed the door and picked up her mobile from the coffee table. *Call me. Need to know where you are xx.*

The distant hubbub of voices, scrapes of chairs, clinks of glasses, movement of cutlery and china and the occasional whine of a small child suddenly died down a little. *What now?* Elaine pushed herself to her feet, realising how tired she was. She pushed loose strands of hair back off her face and went back to the bar. A uniformed policeman, broad and unsmiling, had come through the door, accompanied by another man, tall, thin and red-haired, whose creased suit, off-white shirt and grey tie looked out of place. They made their way straight towards Elaine.

'A word?' said the ginger one.

She nodded towards the living room and raised the flap so that he could come through. The uniformed one stayed, looking round the bar, while the customers spoke to each other in subdued voices.

She shut the door and turned to face him. 'Is it…?'

He raised a ginger eyebrow.

'My son. Is this to do…?'

'Not unless your boy was out with an axe last night and came home drenched in blood this morning.' He gave a short laugh. She stretched her lips into a copy of a smile.

'Sorry, Ms… er… Maple. Really not a laughing matter. There has been an unexplained death and we need to contain the area.'

'Death? Who's died?'

He didn't reply, exactly. 'You know the people who run the caravan site, do you?'

Elaine felt a ridiculous surge of relief. 'Well, of course. I mean, they don't come up here much. They don't seem to like to mix. The village… you know…'

'Hostility, was there?'

She was saved from having to go into the whole complicated story of the low-level animosity that festered between the caravan site and the rest of the village by a sudden babble of raised voices coming from the bar. He moved back in there fast and she could hear him calming, explaining. Elaine took the opportunity to snatch up her phone and check for messages. Nothing.

When she walked back through she discovered that there were now several police in the pub, organising the customers into groups and writing down details.

Dave was outraged. 'Haven't they heard of civil rights?'

'Haven't you heard of the police being allowed to do their job and catch murderers?' she snapped back.

He took a step sideways and held up his palms. 'Whoa. Only saying.'

They stood side by side and watched. 'So who got murdered then?' he asked.

'Don't know. But he was asking about the Langeveldts.'

'Oh, well that wouldn't be a surprise. See that little guy over there – the one waving his arms about? Looks a bit hyper?'

She looked across. A ferret of a man, cocky-looking and twitchy, keeping his restless kids in order by snapping his fingers and shouting orders at them.

'He was mouthing off about him the other day. Said their caravan was leaking gas or something and that Langeveldt guy wouldn't do anything about it. Wouldn't surprise me if he was the one that got offed. He's not popular.'

'No, he isn't,' said Elaine. But not liking someone much was hardly a reason for… offing… someone. What was the place coming to? She shook her head and took a deep breath.

CHAPTER NINETEEN

MAGNUS WAS IN THE BIG SHED, WITH THE ENGINE COVER OF the John Deere open and the socket set laid out beside him on the bench. With the weather calmed down, at least for now, he could get on with some maintenance at last. He wiped his hands on the rag, then sniffed at them, breathing in that grounded smell of engine oil. He reached up to the big old arc light and angled it better at the battery terminals. Toby was lying on his side on an old blanket and would raise his head slightly every time Magnus dropped a tool back on the bench.

The phone rang in the house, magnified through the yard by the loudspeaker system he'd rigged up. After a while it stopped. Magnus wasn't interested in who might be calling, though it was usually a feed supplier or market dealer and Brenda could handle them. This time, though, he could hear her shouting from the door of the house. Toby raised his head a little and growled.

'Quiet.'

He walked towards the house, wiping his hands on the sides of his once-blue overalls. Brenda was standing in the shadows, just inside the door. Her dark shape was still, watching him carefully. 'Who is it?'

'It's them at Laurel Dene.'

He picked up the phone; he listened, nodded, grunted a few words, put the phone down.

'Is that it? She's gone, then?'

Magnus nodded and turned away.

'You'll need to get her stuff sorted, then,' Brenda went on.

He looked at his feet. 'Give me a chance – it's only just happened!' His voice came out gruff. He cleared his throat. Yes, there would be plenty to do, to organise, but there was no great rush, surely.

'I'm just saying,' she added.

Magnus walked through to the kitchen and stared, unseeing, through the window. The brightness of the pale sky made his eyes sting. He stood, his hands hanging loose at his sides, looking out across the land that had been owned and farmed by Bostocks for hundreds of years. Land that would now officially be his, though he felt no pleasure from that. It was yet another burden.

Brenda was bustling around in the hall, taking out the vacuum cleaner. She seemed completely unmoved. This was a huge sea change in his life. Nothing would ever be the same again, he realised, and a surge of loneliness spread through him. A loneliness that Brenda would never understand, obsessed as she was with market prices and subsidy applications. For her, everything had to be productive, or it had to go.

Grandmothers and their granddaughters-in-law – was it always so difficult? He lifted the kettle, swung it to make sure there was enough water, put it on the range to heat. All over now, anyway. He gripped the edge of the sink, felt the cold smooth of the stainless steel under his palms, raised his head to stare out of the window. It was just that they came from such different beginnings – Brenda and Grandma. Brenda had no family, no history – never had – it wasn't her fault that she'd never understood the power of these connections. Years ago he'd heard the phrase "the weight of history" – in some TV documentary, probably – and felt he understood what that meant in a way few people might.

'There'll be papers to sign – people to tell.' She had followed him in.

But would there? There weren't many left of her generation that he knew about. Not that his parents had had many friends, anyway, when he and Nick were growing up. He and Nick – and not Louise.

'Not really.'

'No, not really, I suppose. Will they ring your brother?'

Magnus swung his head from side to side, like a bull in the ring with the matador to one side, picadors to the other, wishing they all weren't there.

'I'll do it if you like.'

He nodded.

'And they want you to go up to Laurel Dene now.'

'What?'

He stood just inside the door of the big bedroom with his hand stuffed in his jacket pockets.

'Go on in, Magnus, go on in.' The manager was shooing him with her hands, like he was a child or a dog or something. And just like a child he dug his heels in. He could actually feel his heels press into the dark floorboards. Part of him wanted to lunge forward, to grab her and shake her: *Tell me, Grandma! What is it with this family?* And part of him wanted to run away; run down the wide staircase, through the too-slow automatic doors, down the drive and across the fields.

She was dressed in a brown dressing gown. It was her colour. Not a rich, earthy brown, nor a warm gold, just dull, dead and functional. He moved crab-like along the wall to reach the chair, where he sat, stiffly, staring at her. Where had she gone in those ninety years? Of course he knew that physically she had gone far.

The time she had spent in India with his grandfather. He knew nothing of that apart from the stiffly posed photographs of men in pale suits and women carrying parasols. When he was little, on a rainy day, he might look through the old photo album of their time there. Then he could picture the jewel colours of the fabrics, the rich reds of the dresses and vibrant turquoise of the lace trimmings.

–

Towards the end of that very long day, Nick and Magnus sat on a bench in the manicured gardens of Laurel Dene, looking down, under the darkening sky, over the sloping lawn towards the shrubs which ran across the bottom, barring the residents from the fields, marshes and coastline beyond.

Connie, the manager, and Milos, the caretaker, were efficient, kind and understanding, and had helped them organise the undertakers and had then offered to finish boxing up all their grandmother's belongings. Nick wouldn't have had a clue about stuff like organising funerals and making appointments with registrars, and looking at his brother he knew he wouldn't have known where to start, either.

For once, neither of them wanted to argue. They were too drained.

'She made a will,' said Magnus.

Nick nodded.

'She wanted it to be fair – about Slegholm and everything. The will sorts out the ownership properly and compensation for you.'

Nick nodded again. There had been times, very recently, when he would have felt smug and very pleased to get his hands on his fair share of what was due to him. But at the moment he hardly cared. Maybe people were more important than money.

'The will's at the solicitor's office, but there are all sorts of documents – family papers – up in the attic at the farm. If you've got time…' he sounded a bit sheepish, almost pleading, '…it would be good if you'd come over sometime and we could look at them together.'

Nick sat up straight and turned to look at his brother. 'Sure, yes, I've got the time. Loads of time,' he added morosely. Magnus didn't seem to have noticed that Nick had problems of his own – and he wasn't going to start telling him now all about Stacey.

'I've never looked at them,' Magnus was saying. 'They've been there forever. I've just never really wanted to look at them so I never go up there. Brenda goes up there sometimes and fiddles around.'

Nick had almost forgotten about the attic rooms in the farmhouse. He could picture now the narrow, steep staircase with its hard brown carpet, rough on the hands and knees of a small boy. Two rooms, one each side of the top of the staircase, were badly lit by dirty skylights. There had been little furniture up there, he thought, thinking back to the times he had been sent up there as a small child. *Go up there and stay up there until you learn how to behave!*

'There is something – there is, er, something,' Magnus was saying. Nick would normally mock his brother for his lack of fluency, but this time he waited.

'What do you know about Louise?' Magnus blurted out.

'Louise? Louise who?'

Magnus took a deep breath. *Let it all go – or pursue it?* And perhaps for the first time in his life he was going to pursue it.

'I don't know much – but she was our sister.'

'What? What sister? We never had a sister!'

'We did. Yeah, I think we did. You won't remember. You were only a baby.' He leant back and looked up into the void. 'There was this one day. You remember Miss Edie – one of those McAllister sisters who lived along at Home Farm? She came in to look after us.'

'Oh yeah, I remember her. Little fat woman with scraggy hair? She came and did the laundry sometimes.'

'She came rushing in that day. There was a panic on. Mum and Dad went off in the car with a suitcase, and I was crying because I thought they were never coming back. I remember sitting at the kitchen table and Miss Edie feeding me boiled egg and soldiers. You were in the pram outside the kitchen door. One of those prams with big wheels and a net stretched across to keep cats off.'

He hunched forward and rested his forearms on his thighs. 'Then I woke up early next morning and ran through to Mum and Dad's room. Huge relief they were back – at least Dad was. I threw myself on him.' It was all coming out in a rush now. 'Usually he'd have been cross and told me to be a man, but this time he hugged me tight and was rocking me backwards and forwards and that was scary because he was crying.'

Nick turned to look at his brother. He had no memory of his father hugging – or crying.

'And he said she died. "The little mite died," he said. And he called her Louise. "My little Louise." And he said that she couldn't live because no little girls could live in our family. And that stuck in my head because those few times we had girls round to visit or to play I would remember that and wonder if they might drop dead or something.'

CHAPTER TWENTY

The phone in the main bar rang. Elaine snatched it up. 'Yes?'

'God, you sound stressed.' It was Suze.

Elaine breathed out a huge sigh. 'Ha. That's putting it mildly. I thought you were the school again. They keep ringing and saying, "Are you aware that your son is not at school today?" And I say, "Yes, you morons, of course I'm fucking aware."'

'I'll bet you don't.'

'Okay, no, I don't put it quite like that.'

'Well then, I've got one piece of good news for you. Alex is with me.'

'What? Oh, thank God!'

'Yes. I found him in a house in Woodbridge.'

'How did he get—'

'One of the kids from school lives in this big house. Had a house party, parents away for a couple of days, you know how it goes.'

'Is the causeway clear, then?'

'Yup, they've managed to sort it. So I went to collect Chloe and Alex was there too. So I suggested to him it was maybe time to come home.'

'Oh, Suze, you are a total star!'

'I know. You owe me an extremely large glass of red wine. One day.'

'Too right.'

'So we're just setting off. Thought I'd warn you first – maybe give you a moment to get your thoughts together before you see Alex? Hmm?'

'Ha. Yes, all right. I'll try to stay calm.'

'See you in a few minutes.'

By the time Alex and Suzanne walked through the door, Elaine had taken many deep breaths, made a pot of coffee and toasted some hot cross buns. As soon as Alex walked into the kitchen she could see his boy-stomach radar pulling him towards the fresh, spicy smell and saw in the same moment the way he pulled himself back. He turned away, looking sad, ashamed – she didn't really know what – she just felt an overwhelming urge to rush and put her arms round him. And this time, she didn't hold back.

'Mum.' The usual moan that meant "Don't hug me, particularly don't hug me in front of other people", but it came out very half-hearted.

'I'm not angry,' said Elaine. She was fuming. 'But this is not the time to go missing. You need to think of other people for once. You need…' She closed her mouth firmly.

'Yeah, I know. Suze has been telling me.'

'Coffee! Great.' Suzanne pulled out a chair and started to pour coffee into mugs. 'And hot cross buns! Jumping the gun a bit, aren't you, Elaine?' She sat down and started to butter one.

Elaine let go of Alex and sat down as well. 'You know what it's like. The minute Christmas is over we have to start Easter.'

Alex tentatively reached out to take one. Elaine put her hand on his arm. 'Sit down first, Alex,' she said. 'Please.'

He did. For a few minutes they all just buttered buns, put milk in coffee and passed the jam.

'Have you heard anything?' Elaine asked Suzanne.

'Well, I have, yes. But you must bear in mind it's all gossip – just what I've heard, you know, chatting here and there.'

'Sure.'

'So. It seems that Ethan Langeveldt was out and about on the caravan site. Apparently his wife said he'd had a phone call from someone in the launderette saying a machine was overflowing. Which was odd, because there is hardly anyone there this time of year and they knew most of them. But he set off to see – and never came back.'

'Wow.' Elaine stared at her friend. Alex was looking at his mug. 'Go on.'

'So she took the dog with her – the dog they've still got, that is – and went out to look for him. It was very dark and there was no moon, remember.'

'And she found him.'

'Yup. She found him. On one of the paths. They'd jumped out on him, took him totally by surprise and slashed him. Just like with that Rokesmith chap.'

There was silence for a few moments.

'Who is it?' asked Elaine. 'Is it a revenge thing? A gang thing? Or just some random psycho?'

Then Alex said, 'Them. It. We don't know what it is.'

'Well, it's got to be someone with a huge grudge—'

Alex's voice was high, unnecessarily loud. 'Someone? We don't even know it's a someone. It might be a something! Don't you get it? There's all sorts of… of… forces out there we know nothing about.' He looked about him wildly. 'It's this place!' He pushed back his chair and stomped off to his room.

Elaine took a deep breath, but the warm smells of toasted bun, melted butter and coffee did nothing to get rid of the cold chill she felt down her back. She knew that when Alex said "this place" he wasn't talking about the kitchen, or the pub. 'For the first time, Suze, in ages, I think I want to leave this place.'

'Leave the pub?'

'I don't mean – Alex doesn't mean – the pub. He means the island. Maybe we should get right away from St Cedd. Maybe it's not good for us.'

–

Later that week Nick was in Colchester, standing at the edge of the little children's playground. It had a slide, a roundabout, a fort to climb up and brightly coloured animals on springs fixed into the ground. It was all fenced in, but he felt some of the mothers or child-minders or whatever were still giving him the odd, hostile glance.

Why was everyone so suspicious of everyone else? Every loitering person was a thief, every person who ever said they hated someone was a murderer, every person who stood on a seashore and ranted at the sky was a nutter, every lone man in a park was a paedophile.

He realised he must look dodgy, though. He'd held it together until the funeral was over: showering, washing his clothes, shaving, getting his hair cut. Christ, he'd even ironed a shirt for the funeral, though that was a mission because he discovered Stacey had taken the iron. Fair enough, she had probably paid for it. The woman who serviced the laundrette downstairs had lent him one.

But now, he'd let it all go. He scratched the stubble on his chin, looked down at his stained jeans and muddy trainers. Did he want Stacey to see him like this? He hadn't thought it through as he drove over from the island. He'd noticed the scars on the tarmac caused by the fallen lorry, and the heavy machinery they'd needed to drag it back upright, and thought how ugly they were. It hadn't occurred to him to look in a mirror.

He looked across the road to Stacey's mum's house. It was where Stacey had grown up. Her mum, sister and one of her brothers, Carl, still lived there. Carl was the sort of boy who looked like he was never going to get off his arse and find a job, let alone finding his own place to live or doing his own cooking and washing. But his mum and Stacey and her sister and other brother didn't seem to mind him doing that. They went along with his dopiness and took it in turns to drive him to dyslexia and – what did they call it? – personal development classes, and didn't go on at him for being a bit slow. No one shouted at him and called him stupid.

The mid-terrace house was painted white and the front door and sash-window frames were a bright, sky blue. There was a brass knocker shaped like a hedgehog that Stacey's mum found in a car boot sale, and a pink china cat in the front room window.

Nick's face wobbled; he wanted to cry. He felt a real, stabbing pull in his heart; a yearning, not just for Stacey, but for a whole life where people actually cared about each other. Where if someone was sad their brother or sister asked them what was wrong, or tickled them till they couldn't help but laugh; a life where if someone messed up, the others would rally round and help put things right.

He turned away and looked back towards the playground, where the women were calling the children to them, packing up the toys and plastic cups into bags that hung off the buggies. And what was he going to say to Stacey, even if she was there? That he hoped to find out, at last, what this stupid fear was all about? Where it had started? Why it had started? That he could make things all right?

–

The weather forecaster was talking of further heavy rains, north-easterly winds with gusts of up to a hundred miles an hour, red warnings of floods. Magnus Bostock turned off the radio when the calm voice started warning of gales at sea for German Bight, Humber, Thames and Dover.

The tide was likely to be the highest of the year. The lower fields were bound to flood, so Magnus and Baltasar needed to bring the livestock up to the higher ground. That much was fine; it was the price you paid for trying to run a farm in such a place. But he had sent Balt off to check out his own cottage – it was vulnerable down there on the edge of the ten-acre. He was about to leave the kitchen when the phone rang, and he dashed back and grabbed it up. 'Hello?'

It took him a while to work out who this woman was – this woman who seemed to know all about him and his grandmother and the farm. And about the attic. He listened, he stared at the floor and he listened further. Finally, he said, 'Well, I suppose if she said this stuff is up there, then it must be.' Further listening. 'If you really want to come round, I suppose that's all right.' He listened further, said goodbye and hung up. As he turned to head for the door he almost crashed into Brenda who was standing right behind him, immovable as a stone statue.

'Who was that?'

'Oh, just that historian woman. The one who was talking to Grandma. She wants to look at stuff.'

CHAPTER TWENTY-ONE

THE LANE TO THE OLD FARMHOUSE WAS PITTED WITH POTHOLES and ruts. Jasmin swore at each one as the Golf plunged into them and then swore at the thorny, bare hedge that reached out and scratched her paintwork with a high, screaming noise.

She rounded a final bend and came to rest where the lane widened out in front of the farmhouse. Through the rain-streaked windscreen she stared at the building. It was large and forbidding, built of uncompromising grey stone. Its square windows stared out over and beyond her as though saying, *We care nothing about you and your little ways and little problems.* A paling fence, faded to silver, enclosed a brown, twiggy garden, dull and overgrown, which flanked the path to the front door.

Jasmin sat in the car, staring at the house. Then she shook her head, plumped up her hair with her hands and stepped out of the car.

The man who opened the front door was big and Jasmin expected resistance; yet he was bowed, passive, resigned to her intruding. He shook hands in a way that suggested he was making a big effort not to crush her hand, then seemed unsure whether to invite her into the kitchen or the unused-looking living room. She took charge.

'Shall we go into the kitchen?'

He looked relieved at the decision and led her through. Her sharp heels clicking on the tiles of the floor shattered a silence otherwise only broken by the gentle tock of a grandfather clock. He held out a chair for her to sit down at the table.

'I'm sorry for your loss.' She thought this was the right thing to say.

This man certainly looked lost and didn't seem to know what to do with himself. Finally, he sat down opposite her. 'Yes.'

This was going to be an uphill struggle. Jasmin was out of place in this room of unvarnished pine, smoothed silver with age. Everything around her, including the farmer himself, lacked colour and crispness. Her peacock blue jacket, jet black hair and the rings on her fingers seemed very alien.

Did she have the right to intrude on his grief? She looked across at this big man with his bland face. He wouldn't have a worry in the world apart from deciding when to get the sheep sheared or what time to milk the cows or whatever. And the dreary wife, hovering almost out of sight behind the kitchen door, what did she have to do all day apart from baking apple cakes or crocheting mats or collecting eggs? These people would have no idea of the pressures of academic life; of having to produce written results and justify every expense.

She smoothed back her hair and felt her chair wobble on the uneven stone floor. She grasped the edge of the table. She cleared her throat. 'I don't know how much your grandmother told you about my research.' The man shook his head, whether to show he did not know or did not care was unclear. She ploughed on. 'I am a historian, trying to make sense of the role of the British army in the Indian mutiny. Your great-great-grandfather was there.' Now he was nodding. 'As was mine,' she went on.

There was an ugly scraping noise as the door into the hall was pushed back, rubbing on the floor. The wife – what was her name? – came into the room and stood, square on.

'My husband doesn't need to be bothered with this now.'

Jasmin held her hands out, palms down, fingers spread; a universal gesture of passivity, of not wanting to be a bother. But the woman's eyes just stared at the rings on her fingers as though they were obscene.

Magnus Bostock pushed back his chair and stood up. 'She only wants to see that old stuff in the attic,' he said. 'It's been there forever – it's about time now someone sorted it.'

He headed for the door, but his wife was immovable, blocking his way. *Christ, what's her problem?* thought Jasmin.

'It needs tidying up, cleaning, before' – she looked at Jasmin as though she had trouble finding the next word – 'anyone goes up there.'

'Cleaning?' Magnus Bostock sounded incredulous and Jasmin was with him there. She didn't want to glance into the corners of the kitchen but had difficulty stopping herself from checking that there were, without doubt, crumbs, grit and cobwebs there.

Husband and wife stood, facing up to each other, and Jasmin felt the vibes of some huge power struggle between them. She had started to rise from her chair to follow Magnus, but sat back down and looked at her hands, trying to be quiet and unobtrusive. She couldn't get involved in this. For several long moments Jasmin felt the tension like a rubber band stretched to its limits. Then:

'Enough, Brenda,' Magnus said in a low voice.

'You don't want—' the wife hissed.

'I do want. Now she's gone, she can't suppress – all this – whatever it is.'

And there must have been something in his face which Jasmin couldn't see, as she looked sideways at them through her curtain of hair, because suddenly the wife backed off, turned and marched out of the house.

Magnus went back to the table, took a last swig from his mug and said to Jasmin, 'Come on. Follow me.'

She rose, and realised he was trying very hard not to look at her body. But she felt self-conscious about her tight-fitting jacket, the plunging neck of the top she wore beneath and the very skinny jeans.

'It will be a bit dusty,' he added.

She pulled her hair back over her shoulders. 'That's fine.' He led the way up the broad stairs to the first floor, then through a door at the end of the landing that led to a much narrower staircase. She almost bumped into him as he stopped, a couple of steps up, clutching the handrail while he stared upwards. His voice was suddenly meek as he said, 'Haven't been up here in a long while. Don't know what state it's in.'

But the attic wasn't in any state, as there wasn't much to make a mess with. Odd pieces of Victorian furniture were dumped at random. Lampshades, cardboard boxes, an ancient sewing machine and unidentifiable heaps under dustsheets formed meaningless piles in both the rooms that Jasmin could see into as she stood at the top of the steep staircase.

'What you want's over here.' He led her across the room on the left. The only light came from two skylights, streaked with dirt. A wooden chest stood under the slope of the eaves. He started to lift the lid and Jasmin half-expected the hinges to creak. Oh, for God's sake, what was she expecting to be in it, Count Dracula? In fact, the lid rose very easily and the chest was just full of papers.

Magnus Bostock moved in the direction of a small table standing against the wall. 'I suppose you can use that,' he said.

She walked across, lifted the table and carried it to the middle of the room.

He came back over and peered into the chest. 'I don't know what's in here. Nothing for a… you know… historian.' His mouth formed the word as though it were trying it out for the first time.

‘That’s fine.’ She pushed up her sleeves, itching to get stuck in.

‘Right, then.’ He hesitated, shuffled away, muttering about having to see to the livestock.

Jasmin lifted a pile of papers from the chest. They didn’t look as though they had been touched for decades. There were school exercise books labelled “History”, “Algebra”, “Geography”; legal documents tied with ribbon, and photograph albums.

She lifted out a pile of folders, took them to the table and opened the top one.

–

Magnus Bostock turned back to look at the woman. He wondered what this smart lady, so out of place, was doing here. Bad things had happened over the last few months – to him and to the whole island. He heard people talking. He saw them turn away. He knew they looked at him, big and blundering as he was, and wondered whether he had slaughtered his own sheep, and those dogs and those cats, in some fit of anger or something. And now people had died as well – human beings – and he hardly dared drive to the shops in case people backed off when they saw him coming.

Had it all started around the time this woman started meddling? He couldn’t remember when Grandma had first told him about her. He’d pictured some fusty old grey-haired, spectacle-wearing, academic type – not this… this, well, what was she? She looked like one of those many-armed Indian goddesses with her serene face, long nose, painted fingernails, almond eyes and high, pointy breasts. She scared him. But at the same time she was a breath of fresh air blowing across this stale place.

And wasn’t it time someone came and shook things up a bit? Time for all this suspicion and secrecy to stop? They’d never been sure that all Brenda’s miscarriages had been female foetuses, but Brenda herself seemed to think so. Maybe whatever it was that had happened in the past should come out.

He turned back into the room. 'And there's something else,' he said.

The woman looked up from the table where she had placed a pile of faded files.

'Hang on a minute, I'll bring it,' he said. He hurried down the steep stairs, wanting to get this done before he had second thoughts. In the bedroom he went straight across to Brenda's wardrobe – the large, carved, dark-oak piece that filled one corner. He opened both doors wide. Her clothes, most of which she had owned for years, hung lifeless and dull. There were the same few things she wore day after day. Here was the heavy, granite-coloured jacket and mid-calf length skirt she hauled out for funerals – dry-cleaned since their recent outing and still smelling of the chemical. He stepped in closer, touched some of the garments. Over at one side, looking garish and out of place, was a yellow and green sundress with large orange flowers. He reached out and felt it. It had a crunchy, artificial feel to it. He raised it to his nose, wondering, for a moment, if it would still smell of that summer's day – years ago now – when they had decided on a whim to drop everything and give themselves a day off. They had driven to Southwold in the old Peugeot, ate fish and chips on the pier and ice-cream on the sandy beach, just like all the other holidaymakers. Then they had driven home in the setting sun and made love – joyful, carefree sex – before life on the island closed in around them once again. Now, the dress had lost that summer fragrance and just smelt musty. Most of the rest of the space was taken up with serviceable cardigans. For a moment, in the gloom, he had a vision of a row of Brendas lined up, one arm of each ready to rise up and point an accusing finger, tell him he had no right to be there.

He found he had drawn back and was gripping the edges of the wardrobe door. Time to find what he was searching for. On the floor below the clothes was an untidy row of shoes and slippers. He knelt down on the creaky floorboards and reached far in. His large fingers clamped round a cardboard box, flatter and wider than a shoebox, and he pulled it out. He lifted the lid, stared inside for a moment. His fingers stretched towards what lay within, then jerked back. He pressed the lid on firmly, stood up, closed the wardrobe door and remounted the narrow stairs.

He crossed the room to where the woman was standing – a question on her face which he couldn't answer. He thrust out the box and said, 'Here. This is what you're really looking for.' As soon as she had taken it from him, he backed off, turned and fled.

CHAPTER TWENTY-TWO

God, these people were weird. As soon as the man had left the room again Jasmin looked down at the box in her hands. It was special – she had no doubt about that from the way he had behaved. She placed it on the table, ran her hands over the lid. It had that soft feel of old cardboard, like the rows of shoeboxes in her mum and dad's bedroom. When she was little, she and Asha used to sneak up there, giggling and excited, fling off the lids and open up the pink tissue paper to pull out the sparkling, high-heeled shoes. Then they would totter round the room in them, laughing and falling over.

No box in this house would contain shiny, pretty things, but she was thrilled by the thought of what she would find. She took off the lid, placed it on the table and stared at the object inside. Here was a beautiful book bound in grey, tooled leather, with inlaid red tracery. She reached out for it. It was heavy. She raised it to her face, closed her eyes and breathed in deeply. A soft, dry, warm odour, as of distant lands, tinged perhaps with spices, filled her nostrils. She pushed the box aside and laid the book reverently on the table before opening it. A slight crackle as the dry pages moved. She could see that some were loose from the bindings, gaps where others had fallen or been torn out. The paper was a pale yellow, lined.

The handwriting was neat, with fancy curls on the capital letters. The ink, dark in some places had faded to the palest of greys in others, like ghost writing. Definitely some sort of diary or logbook. She went back to the beginning. The first few pages were just some fancy doodling, then a gap where pages were missing, then:

Walked round barracks today. Could smell the tension.

Barracks? What barracks?

Men jumpy, restless. Others muttering amongst themselves. Village much the same, people staying in their homes with doors barricaded, or skulking in shadows.

She scanned the words for some clue as to where the writer was.

Riders arriving every hour with further despatches from Lucknow where blasted sepoys in mutiny.

The Indian Mutiny. Yes!

Must be stamped out. Must be.

June 1st. Long talk with the General. Sweat pouring off the man; obviously suffering. Most decidedly one of the hottest seasons we've had here. Suspect heat only part of the reason for the sour drips that were making his uniform tunic even more unbearable than usual.

General Wheeler called for Chaudhary. Wretched man eventually came running. The dimness in the bungalow temporarily blinded Wheeler and he blundered into a table and cursed. Bad to look weak in front of the servants. When the General asked where everyone was, the man shrugged, said perhaps they sleep.

Wheeler, and I, have had so little sleep over the past weeks – find this thought incredible. Perhaps we alone understood seriousness of these various small acts of rebellion that had been going on in other garrison towns. Perhaps we alone had forebodings of the horrors and slaughter ahead.

Oh my God, she thought. Definitely a personal memoir. And surely written by Magnus Bostock's great-great-grandfather, James Bostock. She pulled the table into better light under the grimy skylight and leant over it, turning each dry, fragile page.

Saw the General standing out in the full sun, staring westwards over the barren plain. Can't help recalling, back in May, soldiers of the Bengal army shot their British officers, and marched on Delhi.

Preparations must be made for the action we will take if the men here were to rebel. Every indication this is real possibility. Nine hundred Britons based here in Cawnpore, two-thirds of them wives and children. General Wheeler responsible for the safety of this large number of his countrymen and he needs to make some decisions now. He must. Nearly all soldiers working for the East India Company are sepoys. The gates of hell could be opened.

Major Salisbury, his second, just senior to me, bustling about. It seems to me both lack the decisiveness necessary. With a mutiny, must take a sword, cut off its head.

They argue like silly women about where to put the families. Salisbury says magazine building, Wheeler says new barracks buildings. These unfinished blocks do not have the thick walls, ample ammunition and stores that the magazine has, nor do they contain the treasury, which the magazine does. They are a building site, with little sanitation and only one well.

Jasmin needed to sit down, so looked around for a chair. There was an ornate dining-type chair in the room, so she dragged it over to the table. The seat was padded and upholstered in what was once some richly coloured brocade and she knew that if she pressed down on it a cloud of dust would rise up. Her mother had always reminded her to carry a scarf in her bag – one of those things that might come in handy along with the emergency twenty-pound note – and for once it came in handy. She pulled it out and spread it over the chair seat before sitting down and carrying on reading.

June 4th. Heat unbearable. Officers' wives whining and moaning. Had to abandon their wardrobes, meaningless fripperies that seem so important to them. Gone now those little social functions that made life bearable in India. Games of whist, the regular musical groups – all abandoned. They can't seem to keep the children quiet. Don't seem to realise how dangerous situation is. Thank God Margaret is home in Suffolk.

Jasmin's fingers were stiff with cold. She growled at them. Come on! Turn the pages!

I know I am considered by the men to be a hard man, a stickler for discipline. Fellow officers find me cold, distant. But I am loyal, loyal to the regiment.

Brief discussion with Wheeler. Then went our separate ways to prepare for the night and what the 'morrow might bring. I do not give inspiring talks. He can do that. I have a different way.

Walked down dusty path towards village. Heat and darkness oppressive. Strange feeling in the air. Tension, fear. Realised all was silence. Would have expected sounds from birds and from rats or snakes in undergrowth. Nothing, as though not daring to make a noise. Almost a relief to reach the Jhakri's hut. Small children peeped round corners to watch me approach. Do they never put their children to bed, these people? Yet another indication of total lack of discipline. Could see their eyes shining in the near total darkness. But as I approached the hut they stole away.

A long, low creak seemed to make the whole house shudder in its foundations. Jasmin's head jerked up and she was shocked to find herself still in the present day, in someone's attic. She blinked at the old Singer sewing machine; the faded watercolours of English fields resting against the walls. Whatever had caused the noise had stopped, so she took a deep breath and carried on reading.

The Jhakri sat in centre of hut. Long, deeply lined countenance, broad yellow streak of paint across brow and top of nose, vertical band of red down centre of forehead. Bare arms and chest covered with white paint. Designed to intimidate, I suppose. Masses of long knotted hair hanging down from under cloth wrapped round head. Long matted grey beard.

A strangely, disastrously compelling man. Found myself seeking him out soon after arriving here, when heard of his supposed powers. Local soldiers said he could channel dark forces of evil. Feared him deeply, pathetic weaklings that they are. Natives in village give his hut wide berth unless they need his powers, when they treat him like a god. Revere him and fear him. But I have sat in his hut in semi-darkness, when local night birds and monkeys cry out in echoing voices and the haunting calls of other, stranger beasts would have chilled the soul of a lesser man than I.

He sits on a low, wide stool, which I perceive to be a sign of status; while I sit in discomfort cross-legged on the floor. Behind him in the gloom are ranged artefacts, sculpted from red clay or carved from wood; sharp pronged or curved metal instruments – signs of his powers or tools of his trade. Atop them all, a dull bronze form glints down at me. It stares at me, me alone. I lean forward to see more clearly. It looks like a serpent crouched on a sphere, yet it has wings outstretched as if about to launch out and strike. From its open, greedy mouth protrude long, curved fangs. Malevolence radiates from this beast and I find it compelling.

The Jhakri sees me looking – turns to follow my gaze. When he looks back at me his countenance shows greed, desire. 'Sarpsipahi,' he says.

Tonight, the wild, red dogs make their ka-ka-ka noise that registers a kill. The bulbuls make an ugly squabble high up in the trees. 'Show me,' I demand. 'Show me your powers.'

June 5th. In the barracks buildings, supplies replenished, water stored, prayers said. Messages requesting urgent help sent to other garrisons – but they had their own problems. Then the cursed renegades try to emulate civilised people by sending the General a note, giving time at which they will attack.

June 5th, day's end. Hugh Wheeler drained – physically and spiritually. Air still thick with stench of gunfire and the men's faces grimy with smoke and dust. At sunset he stood down the troops and sent Havelock and me to check on the families – he couldn't face them himself.

June 11th. A week now. The troops are ragged, the women stiff-lipped and complaining and the children whining. Supplies severely rationed – as is drinking water. What little water there is proves hard to reach, as men deployed to approach the well to draw water are often picked off by snipers hiding in the undergrowth.

June 23rd. Three weeks now we've been under siege. Cursed sepoys. God damn them. Life wretched inside the unfinished barracks. Several died from dehydration, mainly children. Even more of the men have died from sunstroke, from having to be exposed for hours on end to the heat pouring down on their uniformed backs as they repeatedly prime and fire the guns to keep those mad rebels back.

June 26th. The ground so hard they cannot dig graves. Dead bodies simply piling up outside buildings, then dragged out in the cool and dark of the night and dumped down the useless, dried-up wells.

CHAPTER TWENTY-THREE

June 27th. Surrender inevitable. Garrison at Lucknow hanging on by a thread. Our forces utterly inadequate to the magnitude of the undertaking. Watched in fury as sepoys prodded our English women with their rifles. They shouted and roared to make them hasten out of their quarters. Rough carts were laid on to carry women, children and their meagre baggage down to the river, where boats waited to take them to safety. But where is safety? I saw their hearts sink as they approached the banks of the sluggish, brown Ganges. Water level so low that descending the muddy banks to get into the boats was fearful.

Looked round at my fellow men. The soldiers, despite the hours spent shining and polishing their equipment and uniforms, were accustomed to being dusty and grimy. But the women? I observed a young woman with a delicate pink lace collar standing close by, up to her delicate, white-stockinged ankles in brown sludge. In her own environment of English women's accomplishments, she was undoubtedly considered brave and talented. Here, though, she was a fawn dropped into a den of lions. She stared ahead with huge round eyes – not seeing, not hearing. Now I understood: this is what the phrase "blind panic" means.

The General and his entourage were the first to climb into a boat. A great deal of confusion and shouting involved in trying to get a crowd of English women in long dresses, crying children and soldiers, many of whom were wounded, into forty boats.

Not sure how chaos descended into nightmare, but a futile gesture of hubris by some of the junior officers still on the bank led them to blast their bugles. The Indian boatmen were startled, fearing they were under attack, and many of them jumped overboard. In this panic, some of the fires on the boats were knocked over and the tinder wood burst into flames.

Who fired the first shot I do not know, but sepoys quick to open murderous fire upon us. Could only watch from the bank as our men tried to swim to shore, but the Indians waded into the water amongst the screaming and confusion and stopped them. The last I saw of General Wheeler was him roaring in rage as his soldiers and civilians were picked off individually with pistols or hacked to death with swords.

June 28th. Slaughter. Four British soldiers survived and escaped. Little more than a hundred women and children left. Most of them wet – all of them terrified – they were taken back to Cawnpore and locked up. Rebels overwhelmed me by sheer force of their bodies piling on me, shrieking. They have shackled my legs. Humiliated. Have at least left me my uniform and these few personal possessions. Chained me up in a horse stall. English women of course appalled at having to watch their husbands or fathers slaughtered. There are far too many of them crammed into the house where they are kept. Given little sustenance or water. Sanitation abysmal.

June 30th. Surely Company forces are fast approaching. The leader of these scum, Sahib, came to me, gloating. Said only kept me alive in order for me to keep our few remaining British soldiers and the women and children in order. Told me he heard I was a strict disciplinarian as he laughed in my face. My suffering was fearful as I was powerless. Amongst the foul smells of excrement and diseased flesh, came seeping under the door the overwhelming odour of failure and defeat.

July 7th, I believe. Have lost track of passage of days. Desperately thirsty all the time. They keep us like animals – worse than they treat their goats. Dysentery sweeping through women and children and now, I fear, cholera. Palpable tension amongst the Indians. They also are frightened. I hear them telling each other the approaching British forces are massacring innocent villagers as they pass through the countryside.

Sahib finally shown himself as the true monster he is. Worst has happened. He has given the order that the women and children indoors should be murdered. I am in my cage, on hands and knees in filthy straw, and can only watch as they are all told to come outside; yet they refuse and barricade themselves indoors, terrified. They huddle in groups, crouched on the floor, as some of the sepoys shoot at them through the walls and windows; yet some of the Indian solders too disgusted by such a massacre and refuse to join in. That painted whore whom Sahib has put in charge of them is furious. She strides amongst them, shouting, spitting and calling them cowards. Strides away, returns shortly after from the town with butchers, bearing their tools. All our surviving women and children hacked to death with meat cleavers.

When all is quiet – when a deathly stillness, in truth, has descended on the House, sweepers are sent in to deal with the corpses. Their orders were to drop them down the disused well, but it was a long, hot job. Hours passed before they dragged out the last bodies. I have watched all; every movement etched into my brain, so am quick to spot a slight movement. My hot, dry eyes stare, but yes, I am not mistaken, that small boy is trying to raise his hand and that woman with the ginger curls moans faintly. The pale, wasted limbs of three women and three small children, their clothing soaked with drying blood, are still moving. I clutch the rough iron bars of my prison so tightly that my fingers start to bleed as I find myself staring at the filthy pink lace collar around the neck of one young woman.

The sweepers call out to the guards – should they give succour to these poor souls? Should they dress their wounds and give them water? No, they are told, no. Throw them down the well with the others.

Am trussed and shackled, can do nothing but watch. If I shout out they beat me with their rifle butts.

Those small children turn my mind to my own sons so far away at home. Augustus and Edmund. Should I never return, I feel certain they will care for their mother as they grow up. My great sorrow, though, is that I have no daughters. I yearn for a daughter even more than Margaret, who seems content with the boys. Sitting here now, wretched, that is what I desire more than anything on this earth. Should I ever return to England I would like Margaret to give me a daughter.

Oh, to think back to my sisters, Elizabeth and Ann, when we were infants, brings a smile even now to my painful, cracked lips. A little older than I, I always admired them, their confidence and delicacy. I picture them now at family parties at Slegholm – New Year or a birthday – bright ribbons tied in their long, shiny curls, dancing and laughing in their best finery, with I standing in a corner, shy and stiff in my suit. They were the greatest joy in my life.

God be praised. Or if not God then a mightier force. Early morning and, thank God, British forces, men of the 84th, reached Cawnpore and have taken back the city. I can hear them down the hill: their disciplined movements, the calm orders. Then the British officers, led by James Neill, set out up the hill towards Bibighar House to find the captives, knowing nothing of what has gone on there.

General Neill and Havelock enter the courtyard, still believing, I can tell, that the wives and children are alive. Through the bars in this tiny stall in which they keep me I see them stand in the dust and the dirt and the chaos of Cawnpore and look around them. The fighting has left nothing but a mess of broken things and broken people. I see them wondering where the legendary coolness is. I laugh, perhaps out loud, to think they search in vain for the serenity of the gently flowing fountains and the shade of the coral trees.

A roar – an inhuman, almost unearthly cry of anguish that echoes deeply down the hill signals their gruesome discovery at the house. Neill stands rigid, his arms raised, his face frozen in disgust or horror. His men form a loose semicircle round him, alarmed by his roars.

They face the mouth of the wide well. The sun, now overhead, shines down the shaft and lights up, all too clearly, an image that I know they will never be able to rid from their minds. The stench already almost unbearable and the buzzing of the gorging flies almost deafening.

They have found me and released me from my shackles. I can see, reflected in the looks on their faces, how sorry is my appearance. They pity me, which I detest, and are wary of me. My voice croaky from lack of water and sustenance as I try to report. They tell me I must rest. The lack of opportunity to explain why I am still alive while all my fellow officers are dead infuriates me. Do they think I collaborated in some way? This increases fivefold my hatred of these rebels. I see Havelock and Neill as they stand in the shade cast by the house, watching the sepoys scrubbing the yard. Neill has ordered them to clean every drop of blood from the house, the garden and the area round the well. At gunpoint, they are not allowed to rest even for a moment; the sweat pours off them yet they are given no water. Just as I have been given no water. I step outside. They turn to look at me. I ask Neill what will happen to them. 'Of course those responsible will be hanged.'

A few terse sentences of mine can barely suffice to describe my fury. I dearly want revenge against the sepoys already under arrest, the ones I can picture shooting at point blank range the soft bodies in the flowered-print dresses or stabbing and hacking at those white limbs previously so carefully protected from the harsh Indian sun.

CHAPTER TWENTY-FOUR

JASMIN STRAIGHTENED UP. HER BACK WAS ALMOST LOCKED into place with bending over so long, but she did nothing to ease the stiffness, simply stared, unseeing, at the peeling wallpaper in front of her. How long had she been engrossed in these papers? This was an extraordinary find: a first-hand account of an atrocity – no, atrocities – that had been recorded before, for sure, but never in such a brutal, vivid way. So many pictures swirled in her head – the raw violence, the arrogance of the British. James Bostock's ravings were personal, immediate and real. This was more than just a find of historical interest.

She grabbed at the leather-bound book – desperate to possess it, to take it away and consume every square inch of it. She wanted now to get it straight back to the university and show her professor. She stared around her in the dim attic. The family had left all this material in here for decades. Would they be happy with her taking it away now? Did they even know the importance of it? Certainly someone had been looking at this logbook in the last hundred and sixty years. Well, all she could do was try to persuade them to let her take it.

The stairs creaked as she headed down to the ground floor, where all was silence. No one was in the kitchen, nor in the lounge when she ducked her head in there. The little back room that seemed to be used as an office was also deserted. Having emerged from that living, visceral account of the heat, the blood, the sweat, the fear and the hatred of Cawnpore to the here and now, it felt weird that there was no other living soul, nor beast, anywhere around. And yet, Jasmin had a feeling of eyes upon her. She looked through the window and spotted Magnus Bostock and another man, even bigger than Bostock – a bear-like man she guessed to be a farmhand, standing by a trailer at the far side of the yard. They were sorting through some tools. She made her way towards them, resolutely clutching the logbook. They both looked round as she approached; the farmhand quickly looked away again and busied himself with the tools.

'I would really like to have a bit more time to look at this.' She looked Magnus Bostock straight in the face, her chin lifted, thinking a firm, positive attitude would win the day. Positive and cool; she needed to come over cool, let him think she didn't really care one way or the other. It was hard to tell what was going on in his head, though. That face, skin thickened by sun and wind, had a permanent row of frown creases on its forehead.

She tapped the logbook. 'Obviously I'll bring it back very soon; it's just that I would like to be able to study it further – it's quite a useful historical document.' *Quite useful.* That made her want to laugh – laugh hysterically, in fact. Shout and scream, even. *Quite useful.*

He began to nod slowly. She clutched the book more tightly. *Was that a yes?*

'You'll look after it?'

'Absolutely. Of course.'

'It's maybe time it was away from here,' he added.

An odd thing to say, but Jasmin didn't pursue it. She was desperate now to leave. She tried to move casually as she backed off, said, 'Many thanks. See you soon,' turned and set off across the yard, slipping the logbook into her shoulder bag as she walked. She rounded the side of the house to where her car was parked at the front. Opening the boot, she placed her bag inside it and took out her phone, itching to call Howard at the university. But no, that could wait until she'd finished reading the book; she had yet to find out how much farther it went into the events of that time. She slipped the phone back into the bag.

For a brief, split second, she was aware of a dark shape approaching fast behind her shoulder. Then there was a massive blow to the back of her head.

God, the pain! She found herself sprawled half inside the boot, gasping. She tried to raise a hand to feel her head, which felt cleaved in two, but her arms were so weak and her legs had crumpled. She couldn't even start to push herself up. Even while she realised this, her hands were grabbed, yanked behind her and roughly and tightly tied together with a coarse rope or something. She tried to speak, to ask, to shout, but realised there was just a wordless mumbling coming out of her mouth. Then a dark, thick, cloth bag was forced over her head and yanked tight round her neck. With a grunt her attacker heaved her out of the boot and swung her body round and onto something metal, whose sharp edges struck her head – on the side this time – and her thighs.

The ground crunched under the wheels and she was tossed painfully around; but the journey was only a few moments. The sound of the wheels grew into an echo, then the cart, or whatever, was abruptly tipped on its side and she crashed onto the ground. The shock of hitting concrete when you couldn't see it coming was horrendous. A few minutes later she heard the sliding and clanging shut of heavy metal doors. She was pushed over onto her back and felt damp concrete under her hands. Now some sort of strap was tied round her ankles. There was fumbling around her neck and the hood was yanked away. She thought she'd gone blind, but then saw thin, bright slivers of light sneaking round the edges of the doors and through a few narrow gaps where walls and roof did not quite meet.

'Meddling bitch.' The voice was poisonous, grating. The figure turned back to the cart and Jasmin soon found herself showered with the contents of her bag. Then something was held up, shaken furiously in Jasmin's face. 'You should not have seen this! Now you'll watch it destroyed. It and you together.' The pages were being wrenched from their bindings, tossed wildly into the air. Each page, filled with words in that controlled script, so laboriously written with pen and ink, was scrunched or ripped. Finally, the empty cover was flung into a far corner of the barn and Jasmin, lying awkwardly, her hands trapped painfully under her back, was littered with ripped sheets of paper, like ragged snowflakes.

Now something was being pulled out of the pocket of the heavy coat. Jasmin saw it was a syringe, and as her assailant came towards her she found herself whimpering and lashing out with her bound legs, like a floundering mermaid. No use. The shadowy figure simply circled behind her, then lunged. Jasmin felt the stab of the needle in her neck. *Oh, Christ, what have I been injected with?* Then the heavy metal door was being clanked open a little, the figure passed out through it and it clanged shut. Jasmin needed to move – she couldn't just stay here. She rolled onto her side, planning to get onto her knees, then maybe her feet, but suddenly felt she couldn't be bothered. Her feet and legs went spongy and warm. Her face felt like it was melting into a soft puddle of its own making.

CHAPTER TWENTY-FIVE

TIME PASSED; OR HAD IT? JASMIN REALLY DIDN'T KNOW – DIDN'T much care. This floor was quite soft, now she came to think about it. Like a fluffy white cloud. She made the effort to open her eyes, though. Perhaps best not to go to sleep. Right in front of her face lay a chunk of the discarded pages and she thought that maybe she would just have a little read of those before getting up. Or going back to sleep. A little light bedtime reading. With her teeth, she dragged them towards her, into the tiny shaft of light.

> *As daylight fades, Havelock and Neill make their way back down the hill to the old barracks. Their men have been busy clearing up the mess caused by the fighting, unpacking the supplies which are only now arriving, cleaning out the cookhouse and sorting out food and water. All trust between the British and the Indians has gone; the townspeople disappeared into their houses, firmly shutting the doors, as the troops marched in.*

Once at the barracks, Neill dredges up some new energy from somewhere and instantly sets about sending off dispatches, to let the other garrisons know that Cawnpore is freed – and at what price.

Yet their emotions are nothing as compared to mine. They largely ignore me – possibly despise me for being weak and for surviving. Yet they have not seen what I have seen. The time has passed for civilised retribution to suffice. Military law will not be sufficiently harsh; consequently, as dusk falls I slip away and make my way down through the trees to the Jhakri's hovel. I push my way in. He is seated cross-legged, enveloped in his noxious, nightmare-inducing smoke. He stiffens when he sees me. Perhaps he believes me dead. I squat down opposite him.

'This evil spirit – this Sarpsipahi,' I say. His black eyes stare into mine. I make demands. I make promises. He asks what it is I desire more than anything else in this world. In my hatred I agree to relinquish that. I am giving up my chance of a daughter. Call it a Faustian pact if you must. I call it revenge of the sweetest, most dreadful kind. I will have the power, yet in return I am cursed. My bloodline is cursed. The evil will pass down the male bloodline and all the female descendants will die.

Early this morning it began. I wake, stiff and bleary-eyed from the deepest of slumbers. Nor has it been restful for I was tormented by the wildest of dreams. If, indeed, they were dreams. What roused me was a great deal of shouting coming from the lower town. As I start along the road to see what befalls, I am met by an extraordinary sight. Dozens of prisoners have been roped together and are hauling the giant cannon up the windy road from the old bastion down by the river.

I have heard stories of reprisals by our men against rebels who have dared to rise up in other parts of India – Muslim sepoys being sewn into pig skins before being hanged, for instance. That shall not happen – not here, not today. There are no pigs in Cawnpore, or if there were they have been well concealed.

There is summoned into my mind a clear picture of a watercolour tint in a religious book from my childhood. Our Lord Jesus, with a rose tinge to his cheeks and long flowing locks, is hauling the cross on Calvary. I had always been unmoved by this. He looked so serene, unsuffering, uncomplaining. I found it unrealistic. These men do not lack authenticity. They are filthy, smelly, greasy. There is a fitting agony in these sepoys' every step, as they stumble and are repeatedly prodded back to their feet by bayonets. Slowly I follow the procession up the hill.

Once at the top the cannon is fixed into place. It points out blindly over the dry, brown plain below. One of the Indians is dragged forward, lifted up and tied across the mouth of the cannon. Our men are ordered to load it, prime it and fire. Neill's eyes are stony black now with a blank emptiness; many of the men, though, find it distressing – a few of them turn away to vomit onto the dusty soil.

Those men of whom there was no doubt about their involvement in the killings of the women are executed. I fail to understand why they cannot all die, but those considered to be less deeply involved will be given less severe punishments. This is disgraceful – monstrous. They are shackled in the jail for the night. The non-military Indian townspeople and families stayed indoors, afraid of being accused of complicity or encouragement.

The night is unsettled and unsettling. As I write this, by the sputtering light of a few candle ends, Havelock is moving around among the men as they settle themselves to rest after their evening meal. The tension is high. There is a smell of edginess in the air that makes people turn their heads quickly, only to find nothing there. Friend begins to mistrust friend and be wary of turning their back on each other. Distant, eerie sounds echo down from the hills, but the soldiers sitting outside their tents – for there are far too many of them now for them all to be housed in the barracks – cannot agree on the source of these noises. I sit in the dark and listen.

'It's wolves – that's wolves howling for sure,' one sapper declares.

'There's no wolves here, you fool,' scoffs another. 'Don't you know anything?' The 13th Rifles have not long been in India and it is evident they know nothing of the fauna.

'Well then, it's tigers,' announces the first, with total conviction. No one will argue with him. They peer nervously into the darkness, comforted only by their campfires that would keep all outlandish animals at bay. As the evening becomes night, the town and the camp gradually settle down until most people are asleep.

Yet the drenching heat of the night, hotter even than is usual, is not the only cause of their sleep being uneasy and disturbed. People wake intermittently, not knowing if they are having a bad dream or have heard some unearthly noise. Those who are supposed to be awake on guard duty find themselves more alert than usual – twitching and jumping at every shadow, pointing their guns into the darkness yet finding themselves staring into nothing.

Now is the time. I take from my pocket the small vial the Jhakri has given me. I trust I know what I am doing. I trust he knows what he has done. I drink the foul liquid.

I wait. Hours pass, the quarter moon rises and sets. Then I notice an itching, a crawling sensation, in my arms and legs, as of a thousand ants creeping towards my groin, my armpits. Oh, my eyes. I cannot see properly. I focus with desperation on the flame of the last candle on the low table beside me. This must be the awakening. Tremors wrack my body, I have a feeling of intense cold, despite the heat and humidity of the night. What is happening? There is now an almighty pressure inside my skull as though my brain will explode. I stare at the candle flame – the one thing I know is real. And now I experience a feeling of intense energy, as of a lightning bolt swirling down my spine – setting fire to my loins. Desire of the most disturbing kind fills me. My whole body shakes now. As every inch of my skin is aware of the most intense of pleasures, the heat rises up from deep inside me, culminating in the most powerful of climaxes that goes on and on. It ceases. I sag in exhaustion. Record this. Before the second stage takes hold. Already as I look at the back of my hand, as it holds this pen, my skin is darkening, then starting to take on a shiny, scaly appearance. The transformation has begun.

I come to myself before dawn. All is silent – an unearthly silence. No dogs barking, no winds rustling the dry leaves on the sparse trees. Then come the first horrified shouts.

I rise to my feet, look down at myself, straighten my jacket, then follow the sentries and stumble up the slope towards the jail. There I see the first three bodies, though it takes me a moment to recognise that these once had been human beings. Their throats are ripped asunder and the black of their blood stained the paler earth. All have their bellies torn apart – their guts spilling untidily onto the ground. The stench rises up towards our faces and we retch. From the scraps of uniform on the limbs I recognise these as some of our own men who were deployed on guard duty outside the jail.

The jails cells are in a long row. Each is open-fronted – except for the stout bars that run from floor to ceiling. Havelock is there before me. He gropes for a lamp. When, at last, he finds one and lights it he turns towards the cells and holds it high. He said afterwards that the sight before him was so hard to comprehend that his mind started trying to rectify matters – his eyes attempted to straighten the twisted metal bars, to reassemble the hideously mangled bodies; his ears to bring into the deathly silence the rhythmic breathing of people sleeping; his nose to erase the stench of blood and replace it with warm spices and roasting mutton.

Only too soon is it discovered that the homes of the Indian townspeople down the hill have also been assailed. In the stillness of the night, in their huts behind what they believed were secured doors, men, women, children, babes in arms and the old have been savagely mauled – dozens, scores of them – and the very few survivors are, it seems, burbling about a djinn that may have roared, or may have shrieked, that may have had a forked tail or two heads, been black, or red. All agree, though, that it had giant, immensely long, strong and sharp claws; and curved, parallel fangs; and resembled more than anything else a massive, winged snake.

I have a terrible pain in my head. Terrible. I stumble down to what remains of the village and to the Jhakri's hut. Still my head is fit to explode. They tell me later that he, too, has been slashed with those foul, deeply penetrating, parallel gouges, he too…

Jasmin's eyes could no longer focus on the writing, that handwriting, which at first had been precise, neat and elegant – almost feminine – had now deteriorated into a frenzied scrawl.

She had the pure sensation of her body being weightless, directionless, formless. She knew why. She was becoming it. It was her. She was that serpent with the huge fangs. But not from her own choice; no free will on her part. She was a small part of a grand plan – a great sweep of evil and destruction. All these little people who'd got sucked up into this would be swept away.

She had been the one to awaken this monstrous entity. She *was* the monstrous entity. She was the Sarpsipahi. She was the death and the destruction. All out of her control. All down to the blood in her body.

CHAPTER TWENTY-SIX

The Dog and Whistle was quiet, for a change, with nearly everyone from the caravan site packed up and gone. Storms, with more to come, plus a nasty murder only yards from your caravan door were not most people's idea of a fun time, though Elaine Maple suspected that those who lingered were relishing a bit of murder tourism.

She stood in the centre of the main bar, put her hands on her hips and looked around. Now was her chance to give the place a really good clean. She needed some activity to take her mind off things – and that meant activity on the part of anyone who came into firing range. She set the grungies to scrubbing the worktops in the kitchen, cleaning out the deep-fat fryer, changing the filters in the extractor fans and turning out all the cupboards. She would know if they slacked off because the banging and crashing would stop. Elaine herself, with the help of Melania the cleaner, had decided to give the carpet in the bar a good going-over; though it was soon obvious they had different notions of what carpet-cleaning involved. Elaine would have moved all the furniture to one end, then back to the other. Melania was sporty and fit, tall and lithe, and seemed to spend all her spare time at a gym in Colchester. Her plan was to pile all the furniture in the centre of the room in a giant pyramid. When Elaine came in with the Rug Doctor she found Melania already close to the ceiling, lifting a chair up with one hand.

'Oh my God, Mel, that's so dangerous!'

'No, no. I am fine. I do this often in my hotel back home.'

Melania's parents ran a small hotel in Brno and she'd brought with her to England all the tricks she'd learnt there. The words "Health and Safety Inspector" ran around in Elaine's head, but she decided not to interfere. At least this way the job would get done – and with enthusiasm. Mel relished any change from routine, so threw herself into the carpet-cleaning with gusto. Elaine struggled to keep up. But it was only when she retired to her sitting room, on the pretext of getting a drink of water, but actually to have a two-minute sit down and catch her breath, that she caught sight of herself in the mirror – the round, red cheeks, the dishevelled hair escaping in all directions from band and clips – and she realised that for at least an hour she hadn't thought about Alex.

He had, at least, sent a text: *Be home soon.* Ridiculously reassuring. She was such an idiot for being grateful for a tiny message; but she couldn't help it – she was grateful. She supposed she should get back and help Mel, so headed for the bar. Would her cleaner be swinging from the light fittings by now? No, she was outside having a smoke, though it didn't look much fun as the wind had got up again and was blowing her hair all over the place. The phone rang. It was Gerry Lucas from the parish council.

'Hello, Gerry,' she said wearily.

He relished bearing bad tidings. 'Haven't you seen the forecasts, Elaine?'

She hadn't. She'd been too wrapped up in her own world to worry about the one outside.

'If you thought last night was bad,' he announced – and she could almost see his chest expand with the self-importance of prior knowledge, 'tonight's going to be a whole lot worse. It's the mixture of factors all coming at once that's the problem. High spring tide and a massive storm out at sea means there's going to be a storm tide. Could be as bad as in '53, they're saying. And that's massive. It means a water level of over five metres above sea level…'

His voice droned on, but Elaine stopped listening. She turned and looked at Mel's furniture tower, her gaze moving up and up the column. Five metres would indeed be "massive" – obviously Gerry Lucas's favourite word of the moment.

'Thanks, Gerry.' She hung up, called Mel back in, grabbed her phone and sent a message to Alex. *Wd be luvly if u came home soon. Massive storm on way xx.*

–

No way was Nick prepared for the chaos that filled his vision. The harbourmaster had said he should get down there, but he hadn't said it would be apocalyptic. Low tide now and the stinking mudflats were a flattened graveyard of rubbish and detritus – from the land and from the sea.

He'd always thought St Cedd boats escaped the worst of the destruction the North Sea could throw at them. When a storm like this hit, the mass of banks and estuaries were their protection. But last night was too much. It looked like a giant had waded in from the sea, scooped up all the boats in his hands, tossed them in the air, like a toddler playing in the bath, then turned round and strode away.

Nick stood on the concrete walkway and stared around him. The rain had calmed to a steady, vertical downpour and he wiped his eyes clear. Where were his boats? *Oh God, they can't have sunk.* Idiots who hadn't tethered their boats properly were going to find them smashed. Chopped into so much scrap wood, metal or fibreglass by being rammed by the huge waves into each other or into the harbour wall. One had turned all the way over, showing its sad, slimy hull to the sky.

A blue Cygnus he recognised lay on its side – wheelhouse, radar, swept away. *Christ, that was fifty grand down the pan for Chris Rodgers.* It had hit the foot of the jetty. Nick bent down and looked along. The iron framework of the jetty was buckled, the wooden planking smashed. *Christ alive.* Thank God the *Star* looked okay. There she lay, across the harbour to the right, sheltered by the wall and safely far from other vessels.

The harbourmaster charged out of his office, mobile in hand. He looked like he hadn't slept all night either. 'Look to the *Lady*!' he shouted to Nick. 'Be quick, lad, or you'll lose her.' Nick stared where the man was pointing, far over to the left. The *Lady* was nowhere near where he'd moored her; and she was listing strangely, far too low in the water.

No, no, no. He couldn't afford this. Nick's fists balled up tight. He needed both boats to keep the business running, and he couldn't afford huge repairs. He ran towards the steps.

'Take the dinghy,' shouted the harbourmaster, rushing back into the office to answer the phone.

Yes, if he got to her quick, maybe he could strip out what was valuable, get her into dry dock and fix her up. He charged down the steps, his feet tangling in the mix of seaweed, twine and bits of plastic dumped there by the storm, and jumped down into the dinghy. His feet slipped where the endless rain formed slick puddles. He grasped the rope of the starter and yanked on it. A bit of a cough. He yanked again. Still nothing more than a stutter. 'Come on, you fucker – come on!' At last the engine took and he spun the boat round and headed for the *Lady*.

Steering the dinghy through the debris was a nightmare. Unidentifiable bits of wood – some with sharp metal sticking out of them – littered the waters. He had to take it slowly, though he was desperate to get to his boat. Once he reached the *Lady* he leapt on board. She was taking on water. He unlocked the wheelhouse and started to gather up the rods, the log, the lifejackets and anything else removable.

He stood a moment, then let them all crash to the floor. He slumped into the seat and stared ahead, towards the open sea. What was the point? He didn't care. He didn't care about anything anymore. Distant shouting made him turn his head and peer towards the shore. The harbourmaster was waving his arm.

'Get a move on, Bostock!'

Of course. The poor bastard needed his dinghy. Other people had to get on with their lives even if his was over.

He loaded the gear into the little boat and pushed off, abandoning the *Lady*, who sat, rocking sadly in the swell. At the steps he cut the engine and stuffed his arms with as much of the equipment as he could carry, to climb the steep steps up the harbour wall. Pieces of tackle tried to trip him up and one rod end was trying to poke his eye out. 'Shit. Shit. Shit.'

'Go on, pass them over, you go back and get the rest.'

His head jerked up. Still the rain fell heavily and blurred the edges of the person above. *Stacey. Christ, it was Stacey.* She was reaching out impatiently to take the rods from him.

Stacey.

'Come on, get a move on.'

He knew he was just staring stupidly, but for that moment, he could not move. She was wearing a dark pink puffer jacket he hadn't seen before and a black beanie. The rain streamed off her long hair that was dulled and darkened by the wetness. She would be hating that. She never saw any point in being out in bad weather and she hated boats. His legs started to push him up the steps.

'C'mon. Give me those.'

She reached out and took the rods, and he turned back, dazed, to go down the steps to bring up the rest. He told himself this might not mean anything. She might have come to sort out boring stuff about car insurance or something. Once back up the steps he stood in front of her. He didn't dare to speak. He'd only say the wrong thing, as usual.

She put a hand lightly on his chest. 'Look at you – you're a wreck.'

He looked down at his unwashed clothes and rubbed one hand over his stubbly chin.

'Can't live with me, can't live without me, eh? Isn't that what they say?' she asked. And now he could see her lower lip was trembling. She suddenly reached out, grabbed hold of his jacket and pulled him to her, pulling his forehead down on to hers. 'You're such an idiot, Nick Bostock,' she whispered.

He found himself sniffing and gulping and his eyes were blinded with water.

'Hey, you great wally. And get off! Your bristles are hurting.'

All he could do was nod and nod and sniff. He still didn't dare speak.

'We need to make some calls,' she said. Ever-practical. 'Look at the poor old girl.' She stepped to the railing and looked across to where the *Lady* sagged in distress.

–

Morgan woke to the sound of groaning. She pushed the covers off and sat up. That storm – had it conjured up one of those horrible wild things that spilt over from her dreams? She crept on cold, bare tiptoes to the top of the stairs. The room below was dark. She remembered pulling the curtains against the rain-spattered windowpanes, to muffle the sound of their rattling in the ferocious winds.

The groans were coming from a dark shape curled up in front of the fire, long since gone out. The shape started to uncoil itself and rise up, with one, large, clawed hand rearing above its head.

She charged down the stairs and through the kitchen, flung open the door and flew the length of the garden before she paused. She grabbed the trunk of the old apple tree. Her chest heaved; her mind whirred. She clutched on to the words Jasmin had used; held on to the image of Jasmin grasping her by the shoulders and speaking the words to her over and over until she promised to understand. '*What you think you're seeing might not be real. What you think you're seeing might not be real.*' Still breathing hard, she forced herself to stop. She turned and looked back.

Alex stood in the doorway, blinking out at her. He too had bare feet. He wore saggy jeans and a crumpled grey tee shirt and had a hand to his head where he was trying to smooth his mad hair.

'Y'alright?'

She stared, while her breathing slowed.

'Er, sorry.' He came into the garden. 'I was sick of home – couldn't think of anywhere else to go last night. I was out on the beach, but then the storm came – so I thought of coming here. Remembered the key under the stone.' He rubbed his head vigorously with his hands. 'Pretty wasted, to be honest. Just kind of passed out in front of the fire.' He coughed up an evening of weed-smoking. 'Would've gone into town, but the road was blocked with another overturned lorry or something. So we're all stuck here.'

She had slept through all this. She had yearned for Jasmin to be there, mourned her empty bed, but hadn't even noticed this hulking great boy stomping about downstairs. Well, maybe he wasn't actually a hulk, and he didn't stomp.

'You got any paracetamol?'

She looked down at the herb beds and pots around her, the plants now just a brown slush. 'I would have feverfew, in the summer,' she said. 'That's good for headaches.'

'Oh.'

He didn't look too pleased, so she said, 'I can make some tea, though?'

'Er, right, ta.' He was looking down at his bare feet. The toes had squelched into the muddy lawn and the wet from the sodden ground was wicking up the unhemmed bottoms of his jeans.

'I can light the fire, too. You can get dry and warm.'

He went into the bathroom, and Morgan laid the fire and filled the kettle. The run of the taps, the creak of floorboards made her think of Jasmin and wonder when she would be back. If she would be back. She'd seemed pretty keen to get off in a hurry.

It was a strange breakfast of oatcakes, chopped apple, dried apricots, dry-roasted peanuts and tea. They sat on the rug in front of the fire, which was now cheerful and crackling. Morgan could tell that Alex was a bit more relaxed now and also that he wanted to talk. He kept half-looking at her, then looking away. Finally:

'So you spend a lot of time out on the beach, then, or on the marshland?'

'Yes. I like the open air, open spaces. And the animals, and the birds and—'

'Yeah – the birds. So how does that work? A mate of mine saw you on the shore once, not long ago, and there was a whole flock of some small birds, and they were coming right up to you, he said, like even landing on your arms and stuff. I don't mean he was spying on you or nothing,' he added quickly. 'Just that he happened to see you. So how does that work?'

Could she tell him? Could she confide in this odd boy?

Well, she could try. So she started to explain about how she went down on the shore, for instance, amongst the birds, and spread her arms and maybe spun around. How she would find herself somewhere else – some*thing* else. How she could spread her wings and soar. Finally, she looked up. While she had been talking she had been watching her fingers pulling woollen threads through holes in the hearthrug. She had expected to see fear on his face, amazement, perhaps admiration or envy, but was surprised to see just doubt.

'Are you sure?' was all he said.

The phone rang. She jumped up. Perhaps it was Jasmin. But it was Auntie Anne, her voice shrill. 'We've been seeing all about it on the news. You're stranded on an island with a serial killer on the loose, Morgan. Do be careful. You must be very careful.'

'I'll be perfectly fine, Anne.'

'But you don't know that! This madman – he could be anyone!'

Morgan looked down at her torn, grubby fingernails, and the scratches, old and new, on the back of her hand. Madwoman, maybe. Then she turned to look at Alex, hunched over, staring at his feet. Or perhaps madman.

—

All day Elaine worked to bring the pub back to something like normal. And all day people delighted in telling her there was worse to come. At one point, the uniformed policeman, and the gangly, red-haired, plainclothes one came back in. They didn't seem much interested in talking to anyone this time. They took their sandwiches to a far corner. Jaggers crouched near the fireplace, glaring at them, his orange striped tail beating the carpet in a slow rhythm. In the end, Elaine's curiosity got the better of her and she went over to speak to them.

'Looks like you're stuck here for a while, lads,' she said as an opener. 'Until the causeway's cleared.' They both looked up at her, but carried on chewing, so she pretended a nearby table needed wiping. 'Though I suppose of course they have police helicopters and police speedboats and suchlike that could get you out of here quick enough if you wanted.'

'They have them, yes,' said the ginger one finally. 'But they're not too handy when there's a bloody great gale blowing.'

'Ah. Right. Yes.' She took herself off, feeling stupid. Those two were stuck here, along with the rest of them. It hadn't really sunk in before that they were cut off in all directions. People couldn't get in.

They also couldn't get out.

'Dave!' she shrieked, unnecessarily loudly, since he was only a few feet away from her. 'Lanterns! Torches! And where's that baseball bat – do we still have that?'

CHAPTER TWENTY-SEVEN

Jasmin could fly. Or perhaps it wasn't so much flying as floating. She could look down upon her own body. It was a sorry sight, forced into an awkward, unnatural position by the monster. But perhaps she didn't need it anymore. She was the beast now – the all-powerful one. She must have been the one who summoned up these punishing winds and cleansing rains that were swirling round and beating down upon this barn. It was exhausting, though. She needed to rest. She needed to rest.

–

Magnus Bostock and Baltasar spent all day preparing for what was coming. On the news they were saying the storm surge would be as bad as it was in '53, if not worse. And that time the sea rose to eighteen feet above sea level. Magnus straightened up from trying to yank a wattle hurdle out of the ground. He and Balt were planning to stack them in the barn.

This field – the Lower Field, they called it – was reclaimed salt marsh. It was below sea level already. If the sea wall was breached, there'd be nothing to stop the waters surging in and reclaiming their own.

'Are you all right, boss?'

He turned to see Balt staring at him. He was a strange man, that Balt. He would disappear for hours on end, then you could turn round and find him working away on some piece of machinery or fencing like he'd been at it for days. Magnus never knew what was going on in his head. But Balt understood the animals and had a control over them that was greater than any herdsman Magnus knew of.

'Don't know if this is going to be any use. It's going to be bad tonight, Balt. Very bad.'

–

The flat looked much better now that all Stacey's stuff was back. Nick picked up a vest top that she'd chucked onto the duvet and held it to his face. She came out of the shower and into the room behind him and pushed him over on to the bed, crushing the vest into his face.

'Go on, you dirty perv, sniff, sniff, sniff.' She straddled him and used the top to tie his wrists together above his head – not very efficiently, but he didn't mind. He wasn't going to mind anything she did, ever again. Ever.

Later, he started to ask her several times why she had come back but couldn't work out how to say it. Whatever had changed her mind about deciding to stick with a loser like him, she was adamant about one thing: they would leave the island. They would get away from this poisonous place, riddled with superstition, suspicion and paranoia. He wasn't going to argue with that – not for a moment. He snuggled down to sleep, his arm around Stacey and her lightly curving belly.

–

Magnus looked up at the clock on the kitchen dresser. Twenty-five past eleven. He was tired. So tired. Balt had gone home long ago. They had done all they could in sorting out the livestock and weather-proofing the grain store and the dry store. Brenda must be asleep upstairs. He hadn't seen much of her that evening; he guessed she'd been busy getting the henhouse and the tool barn ready for the storm.

He made another cup of coffee and took it up to the back bedroom, from where he could look out towards the sea. The marsh grazing land was a dark flatness; the far side of it, which he knew he couldn't really see from here even if it were light, was separated from the beach by just a rough gravel path. It was hard to believe the sea could come right across that and reach the house and barns, yet he knew it was all too possible. The Met Office flood warning was now red, and the Environment Agency was warning of major flooding in the Shadowbrook and Colne estuaries. He sat down on the bed and lay back against the pillows. He had to keep watch; but he would shut his eyes – just for a moment.

A closing door woke him. It wasn't a slam, just a close, but for some reason it broke through into his consciousness despite the roar of the wind and the teeming of the rain. He rubbed his eyes and rose stiffly from the bed. The window streamed with rain; the old sycamore tree across the yard was swaying wildly in a way he had never seen before; the moon showed faintly and fitfully through thinner rakes of cloud but cast little light. As he looked down, though, he saw a shape, a vague, darker figure, cross from the house towards the tool barn.

He charged down the stairs. The clock on the dresser showed nearly three o'clock. Even as he started to open the back door, the wind tried to snatch it from him; he had to hold the knob with both hands. And he was instantly soaked. It was like having a bathful of cold water heaved at you. He closed the door and tried to shake the worst of the drops off his sweater and trousers. This time he put on his waterproof and boots before opening the door and stepping out to look towards the barn. Definitely a faint light there, a wobbly small light as from a torch.

His boots sliding in the mud, he crossed the yard and pushed open the barn door. He stepped in, then stopped, trying to make sense of what he saw. A storm lantern was on the floor, over by the wall. The light it cast failed to penetrate the whole building. Straight ahead of him, by the back wall, an animal lay injured on the floor. What the hell was it? A sheep? It was stirring about and bleating. But he knew none of the sheep could have got into here. He stared at it, knowing how a wounded creature could lash out. He forced himself towards the lantern to pick it up. A slight noise from the shadows behind made him start to turn; he caught one glimpse of the massive broad blade of a shovel before it came down on the side of his head and he crashed to the ground.

The echo of the metal bouncing off his head was so loud it made his brain scream – and it went on and on. He pushed his hands against the gritty, damp concrete to try to stand up, but his legs and arms were so weak they would not do what he told them. He tried to speak, but a weak moan came out of his mouth. Blood dripped down the side of his face and into his eyes, and he tasted the metallic tang of it running into the corner of his mouth.

He could barely see anything – his vision was blurry, with flashes of brilliant silver round the edges. The wielder of the shovel, wearing a big, hooded cloak, now moved over to the animal by the back wall, and seemed to be trying to pull it along the floor. Magnus went to drag himself forward, but only seemed to have strength in one arm – and not much there. The hooded figure swung back towards him, grabbed up the shovel again and raised it.

'Stay back. Stay back or I'll have to smash your head in. Stay back!'

He lay motionless, speechless.

'Stay back, Magnus – stay out of this.' The voice was shrill, manic. 'That Indian woman, she should never have come here! You couldn't know – you'd not have coped. I had to do it all.'

Magnus just stared. His mouth opened to ask questions, but all he could do was drag air into his lungs.

'Oh, it was all there in the attic. All that stuff had been up there for years and years. And I found it and I read it. And I know about how he gave you all bad blood. Bad blood that ruined everything. Ruined my life.'

The shovel crashed down onto the floor.

'And now this meddler has to turn up – couldn't stay away, couldn't mind her own business.'

The figure turned and the cloak swung open. Inside was a huge metal claw.

CHAPTER TWENTY-EIGHT

Elaine knew that Alex had tried to creep in without her noticing; but he wasn't going to get away with that. She thrust his door open while barely bothering to knock and found him sorting through the clothes that were on his floor and his chair. She felt a huge sigh of relief sink through her body, though she wasn't going to let him see it.

'Well, if you think I've got time to put a load of washing on, you can think again. I guess you can work out how to use the machine – you've seen me do it often enough.'

'Yes. Yes. I know how to use the machine.'

'Don't you get uppity with me! Do you realise how much I have to do around here without very much help, thank you? Do you?'

'Yes! Give it a rest.'

'Well, in case you haven't noticed, there's a red storm warning. There's going to be a massively high tide tonight. Gales. Rain.' She found herself grasping her hair in great fistfuls and thought, *Right, get a grip, woman. He's here, he's safe.* 'But no more going out for you, my lad. You're to stay in – you hear me? Stay in!'

–

Darkness fell early that afternoon and Morgan had done all she could to seal herself off from the outside world. She had gone out to the henhouse and chased around, catching each bird and carrying them one at a time up to the kitchen. They clucked around, pecking the floor, disappointed at the lack of crumbs. But at least they were safe and dry in here. And they were company, of a sort.

That last storm had been wildly exhilarating. She had stood under the low, black, fast-moving clouds, felt the wind grasp at her hair and her clothes, flinging them wildly up and around, snatching her breath out of her body, trying to suck her consciousness from her.

But this wind was different. It was angry, she could feel that. It wanted something. And the sea seemed to be rising higher than it ever had. From the cottage she could see the waves, huge and flashing silver, closer than they should be. She cooked an omelette for her supper and sat in front of the fire to eat it. She found that if she kept the light turned off in the kitchen the chickens quietened down and settled in a huddle in one corner.

In some ways she wished Alex had stayed. He was clumsy and too tall for the cottage and he smelt of teenage boy. But there were times when it was nice to have another human being around. Certainly when the winds were so angry like this. It was Jasmin she really wanted, though. Jasmin would know what to do to keep the waters at bay – she knew everything. Morgan had never met anyone so cool. Jasmin didn't put up with any nonsense from anyone; she didn't let them all tell her what she should be doing and not doing. And she had a pierced nose and three earrings in each ear and a stud in her navel. Morgan had once gone along to a hairdresser's in Ipswich that advertised ear-piercing but jumped out of the chair and ran away as soon as the woman came near her with the instrument.

Why had Jasmin gone? There was an untidy pile of papers that she had left on one end of the dresser and Morgan idly picked them up and took them to her place in front of the fire. She started to fold one into a swan, but it ended up looking more like a duck. She took another sheet and made a dart, which she glided into the flames. She then tried to make a dog, but that failed, so she picked up yet another piece of paper. Jasmin wouldn't need them anymore or she wouldn't have left them. One word, though, was repeated so often that it gradually impressed itself on her consciousness: Bostock. She kept seeing it; every page was talking about the Bostocks. But they were the farmers who lived up at that big gloomy farmhouse up the hill, weren't they?

A deafening, reverberating, metallic crash had her scuttling into the corner of the room, screwed up like a ball, her hands over her head. There was no further noise, and gradually her breathing slowed and she dared to stand up. The chickens were silent and still, their necks stretched to the utmost, their eyes bulging. Morgan crept to the window and peered round the curtain. There was a moon, but the thick, woolly blankets of clouds rarely let it see through for more than a second or two at a time. A few feet in front of the window a huge sheet of corrugated iron leant at a crazy angle. It must have blown off one of the old sheds along the lane.

But what was also there that shouldn't be was a shimmering, shiny lake. The whole world was underwater – not much, maybe, but nevertheless everywhere. Upstairs. She must go upstairs. She turned to look back towards the kitchen and found the chickens were paddling. Each of them was strutting around unhappily lifting first one foot then the other high out of the water seeping under the back door. Chickens might have trouble walking up stairs. They might flap their wings and squawk a lot and make it up the first three or four, but then they would all be jostling for space and end up turning round and fluttering back down. So once again, she picked them up, two at a time now, and carried them up to the bedroom.

The window fitted more snugly up there, so the roaring of the wind was not so angry. Once she pulled the duvet tight round her and piled the pillows in a kind of pyramid round her head and could manoeuvre the tartan blanket on top of all that, the outside world felt like a distant dream.

And eventually she fell asleep and had a dream – one of her wild ones with extraordinary creatures swirling through the skies. They had sharp, gleaming teeth, wings, claws and long, lashing tails and plunged out of the skies on some small, helpless being down below. But this time it wasn't some shadowy victim. It was very real and it was Jasmin. It was Jasmin who was being slashed by the huge bloody claws.

Had she been asleep for minutes or for hours when a new noise penetrated her cocoon? Ferocious banging and a man shouting. Had the storm and the wind worked itself into such a frenzy that it had solidified into a man? A wild, angry murderous man – the one who was doing all this damage and all this killing on the island? She tried to quieten her whimpering by stuffing a corner of the pillow into her mouth, but now he was on the stairs – she could hear the old wood creaking. The hens, who had settled down in a cosy heap in the corner, launched into their panic squawk.

'Are you in there?'

Even though her fists were balled in her ears, she couldn't keep the voice out.

'Hey... Morgan... are you there?'

It knew her name.

And now it was coming closer. It was in the room.

—

Nick was once again standing at the window of the flat above the launderette in the middle of the night, in the pitch black, with the rain again spouting wildly out of the blocked gutter. But this time his head wasn't throbbing fit to burst with a hangover, and this time he wasn't trying to forget. He had his Stacey back – unless he went and messed up yet again. He was thinking more clearly, though, than he had done in a long, long time.

He saw himself back in his grandmother's room at the home, when he had told her that Stacey was pregnant. Dorothea had stared into the distance as though she were staring into the abyss. She had refused to answer his questions then, but now she was dead. He saw that all his life she had been like a dirty window that blocked out most of his view of himself, his life, his past. Magnus's revelation about little Louise had caused everything he thought he knew to come tumbling down. Now the window was smashed. Nothing could stop him from seeing the truth. As soon as this bleeding rain ever stopped, he'd go up to Slegholm and go through the family papers with Magnus and find out what the hell it was all about.

–

'Hey, hey, it's only me.'

The voice was saying this over and over again. Slowly, ever so slowly, its message got through to Morgan. She fought off the tartan blanket and the layers of duvet and sat up. Enough light spilt in from the landing to show her clearly that this was the one she still thought of as the pale boy. *Alex. What a relief.*

'You need to get out,' he was saying. 'Come on – we have to go now.'

Why? Why go? Why go out into that dreadful night?

'Something evil came with that storm,' he said.

She looked closely into his face. 'I believe it was already here.'

'I had to wade up to my waist to get in here. Don't you realise the water's halfway up your stairs?'

Morgan jumped from the bed and raced to the window. There was nothing but sea. It was like they were in some sort of Noah's ark that was floating along across a never-ending expanse of water. She giggled.

'Fuck's sake – this ain't funny!'

She turned quickly and looked at him – scrawny, pale and anxious. 'No… I only meant—'

'Whatever. We need to think of somewhere to go. Get your boots on. No use trying to get back to the pub, 'cos that's downhill – it'll be even deeper.'

Morgan turned back to the window and pointed out into the blackness. 'We'll go up to that farmhouse – Slegholm, is it? Jasmin's there. She needs me.'

He turned and looked into the darkness. She could see he looked doubtful. Like a lot of people round here he probably thought that gloomy old farmhouse was a bit spooky. She started to gather up the chickens once more.

'We can't take those – are you crazy?'

'Well, I'm not leaving them behind to drown.'

'They won't drown,' he said. Then, 'Chickens can swim. I've seen them.'

Could they swim? Morgan wasn't sure if he was making that up off the top of his head.

'Look,' he was saying. 'We'll leave the window fixed open, then if the water comes that high, they can just step out and float off. Simple.'

She thought it through. It sounded good enough and Alex was getting really twitchy, obviously keen to get away. And he must be frozen in those wet jeans. So she was happy to follow him down the stairs.

The water was cold – unbelievably cold. But not just that. It was swirling, powerful, and it had stuff floating in it that banged into them as they waded through. Hard stuff, disturbingly squidgy soft stuff and sharp stuff. Gradually, though, it became shallower, and as they forged their way up one long, sloping field they found themselves on drier land. It was still spongy and saturated, but not underwater. Exhausted, they found a fallen trunk on the edge of a band of trees and sat for a moment to regain their breath and their composure. It was too cold to stay long and Morgan was desperate to keep moving.

'Come on, come on,' she urged.

Alex would have been happy to be inside any building, right now. His pallid skin was all she could see of him – it almost glowed in the dark like those stick-on moons and planets you could get for a kid's bedroom ceiling. They were approaching the big house from behind and there were no lights on in there, so they made their way to the front. This was hard, since as soon as they were in the shadow of the great stone building the dark was nearly absolute. Morgan's feet, in her sodden canvas ankle boots, were so cold they hurt.

The front door was slightly open. They both called out as they stood in the hallway, but their voices echoed back at them from dead walls.

'She is here – I know she's here!' said Morgan.

'Who?'

'Jasmin.' Didn't he listen to anything? He was touching the ornate frame of one of those murky old pictures that show a field full of cows, or something. He started to outline the hills in the background with his finger. She grasped him by the sleeve and dragged him to the foot of the stairs.

'What are we looking for? Can't we just find some towels and stuff?' he asked.

He didn't get it. He didn't get the overwhelming, suffocating, clenching urgency with which they had to find Jasmin. In the end, she left him behind and plunged from room to room, downstairs and up. Nobody; nothing.

From the top of the stairs she saw Alex still in the hallway. He was pointing at something on the floor, by the door to the living room. 'That's that thing! That's that statue—'

But Morgan didn't have time to listen to this. 'Out! Outside! We'll look in the sheds and barns. If she's not here, she must be there.'

She wished he wouldn't look at her like she was so bonkers.

'You saying we have to go out there again? Just when we've got a chance of getting warm and dry?'

She wasn't going to argue. She simply ran down the stairs, out of the front door and round to the back of the house. There was a large yard, dark buildings, sheds or barns, overshadowing the lesser darkness of the open ground.

To her right was a long, low building with an open front. There seemed to be nothing in it, so she ran from the end of that to a much larger barn. Snuffling noises, heavy breathing and blowing, and the rustle of straw suggested cows. And they smelt like cows. Morgan peered in through a wide opening in the door. An enormous bull stared straight back at her. He was huge. His head and neck were about the size of her entire body. She jumped back, even though he obviously couldn't get to her.

Another building had an open front and looked like a vehicle store. An old car, a pickup truck and a small tractor were lined up. So that left one more barn. As Morgan moved closer to the big sliding door of this place she heard anger. For her, the wind and the rain would be angry. They would spin around her head and fill her ears – but this was something more, something horrible. Yet Jasmin was there – she knew it. She grasped the edge of the door and with all her power pushed it open.

A storm lantern hung from a beam and gave off a fiery glow that cast huge, swaying shadows. Morgan didn't know what hell was like; she didn't know if she believed in it. But one of the art teachers at school had once taken her aside and shown her a giant book containing paintings by William Blake. Tortured, twisted bodies in deep gloom shrieked out of the page at her. They crept on hands and knees, their limbs straining in pain. Their naked muscles and sinews twisted to breaking point, mouths open in that never-to-be-heard, never-ending howl of perpetual torment. This was that. She pulled the wet strands of hair away from her face where the wind had flung them and found her hand shaking badly.

A man was crawling across the floor. One side of his head glistened with a dark mass. It looked like raspberry jam. Her mind wrenched away from Blake as she focused on this. Why would he have raspberry jam on the side of his head? He was lopsided, moving crab-like, one arm dragging a shovel, the other reaching out across the floor towards a wild creature standing with its back to him, which now raised its arms above its head and shrieked an unholy shriek. At its feet was a bundle, but the bundle too was moving slightly. The savage creature loomed over it. Instead of hands it had one massive claw, raised high, gathering momentum, about to slash down in an almighty, savage blow.

The bundle shifted a little, even as the huge claw began its slicing movement. It tried to push up onto one elbow and Morgan glimpsed a fall of black hair, a shiny reflection from the lamp on silver ear studs and a silver hoop. She flew. In less than one breath's time she pushed hard against the monster, then flung herself over defenceless Jasmin. She tried to spread herself to cover as much as she could of the body of her friend; she pressed her cheek into Jasmin's cold, clammy face. A sudden burning, horrific pain burst through her back. So sharp it ripped the air out of her lungs. She felt it go – and couldn't breathe in to get it back. She felt Jasmin push her up a little, she felt Jasmin's arms tighten around her and Jasmin's warm breath against her face.

—

'Morgan!' *What the hell is going on?* thought Jasmin. She was completely back in her own body now – and didn't she know it. She was bruised, grazed and bitterly cold. Her head was on fire, though. Splitting. The floor she lay on was freezing, wet and gritty.

And that sweet girl, Morgan, was now lying in her arms, while a warm, sticky fluid – what, blood? – poured out of her back over Jasmin's hands. She raised her face from where it was pressed into Morgan's cheeks. Her eyes felt like they were taking forever to come into focus, but she could see a gleaming curved blade, or giant claw, being raised up in preparation, she guessed, to strike again.

There was a rush of movement from near the door and a heavy pounding of feet on the concrete floor. A body launched itself at the clawed beast, toppling it to the ground. The beast roared in anger and turned to wrestle off the newcomer. Jasmin strained her eyes through the near darkness to see this person. It was that weird boy who lived in the pub. *Alex. Fuck.* She needed to help him. She tried, gently, to push Morgan off her and realised how light and floppy the girl's body had gone. *Oh, Christ no. No.*

And now there was someone else here. A silent shape had risen slowly from the far corner and was moving their way. Hostile or friendly she had no idea, but it was definitely scary. Big – very big – and it was carrying something – a spade, a shovel? She would have to leave Morgan for a moment. She would have to help Alex. She pushed Morgan off her and onto the ground. Recovery position would be good, but that was a luxury. Or was it just pointless? Alex was pinned down now and the assailant had its hands round his throat. *Jesus!* It was going to strangle him to death.

Even as she tried to push herself up, though, the big man with the shovel gained momentum. She stayed very still. Where was he headed? But he didn't even glance at her. He charged straight past, lifted the shovel high and brought it down without hesitation onto the back of the beast's head. The noise of metal on skull jerked Jasmin back into that night of storytelling back in Morgan's cottage. The stark image of men standing on a dark shore, foul, greedy faces leering through the gloom. She could smell the brackish fog, the sweat on the wreckers, the blood bursting from the heads of the exhausted sailors who floundered on the shoreline, as their skulls were smashed by the piece of wood studded with nails. Jasmin clapped her hands over her mouth. At least Alex was freed now. He was clutching his hands to his throat and making horrible rasping sounds. She crawled across to him and helped him to sit upright.

The big man, she could see, was no threat to anyone anymore. He had dropped the shovel and stood, limp and unmoving, one hand pressed to a wound on the side of his head, which dripped blood. She saw it was Magnus Bostock who stared down at his dead wife on the floor.

EPILOGUE

Elaine Maple stood in the middle of the Lounge Bar (newly renamed – she'd always wanted a Lounge Bar) at the Dog and Whistle and looked around her. The early-morning September sun angled through the new glass in the windows. The builders had taken away the last of their tools and the insurance had paid up.

Now there were fewer internal walls, so she had a lighter, more open space with bleached wood flooring in the dining area, like in posh gastro pubs. She took in a deep breath full of the fresh paint smell – the replastered walls were painted in a pale dove grey. Dead sophisticated. There were only the last few tourists of the season around now, but she'd noticed they were coming from further afield – bothering to make the journey for a night out at the Dog.

She walked over to the corridor leading to the toilets and moved along the row of photographs of the great storm; took one down from the wall and gave it a quick rub with her sleeve before hanging it back alongside the others. They'd become a real talking point.

She looked at people helping each other to climb out of bedroom windows and being ferried away in rowboats. Children passing kittens and hamster cages to firemen before being lifted to safety themselves. Sadder images of debris being swept away by the muddy waters – a rocking chair, an upturned kitchen table.

The aerial photos were astonishing. The one looking down on the Dog and Whistle showed the water up to the ground floor windows, the posts of the car park fence poking up through the waters. Another showed a vast grey sea punctured by roofs of buildings and tops of telegraph poles. Unrecognisable. And here the camera looked down on a forlorn herd of cattle clustered around an old farm building on a tiny island that was all that was left of their field. These were just moments captured in an instant. They never show what happened next. Did the waters rise higher? Was there no boat big enough to carry them? Did the cows drown?

She shuddered, as always, when she thought about the deaths that occurred that night. The dead sheep she had seen floating, bloated in the flooded fields. And all that stuff that happened up at Slegholm Farm – that hideous woman, that poor husband.

A distant scream and cackle of laughter from the sky to the north, the direction of their farm, made her jump. She ran to the window, but it was only a chevron of Brent geese, making a fuss as they headed in from chillier parts.

–

Morgan stood in the lane outside Nan's Cottage and watched the brake lights of the black Golf flash briefly as it turned into the bend. Then it was out of sight.

The salt-laden wind flung Morgan's hair up and made her short skirt flap around her thighs. Her black leather biker boots held her firmly to the ground, though.

'Y'alright, Morg?'

She turned and swept one arm up to clear the corkscrew curls that were whipping round her face. Alex was approaching through the trees. He stopped some distance from her, his hands stuffed into the pockets of his jeans, kicking at the loose earth with the toe of his trainer.

'Yeah,' she said. One last glance at the empty road, then she turned and walked towards the skinny boy with his strange black, spiky hair. She came up close to him and reached out her hands to take hold of his forearms. Then she held his left arm in both her hands and pushed back the sleeve of his Caves sweatshirt. The ugly scars were faded now to a dull purple. She looked into his face and nodded slowly.

'What's with you?' she asked.

He smiled, shook his head. 'My mum still giving me hell. UCAS application now. She's going uni this, uni that.'

'You should. But that's months away, isn't it? Year, even?'

'She likes to plan ahead.'

They sat down on the springy turf. Morgan stretched her head back and felt the sun warming her throat. A swallow soared high above them. She straightened up and rubbed her back.

'Still hurting?' he asked.

'No. I'm all right.' It was the memories – the flashbacks – that were worse than the physical pain. But the counsellor was helping loads with that. She was very…

'Grounded.'

'What?'

'Nothing.' She smiled at Alex.

'And you, eh?' he said. 'Off to Colchester, then?'

She spun round and onto her knees. 'Art and Design, they call it. And it's not just drawing and painting and stuff – you can do textiles and ceramics and photography and—'

'And you'll get off this island.'

'Yep. Off this island.'

'Staying with your auntie and uncle?'

‘Yep. To start with.’

Alex lay back on the lumpy grass and gazed up at the pale blue. Morgan, too, looked up again. Far, far above them, the tiny dot of a plane left a pure white vapour trail, headed off to some distant place. The swallow had been joined by another, and the pair of them swirled in giant, lazy loops. They would be among the last to set off, knowing that darker, colder times were ahead. But not yet.

–

Jasmin glanced for a last time in the rear-view mirror before swinging the car round the bend that led to the causeway. *Bloody hell.* She'd planned to come for three weeks and ended up staying half a year. And that was only because the complicated probate, with the deaths of Dorothea and then Magnus, meant she couldn't take away the family papers. But the new academic term started soon and she needed to get up to speed with her writing up. She opened up her playlist. Turned the volume up high. There was future research to think about; grant applications; networking at the coffee break. True, it was a bit sad to say goodbye to Morgan. She was a sweet girl, a one-off. But she'd be all right.

At the end of the causeway she pulled over and reached forward to set the satnav. *Civilisation? Real world? Normality? Twenty-first century?* What should she put? In went her mother's postcode – tasty food, comfortable bed, reliable washing machine. She opened the door and stepped out to take a last look back at the flat landscape with its hedges, ditches and gates, scattered cattle feeding, the narrow leaden line of the river. Even in summer the predominant colour was grey – the crops in the fields, the water glistening on the marshland, the birds in the sky, and the distant emptiness from which the wind rushed in. And all around – angry, mysterious, threatening, enigmatic, controlling, scary, dominating – was the sea.

–

Nick Bostock dumped the shopping bags on the kitchen floor and started to unpack them. The cupboards were already crammed. The whole damn house was a bit overfull – but that was okay. Stacey's mum was fine with it and they were all managing to rub along sort of all right for now. And it wouldn't be too long before the money came through and they could get their own place.

He found the new packet of nappies and took the stairs two at a time. 'Got them.'

Stacey was lying in the bath. She held a shiny, pink-skinned, plump baby girl tight against her chest. 'Look at her,' said Stacey. 'I think she's really liking this.'

Nick knelt down and splashed some warm water over his baby daughter's back. 'Yeah. Yeah, she is. She's loving it.' He kissed them both. 'See you in a bit.'

He went downstairs and out again through the sky-blue door. The old green Polo fired up the first time – bloody miracle, he'd be pleased to see the back of it – and headed off for St Cedd.

At the junction where the road from Colchester would take him onto the causeway to St Cedd he pulled over. He'd have to wait a short while for the tide to drop. He stepped out of the car and the always chilly breeze off the North Sea caught him in the face while the salt spray stung his eyes. The sunny day had given way to heavy clouds that moved fast across the sky, seeming to dip as they paused over the island. He shivered, and as soon as the road was free of sloshing seawater he forced the car towards the island.

Slegholm Farmhouse, unlived in since that night, seemed to stare out across the marshes, more forbidding than ever. A solitary, greying net curtain had escaped from a gaping upstairs window and flapped in a forlorn way towards the open sea beyond.

Nick parked the car at the front of the house. Muddied strands of yellow and black police tape still hung near the heavy front door. Nick pushed it open. The house was stripped now to the bare bones, brittle and hollow. No coats hung in the hall. He wandered into the kitchen. No table or chairs, washing machine or fridge filled the emptiness. Only the old Welsh dresser still stood against one wall – unwanted by any buyer. He found himself staring down at the flagstones, polished by decades of people coming and going. But there was no sign that it was here that his brother had stood and shot himself. He had walked out of the barn while the other people were still reeling with shock, gone into the house, taken the shotgun out of the gun cupboard and blasted half his head off with it. Nick pulled at the neck of his shirt to try to get some air in and stumbled out of the room.

Back in the hall he looked up the staircase, with its moss-green Wilton carpet that had been there forever. A thousand clouds of vague memories floated into his mind. He could hear himself breathing, fast and shallow. He bashed himself on the side of his head. *Get the fuck out.* Leave here; don't come back.

One last look at the big living room – silent now. No television, no children playing on the Persian rug, no neighbours standing chatting with glasses of sherry – if that ever happened. As he turned to leave the room a violent, intense pain went through his foot. *Jesus! What was that?* He leant against the doorframe while the stabbing pain shot in waves up his leg and looked down to see what he had kicked. That solid bronze statue, the Sarpsithingy, whatever – the winged serpent – used for so long to prop the door open that everyone had stopped noticing it – stared up at him, its dead eye malevolent. Still here.

He walked round to the yard, which used to be perpetually muddy from cows' hooves and tractor wheels but had now dried into cracks and hollows. An imprint of the tyres of the old John Deere, gone for auction, showed clearly in the centre. The silence and stillness were abnormal. This should be a place of industry, men calling to each other, animals lowing or bleating, workers laughing together. But it never had been, not in Nick's memory, and it never would be now. The land was parcelled up and sold, the house soon to go to developers. And now the barn, scene of all that terror and violence, was about to go up in smoke.

Baltasar stood, looking more like a bear than ever, at the corner of the barn.

'Thanks for coming, mate,' said Nick. 'Can't do this alone.'

The big man nodded, long and slow, and helped Nick carry the petrol cans from the car. When they had them lined up outside the barn, Nick straightened up and looked around him. An ugly cry made him jump. Then another. He looked across to where half a dozen large birds were landing in the trees on the edge of the woods.

'Crows,' said Balt. 'They come.'

Nick turned towards the birds and forced a laugh at them. 'Then they'll soon be fucking well going again.'

He grabbed up a petrol can, flung off the lid and let the liquid pour out as he walked rapidly round the building. Balt followed suit. Within minutes the fire was alive; a few minutes more and it was greedily eating away at the creosoted planks of the barn walls.

They stepped back from the heat. Nick turned swiftly and strode back into the house. He came out, moments later, clutching the bronze statue. Balt stood aside to give him space as Nick swung his arm back and flung the statue into the middle of the burning building. 'Bastard! Bastard!' he shouted over the noise of the flames.

He and Balt stood back and watched until the walls collapsed inwards and the roof crashed to the floor. The flames died down to become a column of bitter-smelling black smoke that curled upwards and merged with the low grey clouds.

Yet through it all a glint of shiny bronze stared out at Nick. The Sarpsipahi, refusing to melt, glared back at him, its dead eye glinting in the embers.

ACKNOWLEDGEMENTS

This book would not exist without the unfailing support of my family, Duncan and Zoe, along with cheerful reinforcement from Chi-Ying and Pete. Many, many thanks. I also hope it will give at least a little encouragement to Ellie and Ivy to persevere at whatever they enjoy.

I would also like to thank my alpha readers: Esther Symmonds, Gill Shapton, Linda King and particularly Bob Pomfret for his bird knowledge. And, of course, my other mates at BF: especially Vince Haig, James Hoskins and Sarah Hickingbottom for their no-holds-barred criticism, inspiration and abiding encouragement over the years in several pubs. Thanks to Vince Haig again for the striking cover design.

I also greatly appreciate the positive comments and critiques from Dr James Hawes and Dr Morag Joss at Oxford Brookes University. Lastly I would like to thank the very efficient team at The Book Guild.